P

MW01105596

STANDING
ON THE
PROMISES

"Both *Sweet By and By* and *Standing On the Promises* will stay in my heart for a long time. While Ramona's writing reassuringly expresses the beauty of God's love and forgiveness, it also gives a clear, not-so-comfortable picture of the reality and presence of evil among us. Be blessed in your reading!"

—Charlotte Myrick,
Baptist Bible and Book House,
Laurel, MS

"Complex, engaging story-telling, *Standing On the Promises* is a sequel that easily stands alone."

—Jo Hubbard,
Mt Olive, MS

"Dormant secrets surface, more dark secrets lie in wait, enriching the plot with each passing chapter. With endearing characters and realistic life situations, though set in the late 1800s, the story is ageless."

—Jean H. Holifield,
Business Manager/Co-Owner WBBN Radio Station,
Chairman of the Book Committee for the Jones County
Genealogical and Historical Organization,
Laurel, MS

"A story that shows how even amidst life's darkest challenges, God's mysterious light still shines through. When you begin your journey into *Standing On the Promises*, be sure to have a snack close by!"

—Alison Smith-Walker,
Ellisville, MS

"Reminisce, laugh, cry, and worship. Bursting with the love of God, family, and friends, injected with the intrigue and debauchery of a locally well-known historical character. Read and read again!"

—Kay McQueen,
Collins, MS

"Very enjoyable reading. An unforgettable, weaving tale of love, deceit, prejudice, and forgiveness…all masterfully stitched together."

—Dema H. Patterson,
Pine Belt Quilters Guild,
Sumrall, MS

"*Standing On the Promises* is a compelling, can't-put-down book."

—Barbara White,
Bay Springs, MS

"A lyrical and intricately-woven story of love, life, and death; the characters have a richness and depth not often seen in fictional writing."

—Mona Swayze,
South MS Regional Library,
Columbia, MS

STANDING
ON THE
PROMISES

To: Jan —
Grace, mercy, and peace —
Ramona Bridges

RAMONA BRIDGES

STANDING
ON THE
PROMISES

A story about love

sequel to

SWEET BY AND BY

TATE PUBLISHING
AND ENTERPRISES, LLC

Published by Tate Publishing & Enterprises, LLC
127 E. Trade Center Terrace | Mustang, Oklahoma 73064 USA
1.888.361.9473 | www.tatepublishing.com

Tate Publishing is committed to excellence in the publishing industry. The company reflects the philosophy established by the founders, based on Psalm 68:11,
"The Lord gave the word and great was the company of those who published it."

Published in the United States of America

ISBN: 978-1-61346-706-0
1. Fiction / Christian / Historical
2. Fiction / Christian / Romance
11.10.27

DEDICATION

This book is dedicated, with love, to my husband,
for standing beside me for better and for worse.

PROLOGUE

In the town of Oakdale, two young lovers held each other close. The night brought a cooling breeze that seemed to call, the moonlit clouds to beckon. As the man undid the buttons on the back of the girl's dress, she pulled free and shook her head.

"No...we don't quit doin' dis, we gone go straight to hell."

His lips were on hers again. "Naw, girl...heaven."

In a moment, she stood naked before him in the room; he lowered her eagerly down on the bed. As his breath caressed her warm skin, he set off stirrings within her such as to cause all logic to flee from her mind.

She thought, *He's right...* Loving him filled her with a glorious feeling, unlike anything she'd experienced before. *Like a new heaven and a new earth...*

CHAPTER 1

"When I consider thy heavens, the work of thy fingers, the moon, and the stars which thou hast ordained...what is man?" Psalm 8:3,4

The setting tangerine sun cast a farewell glance toward the sky.

Stell Roberts and Claire Ellis settled into their rocking chairs on the front porch of the small, plain-as-rice farmhouse they shared to gratefully observe the day's end, an event they'd looked forward to all day long.

As the soft sounds and blessed coolness of dusk drew nigh, they indulged their simple vices. Claire, a former schoolteacher, puffed contently on a pipe that had at one time belonged to her late husband, Luke. Stell, an old spinster, had her bottom lip crammed full of snuff.

Just down the wooded lane, at Wesley and Laura Warren's place, a hen squawked. A mule brayed. The pleasant smells of tobacco and woodsmoke and supper cooking were in the air. For a while, there was no spoken exchange between the two elderly women.

Claire reached down beside her chair for a pint jar half full of muscadine wine. She drew a healthy draught from it and then held it out invitingly toward her companion. "Here, have a swig. It'll cure what ails ya."

Not to be unsociable, Stell took the jar and drank without bothering to wipe the rim. Handing it back, she said, "That's a-plenty for me," and closed her eyes, muttering, "that there's stout enough to make a pig squeal."

Stell, who by birthright was self-absorbed, quarrelsome, and outspoken, for the most part considered idle conversation to be a bothersome pastime, having little use for words other than to make her opinions known or to pronounce judgment on those who grated on her nerves. She was habited to speaking her mind militantly with little regard for the feelings of others.

Her mind, known to have begun to wander and forget at times, suddenly remembered. "Dreamed I got bit by a snake last night," she said gruffly.

Claire, with her natural good cheer, philosophized happily in response, "Booger Man's after you."

When Stell didn't open her eyes or comment, Claire reiterated, "That's what old-timers used to say. When you dream about snakes, it means the Booger Man's after you."

Frowning, Stell leaned her rotund little body forward and spat off the porch into a fragrant bed of pink four-o'clocks and grunted. "Horse hockey!" She rocked back, re-shut her eyes, and silently farted.

A moment later, as Claire was reassessing her crudeness for the thousandth time, Stell scoffed, "Don't want me no trouble with the sorry cuss, but the Devil messes with me, sure as you just broke wind, he'll have a mighty fight on his hands!"

Claire snorted. *Foolishness!* The woman was full of it. Three years they'd been acquainted, and not once had she owned up to breaking wind, least not to her recollection. Albeit, while Stell did prove worrisome, over time, Claire had gotten used to her, if such could

be said within the realm of possibility. And so, she kept quiet, seemingly unruffled, letting the comment pass like she didn't even hear it.

Of course now, that was only one side. On the other, given her due, Claire could be just as eloquent in her own requitals when the mood suited her, thusly making her and Stell a perfect match.

Truth be told, it was nothing other than spite—knowing that Stell would be purely disappointed if she didn't say anything back—that now compelled Claire to sit there holding her tongue. She was not about to let the gassy old goat get a rise out of her, would about as soon die as give her the satisfaction.

Taking her thoughts down a livelier path, for a few minutes Claire sought to further amuse herself by conjuring up a more whimsical image of Stell, one absurd, as an angel all gussied up in a halo and wings, plucking on the strings of a harp. Suppressing the urge to laugh out loud, she said, "You know, it's likely the saints won't look kindly on us smokin' an' dippin' up in Heaven."

The music of the day dwindled low, the moon rose to float in a sea of late-June stars. Soothed by the gentle cadence of the rocking chairs, Claire quietly sipped her wine and let herself take in the sounds and smells around her. She looked up. Awe and a feeling of smallness washed through her soul as she inhaled the stillness and majesty of the heavens.

Just when she thought Stell must have dozed off, in a voice barely audible her old friend stated flatly, "Well, if they can't be hospitable, I 'spect I'll cut my stay short."

CHAPTER 2

"Thou maintainest my lot. The lines are fallen unto me in pleasant places; yea, I have a goodly heritage." Psalm 16:5,6

Time, rather than diminishing its appeal with age, lent a certain character to Hiram and Addie Graham's house. The cypress siding was weathered to a shade of misty gray most often captured in winter's early fog, a shade that naturally evoked a sense of peace and quiet.

The passing of time could also be credited for the ancient, sculptured live oak, whose sprawling limbs sheltered the dwelling and, except when barren of its leaves, cast a sun-dappled appearance across most of the yard and porch. Inscribed above the double-door entrance which led into the large front parlor of the house were the words from Psalm 127: *"Except the Lord build the house, they labor in vain that build it."*

In an attitude of comfort, the face of the house was turned to catch the gentle southern winds that moved light and lively across the surrounding meadowlands. It was the pleasantest of places, where a field grew lush with tall, green grass and red clover, a place where wild daisies and larkspur bloomed and delicate blue flowers sat atop slender stalks of flax, intermingled with bee balm and white yarrow.

A picket fence bordered the front of the house, which was located along the winding course of Longview Road in the community of Golden Meadow in the central region of Mississippi, a few miles east of the town of Oakdale. From the corner of the yard, a meandering split-rail fence led past a vegetable garden to the entrance of a woodshop. A stone's throw behind the shop sat a rustic barn constructed of hewn logs.

Cedar Creek flowed through their property, and upstream through the woods was a good-sized swimming hole fed by a trickling artesian spring. The day was oppressively hot, as summer days could be in Mississippi, and the swimming hole was where the woman and boy were headed on this afternoon.

As they walked through an avenue of poplars and beeches, the shaded ground was cool beneath their bare feet. Birds twittered and hopped from tree to tree. A little farther, they came to a place where purple coneflowers bloomed *en mass* alongside the path. Butterflies with gossamer wings fanned the pretty bouquets. Across in the distance, a majestic white oak, a landmark well known, rose like a tower above its surroundings.

They kept to the path and soon heard voices. The boy, whose little hand held tightly onto his mother's, giggled and squealed excitedly, "Papa!"

Addie smiled adoringly at her two-year-old son, Samuel. "I hear Papa too!" she said. The child was named after her beloved late father, Samuel Warren, who, likened to Eli's son Samuel of biblical times, had been a man called of God...*one in favor both with the Lord and also with men.*

As the creek came into view, Addie and Samuel saw them—Emily, Jesse, and Meggie, laughing as they dunked Hiram's head under water. Moments later, he bobbed up, sputtering, feigning defeat, citing unfair disadvantage at being so gravely out-numbered. They relented, exuberant, content in their victory, but just when they forgot him and went back to splashing each other, he suddenly lunged and chased them to the opposite bank, where they climbed, shrieking, to safety onto a diving platform that jutted out over the water.

Seeing Addie and Samuel, Hiram spouted like a whale and floated toward them. Samuel ran across the fine, white sand on short legs and leapt into the security of his father's strong arms, blindly trusting him to protect him from the depth of the creek.

"He woke from his nap asking for his Papa," Addie said.

Hiram grinned and watched with fatherly pride as the young fellow slapped the water. There was no question they were father and son; Samuel was his spitting image.

"Jump in, Mama! Swim with us! Pleeeeeese!" Emily begged.

"Yeah, Mama, jump in," Hiram imitated, pleading with her teasingly.

Though subtle enough for her ears alone, the undertone of his invitation was undeniably suggestive. Addie glanced down at her husband. Water droplets beaded on his wide shoulders and muscular arms and in the dark, matted hair of his chest and beard. His eyes were startlingly blue and crinkled at the corners when he smiled. As her gaze met his, his disarming grin made her recall a day not long ago when the two of them had enjoyed a pleasurable swim here alone. *Most pleasurable indeed...*

Tearing her eyes away from his, her mind wasn't really on what she said to Emily. "Maybe next time, but right now I need to go help your Aunt Laura get ready for tonight...When y'all get home, you help your pa dress your little brother for the party."

In parting, she glanced back down at Hiram, leaving upon his mind an intimate promise. "I'll see *you* directly."

In the kitchen, Laura was extremely busy. She lifted a pan from the oven and deposited it heavily onto the oak table. An enticing aroma filled the air as steam rose from the succulent cured ham, which had been slathered with salt, sugar, and spices back during cold weather when they'd had a hog-killing. The fat rind of the ham sizzled.

"Mmmm…it smells good in here. Tell me what I can do to help," Addie said as she whisked in.

"I could use a tonic for my nerves," Laura replied.

"Well, lucky for you, the doctor will be here soon," Addie asserted cheerfully. Looking around, she asked, "Where is our birthday girl?"

Laura sighed heavily. "You know Sarah Beth; if I had to guess, I'd say she's in her room primpin'." The girl's vanity was renowned. She could sit for hours, contented as a cat licking cream, before a mirror with nothing more than a brush and a comb and a handful of hairpins. "Either that or lyin' across her bed, flippin' through a catalog, wishin' for something off ever' page."

Much to Laura's aggravation, the girl had spent the greater part of the day wandering about the house like a penned heifer in anticipation of her "sweet sixteen" party; however, she hadn't turned a hand to do anything constructive whatsoever in the way of helping her mother with preparations of the event.

After a brief pause, Laura added, "Tonight when she blows out her candles, that girl better be wishin' there's a rich husband hidden away somewhere in her future."

While this made Addie chuckle out loud, all the while she was thinking, *The poor sap better stay in hiding*…To say her neice was spoiled rotten would be a grave understatement.

"Children!" Laura exclaimed. "Who ever can understand them?" Then, "By the way, did you ever talk to Amelia and invite them to come tonight?"

Addie nodded. "This mornin'. Amelia said to give you their regrets; she and Daniel can't make it."

"Oh, I'm sorry to hear that."

Remembering her daughter-in-law's excuse, Addie laughed. "She said Carson's packin' way too much extra lead these days to be turned loose at a party. I will say, that little rascal is a handful, wild as an Indian." Lucky for her, her son Samuel was far less rambunctious than her two-and-a-half-year-old grandson.

Laura smiled. "How well I remember what it's like to run after one his age. Lord knows I've got too old for that." Her and Wesley's youngest, Meggie, had recently turned six.

Two more who seldom attended family gatherings were Laura's lighthearted twin brother, Asher, and his disagreeable wife, Anna. They pretty much kept to themselves. While Asher's absence might be notable, none's presence was more dreaded than Anna's, and she would be forgiven if she decided to stay home.

Their daughter, Libby, was eleven years old, a strange and shy child. From the time she could walk, she would wander off, without a word, alone. Motherhood gave Anna no satisfaction, and she, especially, seemed not to wonder why the girl chose to isolate herself. Having no desire to deal with her, Anna was content to let Libby to do as she pleased, seeing no harm in her solitary wanderings.

Finally thinking of something that Addie could do, Laura said, "When the ham is cool enough, you can slice it for me."

Addie went to a drawer for a knife. "I sure hope Sassie remembers to bring the candles for the cake." Sassie was making Sarah Beth's birthday cake and would be riding out from town with Travis and Abigail for the celebration.

"Speakin' of the doctor, what did Sarah Beth think of Travis's proposal?"

Now that Sarah Beth had finished her schooling, Travis had offered her a job as his assistant in his medical practice. Secretly, Addie found what he'd said about the girl somewhat amusing: "*Sarah Beth has a head full of sense, she just lacks direction.*"

"Oh, as you can imagine, she's on cloud nine." Laura shook her head. "But, as you can also imagine, she's havin' a heck of a time convincin' her father of the idea. Wesley has no problem with her takin' the job, but he's yet to consent to her movin' into town, never you mind that she'd be well chaperoned, livin' with Travis and Abigail. So I guess you could say, at least for the time being, the matter is pending."

Addie understood Wesley's reluctance. Though the circumstances were very different, she remembered how hard it had been for her to accept Daniel's leaving home at fifteen. Too, Addie and Claire initially had their doubts about letting Sassie go so young when she took a job cooking at a restaurant called the Preacher's House and moved into the boarding house in Oakdale. Sassie had always exuded independence, though, and so far the arrangement had turned out well.

Though Sassie wasn't an actual daughter to either Addie or Claire, both would attest that in some instances family had little to do with bloodlines. In this particular instance, the girl's mother, Creenie Boone, had been a cherished friend of theirs. Devastated by her untimely death, there was never any question in their minds as to what to do about Sassie. They took her in, shared guardianship of the girl, and loved her just as they had loved Creenie. It was a decision that raised some eyebrows, since Sassie was part Negro. And, though it wasn't for everyone to know at the time, Claire also taught her to read and write. In any event, the fact that her literacy had been subject to secrecy was a shameful testament to society, in both Addie and Claire's opinions.

Remembering all these things filled Addie with vague yearnings. "My, how quickly time passes; seems like only yesterday Sarah Beth was only Samuel's age." Inwardly, she sighed wistfully, glad that Emily, at thirteen, was still content to put her hair up in pigtails, ride the spinning jenny, and challenge boys to arm-wrestling matches.

Sampling a sliver of the ham, she said, "Need I remind my brother there are two things we give our children? One is roots, the other—wings."

With these words on her tongue, the ham tasted both salty and sweet.

The young folks made a raid on the food and drifted outdoors with their plates to gather around a table underneath an oak illuminated with hanging oil lanterns. Stell and Claire sat in the breezeway with their chairs drawn close, soaking up the activity; Claire's heels hooked over the rung of her rocker, while Stell's rested flat on the floor.

Still full of life well into her sixties, her eyes bright with merriment, Claire observed the party and said dreamily, "Ah, mere sprouts in the springtime of their lives…They're cultivatin' some of their fondest memories right now. Oh, wouldn't it be grand to be that young again—"

Stell shifted irritably in her chair and answered, "No!" She had been an old woman on the day she was born and their youthful energy only made her feel tired. After a pause, she grumbled, "Just watchin' 'em purely wears me out." For her, it was equally gratifying to see company arrive and to see them leave.

Being particularly partial to Addie's sweet potato casserole—a delicious concoction topped with a generous sprinkling of brown sugar, cinnamon, and toasted pecans—for the last hour, Stell had kept vigil over the dish like a bird of prey. She already had her taste buds set on savoring the leftovers at breakfast the next morning. So she watched with regret when Emma Grace Johnson—one of Sarah Beth's silly friends—flounced toward the table eyeing the last helping.

Acting quickly to dissuade her, greed appealed to vanity. "You lookin' to get your money's worth out of that fancy new dress, you best steer clear of them taters. You ain't careful, a'fore the year's out, you'll wake up an' find yourself plumb moon-faced. Mark my words, that girlish figure will slip through your fingers in jig time." To fur-

ther suppress any skepticism, Stell added, "You'll no doubt wonder, but back in the day, I myself was skinny as a hoe handle."

Rolling her eyes disbelievingly, Claire murmured through pursed lips, "A sight, we *all* no doubt wonder."

Not surprisingly, the girl's interest in food promptly waned.

Self-satisfied at having so cleverly saved the casserole for herself, Stell, now unfettered, suddenly felt pressed upon to oblige Claire's catty remark. "Why, I bet time was when even ol' Claire here weren't near so stout—or homely—as she sets before us tonight." Her eyes then wandered to an imaginary speck of lint on her dress, which she picked at while saying, "Pity what unforeseen tragedy can befall the human body…" letting her voice trail off.

This gave rise to righteous indignation. Claire was neither homely nor stout, had never stored an ounce of extra flesh on her body. Furthermore, while she may have come accustomed to Stell's preposterous carryings on and learned to keep her temper with her, she'd duly lie down and die before she let the old gal out-gun her.

Smiling sweetly, to Sarah Beth she said, "Honey, wonder of all wonders, and you can thank the stars for it, is that your granny, dear old soul, has actually *lived* to see another one of your birthdays."

That didn't sit well with Stell. Frowning, she retorted, "Hmph! You're a rusty relic to speak of birthdays!" *Never* would she admit to being almost ten years older than Claire.

Like everyone else in the family, Sarah Beth was used to being caught in the crossfire of the shots, benign as they were, constantly slung between the two old women. Always one to wear her best manners, particularly around her elders, she reached and gave her grandmother's arm a gentle pat.

Demurely, she replied to Claire, "Now Aunt Claire, knowing what a treasure Granny is to us all, *surely* the Lord hasn't a mind to take her from us any time soon." And to Stell, "Granny, I've no doubt you'll live to be a hundred."

The door had been properly cracked open to give Claire occasion to amble on in. Faking endearment, she leaned over and laid her hand on Stell's other arm and quipped, "No need to worry your pretty head over such, Sarah-dear. Sure as the Lord spared Jonah from the belly of the whale, surely he's a mind to spare himself the bellyache of *Granny's* company for a good many years to come. Why, I've no doubt she could quite possibly outlive Abraham." Staring pointedly at Stell's upper lip, she then ended with, "And, if I might add—pity it's not deemed pleasin' for a woman to sport a moustache..." She, in turn, letting *her* voice trail off.

Wilkes Graham, Hiram's younger brother, made a late appearance, arriving to the party at eight-thirty instead of six o'clock. Stopping his horse at a hitching rail, he swung down from the saddle and whipped the reins around a post. Wilkes was very handsome, in a raw-boned way. Impeccably dressed, he tipped his hat to everyone in polite greeting and went directly to the porch, where he spotted Sarah Beth standing, center stage, in a pretty, pink organdy frock.

Presenting her with a bouquet of flowers, he embellished the gesture with a low bow. "Miss Sarah Beth, I offer you my best wishes and am truly honored to be your guest on this special occasion."

"Oh! They're so beautiful! Truly, I feel like a bride!" she gushed, a bit overdramatically, for Sarah Beth certainly had a flair for drama.

The dress she was wearing made obvious the fact that she was no longer a child but a young woman. When Wilkes's eyes finally left her rounding bosom and met her gaze, he said, "And my, don't you look lovely?"

Already an accomplished flirt, she smiled brilliantly. "Why, thank you, kind sir." The entire exchange was like a play.

Whether intentional or not in her timing, just at that moment Stell hawked crudely and spit into her handkerchief, mortifying her granddaughter.

Equally unimpressed with the dramatic display was Sarah Beth's father, Wesley.

Wilkes may have bore a physical resemblance to Hiram, not quite as tall, but any similarity ended there. Wesley knew Hiram to be a good man, and God knew Wesley tried to be. Neither could be said of Wilkes. Wilkes had a tendency to be somewhat arrogant, a bit too proud of himself.

To Wesley's way of thinking, a man should give some thought to his words before he said them, but Wilkes was bold in his talk, liked to brag about things that Wesley didn't care to hear about. By his own admission, the man had a thirst for whiskey, liked to gamble, and was given to whoring. He was an untamed man living an untamed life, and Wesley didn't much like him.

Presently, as Wesley watched his daughter consort so heedlessly with the older man, every hair on the back of his neck stood ready to fight. If only out of respect for Hiram, he struggled for control over his anger, finding enough to restrain him from going over and making an utter ignoramus of himself.

For Sarah Beth's sake, Wilkes pretended not to have noticed Stell's lack of charm. Smiling somewhat sympathetically, he took Sarah Beth's hand and kissed it, making her heart skip a beat. She couldn't help swooning over the man; he made her feel so grown up.

Her smile quickly faded, however, along with the feeling, when her gaze drifted across the yard and met with her father's disapproving glare. For a long moment, his eyes never moved from her face as he made no effort to conceal his displeasure with her, she perfectly aware of the reason why. Caught like a fly in a spider's web, she felt the blood rush to her face, quickly disengaged her hand from Wilkes's, and pretended to fluff out the lace ruffle on the bodice of her dress.

The exchange didn't escape Laura's watchful eyes. From the perturbed look on her husband's face, she knew with absolute clarity that the fat was in the fire. She knew Wesley detested Wilkes,

just like he detested all the boys who vied for his little girl's attention; the same way her father had detested *him* when she was Sarah
Beth's age. She surmised that undoubtedly, sooner or later, he would
knuckle under, get on terms with the ages-old sentiment of fathers
everywhere, and just accept the fact that his little girl was growing
up and becoming a woman.

As Wilkes sauntered over to where the men stood around brag-
ging and smoking, Laura waited until he was just out of earshot and
then strode directly toward Sarah Beth. Irritated with her, she gave
her arm a hard, reprimanding pinch. "What in heaven's name do you
think you're doin'? Do you have no concern at all for your father's
feelings? You must want him to walk the floor all night long with a
headache!"

"*Ouch!*" Sarah Beth winced, rubbing her arm.

"I'll show you ouch, young lady, if you don't stop carryin' on so!
Stop actin' so silly and behave yourself!"

"I'm not silly, Mama. Are you forgetting? I *am* sixteen now."

Laura narrowed her eyes. "Shut up. You are *barely* sixteen, and
believe you me, if you want to live to see seventeen, I suggest you
be more considerate of your reputation and stop battin' those long
lashes at men twice your age!"

Inwardly, Sarah Beth rolled her eyes. *It wouldn't matter if I was
a hundred!* How long must she stand there and endure yet another
dreadful lecture about the importance of having a good reputation?
*I've done nothing wrong! Just because my parents are dull as lard, they
don't want me to have any fun!* She said, "Mama, of all things! I do
wish you wouldn't worry so! Surely you know I wouldn't do anything to disappoint you or Father. Anyway, for pity! Mister Wilkes
is Uncle Hiram's brother; that practically makes the man *family!*"

Laura searched her daughter's face for some sign of sincerity. As
bad as she'd like to believe her, she knew Sarah Beth. She knew her
precious firstborn could quite convincingly sugar her lips when it
behooved her fancy. No, she wouldn't be fooled by her, not for a

minute. For a moment, they stood there unspeaking while Laura subconsciously tapped her foot.

Sarah Beth dared not say anything else, dutifully giving her mother the respect she was entitled to. That, of course, but also more importantly, all this serious talk was spoiling her birthday! She was relieved when Sassie approached the porch for a cup of punch, giving excuse to the tedious argument.

Just as glad to be changing the subject, Laura made a point to say, "Sassie, you really outdid yourself on the cake."

"Thank you, Miz Laura," Sassie replied. "An' jus' in case you'z wonderin', dem lil' black specks in the icing's strawberry seeds, not flies."

Laura smiled at Sassie's rejuvenating honesty and assured her, "Well, strawberries have always been my favorite, seeds and all."

Sarah Beth chimed in, "I loved it, since pink is my very favorite color!"

"And by the way, while I'm thinkin' about it what's this I hear about you havin' a beau, Sassie?" Laura asked. "You should have brought him along tonight. He would be welcome, and I'm sure Travis and Abigail wouldn't have minded him riding out here with y'all."

Sassie's beau was seventeen-year-old Obie Quinn, and a bubble of happiness rose in her just at the mention of him. He and his father, Ezra, farmed and peddled fresh produce; therefore, Obie came by the Preacher's House regularly, making deliveries, which was how they met.

She quickly explained, "At first, Obie say he wuz comin', but today he chicken out. He sorta shy-like an' didn't want ever'body starin' at him on account o' him bein' the only colored person here."

If they themselves even noticed, neither Laura nor Sarah Beth gave thought to the inadvertent disassociation that Sassie, even though mixed, was generally considered to be colored. Laura replied, "Well, we'll look forward to meetin' Obie some other time, then."

Sassie suddenly became conscious of Addie staring at her from the end of the porch. In that moment, she felt some of her happiness evaporate as she remembered the night before. Feeling guilty and uncomfortable, she looked away from Addie's eyes, afraid she might somehow be able to read her private thoughts and know what she had been doing.

Ten-year-old Jesse and another boy his age, Wiley Parker, were seated at a trestle table, wolfing down their third pieces of cake. The two had just come in from sneaking a smoke of rabbit tobacco in their corncob pipes. Jesse cast a quick glance at Sassie, trying to be inconspicuous in his ogling of her. The way she was looking at him with those big, green, exotic eyes…it was enough to make his toes curl.

Jesse was completely enamored with Sassie. In his young mind, she was a total mystery. When she first came to live amongst them he'd quickly decided she was the prettiest girl he'd ever seen and fell desperately in love with her, the way boys his age fall desperately in love with pretty, older girls.

However, instinctively, he knew beyond question he best never let on to another living soul how he felt. He was white, she was not, and based on that simple fact alone, he knew folks would most likely disapprove if they knew what was in his heart. For him to love her was, without question, taboo.

While Jesse fancied himself to be Sassie's prince, he would have been crestfallen to read her ordinary thoughts of him. She saw him stealing glances at her and thought it was sweet how he avoided looking at her directly and how he always got all red in the face when she spoke to him, like he'd been caught naked or something. She smiled at the young boys and said, "Hey, Jesse. Hey, Wiley. How've y'all bin?"

They blushed crimson and sort of mumbled a response, oblivious to the cake crumbs and icing spread across their chins.

A minute later, out underneath the oak, a quartet of young troubadours burst into a rollicking serenade in honor of the birthday girl. Delighted afresh, Sarah Beth tossed the bouquet of flowers Wilkes had given her into the nearest empty chair, any sentiment for their beauty henceforth withered. Grabbing Sassie's arm and pulling her down the steps, the two sashayed off together to enjoy the singing and mingle with her guests.

As Claire continued to watch the scene sprightly from the porch, just when she thought Stell was dead to the world, she scraped her chair back and rose abruptly, saying, "I'm fixin' to go home before the confounded ma'skeeters tote me off!"

Shortly after Travis and Abigail's arrival, Abigail and Addie had excused themselves from the crowd and slipped onto the quieter end of the porch, where they sat down upon a bent-willow settee. It was a warm, gentle night with the heady fragrance of a nearby jasmine vine perfuming the air. As they watched the girls cross the yard, Addie couldn't help but notice that something seemed different about Sassie. The girl seemed to have blossomed since the last time she'd seen her. But hadn't that been just a week ago? Good gracious! She was like a bud that had verily overnight become a flower...

Abigail broke into Addie's thoughts. In a lowered voice, she said, "I know Wilkes is your brother-in-law, and maybe I shouldn't say it, but that man gives me the creeps."

Abigail saw through Wilkes; she saw him for the scamp he was. And, she had seen exactly what he had done. Of course, Sarah Beth was too naïve to realize it, but his overstated flattery of her was simply his way of mocking the poor girl.

Having suffered through a long and regrettable dance with her first no-good husband, if anything, Abigail had learned the hard way how to spot a worthless libertine. Indeed, Wilkes was handsome and polite, but how well she knew dashing looks and genteel manners could be deceiving, merely sheep's clothing. It was her gut feeling—something in his demeanor convinced her of it—underneath that appealing hide of his lurked a whole other sort of animal.

Beside her, Addie had grown still, making Abigail wonder if perhaps she'd gone too far or presumed too much. "I'm sorry. Sometimes I talk too much," she apologized.

Addie shook her head in a way of excusing her friend. She held her own opinion of Wilkes, but like Abigail said, he *was* Hiram's brother. She gave nothing else away except, "I do have to admit, Hiram and Wilkes are different as night and day."...*Cain and Abel...Jacob and Esau...*

When Wilkes joined the circle of men, Wesley acknowledged him—just. If he had been anybody other than Hiram's brother, Wesley would not have been willing to stand on the same piece of dirt with him.

"Me an' Addie 'bout decided you'd lit a shuck an' headed back t'ward Virginia," Hiram addressed his brother. Since coming to Mississippi four weeks before to visit, Wilkes had been staying in the stranger-room on their back porch. The previous night he hadn't come home.

Wilkes shook his head. "Not to be overindulgent of your fine hospitality, I decided to stay in town last night."

Taking the cigar Travis offered but declining a light, Wilkes stashed it in his vest pocket and said, "Obliged...I believe I'll just hold on to this 'til later."

"Hiram tells me you're a tobacco-grower yourself." Travis drew deeply on his cigar and exhaled a big billow of smoke.

Wilkes nodded his head. "After our daddy passed on, me an' a feller formed a partnership, went in on halves. We spent most of the first year colterin' the fields and raisin' a curin' barn. I ain't got rich yet, but meritin' our rich Virginia soil and favorable climate, we

made our investment back with the second harvest. But I won't lie to you, my friend. Growin' tobacco ain't a pastime for the lazy."

Tobacco farming had proved to be a shade more laborious than Wilkes had originally anticpated, but that aside, the profits they reaped had far exceeded that of any other crop per acre, say corn, for instance.

"What time of year do you plant? When do you harvest?" Travis asked.

Wilkes explained, "Sow the seeds in late winter, transplant the seedlings to the field in the spring; harvest begins in August and usually ends some'ers 'round the second week of October."

Never having taken much of an interest in farming but always having taken pause for a fine cigar, Travis listened intently, impressed by the man's broad knowledge on the subject. When Wilkes stopped talking, Travis cocked his head back and blew smoke from his nose. "By God," he said. Now he knew.

After that, for several minutes the men discussed the building of a new general store in Oakdale. Finally, Wilkes excused himself, saying, "Gentlemen, I hate to leave such good company, but my presence has been requested at another party tonight, so I best get goin' and not keep the lady waitin'."

After Wilkes had taken his leave, Travis couldn't wait to tell what he knew. "Hiram, your brother didn't bother with the particulars about *why* he decided to stay in town last night, but I happen to know for a fact that he was locked up in jail."

Hiram appeared unfazed; the news triggered no particular outward reaction or regard from him, and inwardly, not even an inclination to inquire of the matter further. As far back as when they were growing up in Virginia, his ways and his brother's ways had been strange to each other. Hiram was easygoing, fair-minded, and sensible; Wilkes was bad-tempered, resentful, and a bully. Their differences had isolated them from ever becoming close.

Most significantly, when he was twenty-seven years old Hiram reached a pivotal point in his life and chose to follow the risen Christ and had since walked in the Lord. Wilkes, on the other hand, had never paid much attention to anything the Lord had to say. He'd always struck out down a sinful path, and to this very hour seemed idly inclined to overcome the roughness of his youth. All Hiram could come up with to say was, "Wilkes always has been rebellious as a patch of sawbriars. He no doubt earned his stay."

Travis, however, didn't let Hiram's disinterest stop him from elaborating. "Him an' Roscoe Hailes got three sheets in the wind an' was feelin' their oats—least they was 'til they got the sorry notion to play poker."

Travis shook his head. "A stone-blind fool could see that was a poor idea."

The tale continued. "That's when thangs took a bitter turn south. From my understandin', Wilkes caught Roscoe cheatin' an' gave him a pretty fair beatin'. Then, when ol' Sheriff Wiggington stepped in an' tried to break it up, Wilkes, that crazy scamp, commenced to swing at him! End of it all, Sheriff trussed 'em up like turkeys an' hauled 'em in for drunk an' disorderly."

After considering it for another minute, with a shake of his head, Travis said, "By God, I envy them boys!"

CHAPTER 3

"But every man is tempted, when he is drawn away of his own lust, and enticed." James 1: 14

Enshrouded by the night, crossing the yard from the house, the woman hastened across the dew-dampened grass and entered the dark, cavernous barn. Inside, it smelled like hay, sorghum, and manure. Tiny slits of moonlight streamed through a couple of narrow cracks in the roof high above her head. From the towering rafters came a soft, rustling sound. *Roosting swallows, most likely*, she thought. *Or perhaps bats*. She shuddered as a slight tingle of both fear and anticipation ran through her. As she crept past the sagging door of the corncrib, a furry rat brushed her ankle as it scurried away.

All of a sudden, a strong arm struck out from the darkness and grabbed her roughly. At first startled, she gasped. But when the man pulled her savagely against his steel frame, she let out a small, welcoming cry of recognition.

Wilkes put his lips to her ear and murmured huskily, "I'd 'bout decided you weren't comin'."

She shivered at the closeness of him and whispered, "I had to be sure they were asleep." A tiny dart of guilt shot through her mind. She knew she shouldn't be there.

His breath was hot against her skin as he nuzzled the curve of her neck familiarly, making her tremble with delight. "I've been waitin' all day to get my hands on you," he said, his nimble fingers toying with the ribbons of her nightgown.

Feeling somewhat vexed, she drew back slightly and said, "Wait...let's talk a minute...there's something I need to—"

Wilkes was in no mood for conversation. Smothering the words, his mouth claimed possession of hers in a deep kiss. Pushing the gown off her shoulder, his experienced caresses grew more insistent, sending a delicious thrill through her body.

Stop, this is wrong! Beset with inner conflict, she knew they shouldn't be doing this. It *was* wrong. She hardly knew this man. Where was her self-respect? And what if someone were to wake up and find her gone?

Soon the pestering thoughts were vague and far away. What he was doing felt so wonderful; she had never been this happy, desperately in love for the first time in her life. And Wilkes loved her. She was assured of it.

He loves me, and everything is going to be fine...

A sweet wildness filled her senses, her doubts faded, all logic was numbed. She thought, *I'll remember this night forever...my heart belongs to him now...* Pinned beneath his weight upon a bed of hay, she was once again sucked down into the treacherous depths of lust from which she had no will to escape.

It was approaching midnight when Wilkes rose abruptly and began putting on his clothes; his features had grown set and solemn.

With her thoughts and remembrance on the hour passed, softly breaking the tense quiet, the woman pleaded shakily, "Promise to meet me again before you leave?" There was desperation in her voice, not what she wanted him to hear. She wished they hadn't argued. She'd only meant to speak her heart to him, never meant to sound so accusing. After all, she was hardly in a position to accuse him of anything.

Perturbed but trying not to sound so, he replied, "I'm sorry, but I can't. Like we discussed, I'll be settin' out come sunrise Monday mornin'." Not only were there pressing matters for him to tend to, it was no longer worth the risk. For him, the fire of their passion had passed. The time had come for him to move on, home to Virginia.

By the light of the moon, he saw her hand reach out toward him. What she extended as an apologetic gesture, he interpreted as weakness. He took her face in his hands and kissed her convincingly, falsely, managing to shade his contempt for her, and his mistake in judgment. Sickened by both, he left the barn and disappeared into the shadows without so much as a backward glance.

In the fleeting embrace of the warm summer night, overcome by a miserable wave of despair and longing, the woman wondered wildly how she would bear being separated from him. In nights to come, would he ever lie awake and pine for her?

Twisting the gold band on her finger, wishing for impossible things, she fought to hold back her tears and her doubt.

Hiram woke abruptly. A looming silence filled the house, a quietness that held such presence it seemed to accompany him as well. He reached out and ran his hand over the sheet where Addie had lain. It was slightly crumpled and cool to his touch. Hit with a sudden twinge of uncertainty, he wondered, *Where is she?* How long had passed since she got up?

The ticking of the small clock on the bedside table seemed unnaturally loud. As his eyes adjusted to the dark, he stared at the ceiling beam above his head; then he turned over toward the window and waited, listening for the sound of her return.

As the minutes ticked by, try as he might, he couldn't stop his mind from turning back to another such time. Years ago, he'd lain wakeful and tossed upon his bed, listening for his late wife Madeline to return, and knowing that even when she returned, she would still be gone from him, her heart estranged from his. And knowing who she was with had only made his pain deeper; Wilkes—his own brother—had transgressed against him, committed an act with his wife, a betrayal that wrung his heart to this day. Hiram's unleashed thoughts ran loose in the quiet darkness, causing doubt.

After what seemed like an eternity, he heard the sound of Addie's footsteps padding down the wide-planked oak floor of the hall; she entered the room quietly. Hiram lay still as she slipped into their massive, four-poster bed and drew the coverlet over herself, as if taking care not to wake him.

A few minutes later, in a drowsy state, she moved toward the middle of the bed; he rolled over and drew her close. Addie sighed contently. Cocooned in the warmth of her husband's strong embrace, she fell fast asleep with her cheek against his shoulder.

Taking great pleasure in the feel of her body against his, Hiram pressed his lips to her head in a gentle kiss and breathed in the sweet scent of her hair. Her lips were slightly parted; her chest rose and fell softly with her breathing. In the glow of the moonlight, his eyes traced her countenance. He saw her beautiful and innocent. His heart caught, so strong was his love for her.

Addie, my beloved, Addie...

Reminded of the love they shared, regret stirred within him. Hiram was sorry for any doubt he'd entertained, sorry for hesitating, however so slightly, and allowing his trust in her to falter even for an instant. He knew he could trust Addie with his whole heart and soul, and he did. It was Wilkes he didn't trust.

Hiram hadn't realized it until then, but Wilkes's being there had brought up some ugly memories, memories he'd let play on his mind and temporarily overcome his common sense. He knew there

was no comparison between Addie and Madeline. His marriage to Madeline was a whole other life ago; it had been his mistake in choosing her for a wife. The foundation of their relationship had been laid upon the shaky ground of youthful lusts. Having learned a painful lesson, next time he'd put his trust in God and let Him do the choosing. And God chose Addie. Addie was Hiram's true love, his lifemate. They two had made a covenant before the Lord.

Addie would never do what Madeline had done, would never hurt him the way she had. Hiram knew Addie's heart belonged to him; she made him happy, as he did her. They were devoted to each other, totally, wholly.

Understandably, Hiram knew that when a man married, he was bound to discover some traits about his wife that were impossible to predict beforehand. Of intimate matters, whereas he'd held no expectations that Addie would be cold to his physical advances, still he was not prepared at all for the passion waiting to be unbridled on the night of their wedding when she blew out the candles and joined him in bed. Even now, with the passage of time, their desire for each other had not begun to dwindle. If anything, it continued to mount. Sometimes it was like they couldn't get enough of each other, as though they must somehow make up for the hard and lonely years of their prior marriages.

Addie snuggled herself deeper into his embrace. Hiram smiled. Letting all uncertainty flee from his mind and vanish into the night, he finally drifted off to sleep. Sometime after midnight, he woke again, to the sound of Wilkes sneaking in, his booted footfall coming up the steps and crossing the back porch to his room.

Wilkes Graham had discovered at an early age that comely women were abundant. Drawn away of his own lusts, a drinker and a scoundrel, he could however credibly play the role of a gentleman when it so suited him. Chivalry and cavalier manners matched up with his ruggedly handsome face created a façade that most women found irresistible, thus putting him at an advantage when seeking female companionship for pleasurable sport.

Yet, for all improbability and awkward circumstance, this latest dalliance had come to him completely unsolicited, had seemingly fallen from the sky and landed in his lap, like manna from Heaven. Whether that prudish act of hers really fooled everyone or whether they were just all too ignorant to see it, he didn't know. He himself, however, knew an apple from an onion, and he'd known the very moment they were introduced, she was no onion. It had required no words. It was simply in the way she'd looked at him, open, lingering, with eyes that assessed, accepted, inquired. Something in her smile affirmed that she knew he understood, and that his answer was yes.

Since making her acquaintance a month ago, they'd rendez-voused secretly on several occasions and, to say it mildly, with morals not exactly lady-like, she had indeed proved to be an entertaining diversion in this otherwise dull and forsaken place. Even the town here exemplified boredom, he swore, host to but one tamely accommodating saloon! One day last week, his mind was so idle just to have something to do, he went out and set half a dozen traps along the creekbank to see what varmints they might yield, even set out a trot line in hopes of hooking a catfish. Of course he'd since lacked any ambition strong enough to go back and check them.

Presently, Wilkes lay back on the bed. Feeling tense, he stretched his arms and legs, trying to relax. Once comfortable, with an equal share of disdain and amusement, he replayed the last couple of hours in his mind.

He'd run up on somewhat of a problem, so it appeared.

What he'd at first taken to be a few mutually gratuitous romps in the hay had now, all of a sudden, turned a bit prickly. Now that the deed was done, it seemed his lover was trying to grow a conscience. Apparently he'd been so enthralled with her charms he'd failed to realize that those soft, silken limbs of hers were simply part of a clever disguise, one that quite effectively managed to keep her whiny possessiveness hidden, at least until now.

Could it be he'd run up on his female nemesis?

In the confines of his room, now studying the view from a whole new and clearer perspective, Wilkes silently mocked her, crudely and cruelly. What did he care that she was so naïve she'd actually believed he loved her? He smirked in the darkness. Cold and unfeeling, he wondered, *How dumb could one girl be?* What they had was pure, un-adulterated lust. A tryst. Nothing more, nothing less. And, it wasn't like he'd forced her to participate. The little wench had come to him; she had let her hair down and rucked up her skirts willingly. No, she was sorely mistaken if she'd thought even for a minute that he had any intention of ever settling down and getting married. She best get happy and stay with the husband she had.

Mentally, Wilkes shrugged. Ah, well…he had already begun to tire of her anyway; he'd maintained an attitude of gallantry just about as long as he could. Yes sir, he'd had his fill of manna. Come first light Monday morning, he'd be leaving here, thankful to be shed of the whole affair.

In his mind he jiggered a plan, thinking how good it would be to see Virginia again, far away from all these dipped Baptists and the rancid stench of redemption they threw off. Back to his tobacco farm, back to his drinking, and back to his familiar, undemanding whores.

The plaintive sound of a mourning dove echoed across the serene stillness of the meadow as fog settled over the waking day.

While Hiram went to milk the cow and see to the horses, Addie got a fire going in the stove, fixed the coffee, and put on a pot of grits. While the grits bubbled and the coffee brewed, she took a basket from the back porch and rushed out to the henhouse to gather the eggs, the ground beneath her feet an etching of feathery tracks left behind by the guineas and chickens.

Sunday mornings were always hectic. Hurrying back across the yard with the eggs, she started up the steps to the porch. Not expecting to see anyone, at first she didn't give particular notice to the stranger-room door standing ajar.

Suddenly, Wilkes appeared out of the shadow of the room. With his shoulder leaning against the doorjamb, he stood relaxed, rubbing the stubble of his beard. A half gasp escaped Addie and the smile disappeared from her lips as she stared in astonishment at his tall frame filling the doorway. For a brief, embarrassing moment, their eyes met. Shamed to the bone, Addie quickly averted hers, the sudden and unexpected sight of his nakedness leaving her speechless. She felt her face flame with humiliation as she focused her gaze on a nearby trellis, where a hummingbird whirled about, sipping daintily from the flowers of a trumpet vine.

Wilkes, however, seemed completely at ease and made no attempt to retreat. A long minute went by as he let his eyes roam over his brother's wife slowly and appraisingly.

It was then that Addie came to an incredulous realization. What she at first took to be an untimely chance encounter had, in fact, been guilefully staged. *Pure and simple exhibitionism!* Under the weight of his impudent gaze, Addie felt exposed, naked. Automatically, she reached to pull the bodice of her dress together, only to discover herself fully covered. His odious manner was revolting and unnerved her terribly, yet she found it difficult to turn away; her feet were affixed to the floor of the porch. An intense sense of loathing for him took seed within her. Had he no respect whatsoever, no decency?

Wilkes chuckled with amusement when Addie presented her back to him and moved with determination toward the entrance to the kitchen. As she reached for the door handle, in a bantering tone he taunted, "Ain't you even gonna say good mornin', pet?"

She hesitated but for a moment. Over her shoulder, she replied indignantly, "I'll be waking the children for breakfast. I'd be much obliged if you'd clothe yourself before joining us."

She went on into the house. Setting the eggs down on the table, she collapsed onto the nearest chair. Her heart was beating wildly. She took a deep breath and roughly brushed away the hot tears from her cheeks. With the image of his naked body branded across her mind, she felt repulsed, violated. Looking down at her trembling hands, she rebuked herself for allowing him to intimidate her so.

As she sat still and turned it over in her mind, she considered Emily and thought, *Who knows what a man like that might do?* But she didn't have to search long for an answer to that. She already knew. Oh, how well she knew! *Alfred!* The night before, at Sarah Beth's party, she'd almost confessed to Abigail that Wilkes reminded her in some ways of him. Being married to Alfred had proved to be Addie's greatest trial; because of him, she had suffered great agony. She shuddered as she remembered how she'd discovered Alfred watching Emily bathe when she was but eleven years old. *His own little girl! How could a man sink so low?*

Alfred had been a monster, an evil monster who had left his mark firmly imprinted upon them all, especially Addie, Daniel, and Amelia, even Travis. He committed horrific acts of depravity that rent the very fabric of their souls, unthinkable atrocities not easily imagined by those of sound mind. Addie had done everything she could to be a good wife to him, and he'd paid her back by murdering her mother, killing her unborn son, raping Creenie Boone, and raping Amelia. Only God knew what else.

Almost three years. Though sometimes it seemed like yesterday. Then again, sometimes it seemed like a lifetime ago. It had been almost three years since Alfred had come back from being presumed dead to terrorize them; luckily, Travis had happened up at the opportune time and saved them. Faced with no other choice, he'd shot and killed Alfred.

If not for the grace of God, Addie thought. Even when all hope had seemed lost and her faith was faltering, God had been there with her, had helped her endure her most agonizing struggles, struggles that consequently led her on a spiritual pilgrimage, one that strengthened her and eventually led her to a deeper trust in Him.

Right now, though, as for Wilkes, he had been visiting for a month and had, as far as Addie was concerned, long since exhausted his welcome. She had a bate of his erratic comings and goings at all hours of the day and night. Some days it was all she could do not to say something about his thoughtless disregard of their meal times and the children's bedtimes.

She couldn't relax in her own house; she was growing grumpy and longed to recapture some similitude of their customary routine. And now this! She couldn't even cross her own backyard and go to the henhouse without the dread of seeing the naked idiot perched on her porch steps like some pandering peacock! Yes, it was time for Wilkes to go home. If he stayed much longer, she was going to have to leave herself!

Lord, you see what's set before me; calm me and give me wisdom.

Contemplating the situation, she thought, *Given Hiram's past troubles with Wilkes, disclosing such a thing as this to him would only serve to churn up old hurts…most likely set Hiram against his brother afresh, cause him to dismiss from his heart any feelings of kinship he still holds for him. It's doubtful he would be so gracious as to forgive him of such unscrupulous behavior yet again.* Addie tapped her fingertips together lightly. *Wilkes might never be able to right himself in Hiram's eyes.* Of course, it was hard to believe he cared at all for Hiram. *Still, this mustn't come to pass on my account.* She looked through the window. Hiram's feelings were all that mattered to her.

All things considered, Addie decided it would be impractical to say anything to Hiram about what transpired. *This is between me and Wilkes.* Anyway, what was there to tell? That Wilkes was crazy?

It was then that she heard the sound of Samuel running down the hall toward the kitchen. Determined not to let Wilkes cloud the splendor of this Sabbath morning that otherwise promised fair, she rose from her chair and went to the stove to finish breakfast.

CHAPTER 4

"Hatred stirreth up strifes..." Proverbs 10:12

That morning after the service at Mt. Zion Baptist Church, the Negro church where Obie had attended all his life, he drove Sassie, with his thirteen-year-old sister Etta tagging along, back to the Quinn residence for Sunday dinner.

Obie had never brought a girl home before, so when they pulled up to the house the menfolk standing around in the yard looked Sassie over curiously, and were met unexpectedly by what they saw.

Sassie was willowy, in a way, and young yet to be considered a woman. Her long brown hair was pulled back from her face and spilled down her back in a tangle of loose curls. Straight nose, clear green eyes, cream-colored skin that blushed like a ripening peach, she had no idea how radiant she looked as she stood there smiling at them while Obie nervously made the introductions.

He gave a couple of the younger boys a threatening look to quit their snickering, they jabbing each other in the ribs with their bony elbows. His father, Ezra, with whom Sassie was already somewhat acquainted from having seen him a few times delivering produce to the restaurant, bid her polite welcome.

After the exchange of general courtesies, Etta dragged Sassie inside the house to meet everyone else. The screen door creaked as they entered.

Pulling Sassie into the kitchen where the women were set about preparing the meal, Etta announced loudly, "Ever'body, dis iz Sassie Boone!"

Naturally, they all stopped what they were doing and stared at her intently as Etta started around the room introducing them to each other. Sassie hadn't expected to be so nervous, but she was. She was glad she'd taken special pains, starching and ironing her dress the night before.

Finally Etta concluded with, "An' dis iz Daddy's sista, Auntie Beulah, an' behin' her iz our mama, Miz Rosette Quinn."

It was Auntie Beulah, *not* Rosette Quinn, who stepped forward and, beaming at her generously, grabbed Sassie by the hand. "We'z so mighty glad to have you, dear."

"Thank you. It's nice to meet y'all." Sassie looked around. "Miz Quinn, you sho' do have a pretty house," she praised respectfully. Everything was orderly and polished, the windows so clean they looked like they didn't have panes in them.

Rosette nodded curtly but didn't say anything. She turned back to the stove and lifted the lid off a skillet of chicken, and steam rose.

Sassie wondered if it was just her imagination or if Miz Quinn's jaws stayed clamped shut like that all the time. And did she always look so stern? Encouraged by the friendliness of everyone else, though, rather than let her mind leap ahead to an unfair assumption, she made an effort to push her anxiety aside and tried not to let it bother her too much that the woman hadn't uttered the first word to her.

"It sho' smells good in here." At home in a kitchen, Sassie reached for an apron and pitched in to help.

As they cooked, Sassie couldn't help but notice how bossy Miz Quinn acted, like she was used to giving orders. A couple of times, Sassie started to tell her that she wasn't just now learning how to cook, but she held her tongue, not wanting to sound like she was arguing with her, certainly not wanting to get off on the wrong foot.

When dinner was done and spread out on the table, another cousin, Leata, went to the door and hollered to the men, "Ever'thang's on da table. Auntie Rosette say y'all come an' git it while da biscuits be hot!"

Sassie was standing at the sideboard pouring tea when Rosette marched militantly from the kitchen, carrying a platter piled high with the biscuits and cornbread. She looked at Sassie like she was accusing her of something, or at least that's how she made Sassie feel.

Rude in her youthful exuberance, Etta grabbed Sassie's arm and pushed her into a chair and plopped down into the one beside her. "You can sit by me," she said. Obie sat down directly across from her.

Grace was said, food was passed, and plates were filled. As they ate, the talk around the table flowed smoothly, meandering from the sermon they'd heard at church that morning and speculation over the coming week's weather to every last one of Auntie Beulah's complaints and aliments. However, the one person Sassie wanted to please the most acted barely civil toward her, far from hospitable. *Miz Quinn ain't nothin' like I expected,* she thought. What she'd expected, or rather hoped for, was to have been welcomed in with opened arms. Inwardly, she frowned. *Maybe I jus' expected too much, my first time here an' all…*

She said, "Miz Quinn, I never tasted such food in all my life. Ever'thang sho' is delicious." The buttermilk mashed potatoes topped with chopped green onions were especially good, quite possibly the creamiest potatoes she'd ever eaten, and she said so.

Praise for the meal resounded heartily around the table, to which Rosette gave a collective response but ignored Sassie's compliment.

Slighted again! Sassie felt the blood rush to her face. She couldn't figure it out. Was this Miz Quinn's way of testing her in front of everybody, or was she just flat-out snubbing her for some reason? By then, she was starting to feel a little bit touchy over the way she was being treated.

For a moment she stared down at her plate, struggling with her wounded feelings. When Obie tapped her foot with his under the table, she glanced up at him, grateful for his reassuring smile. She picked up her fork and half-heartedly began eating again. As she chewed silently, her mind wandered. What on earth? Had she said or done something to offend the woman? She couldn't imagine what. One thing she did know for certain—unless she was looking to further upset the applecart, it was better not say what she felt like saying right about now.

Auntie Beulah recaptured her attention. "Sassie dear, Etta tells us you's a cook at da Preacher's House in town."

Doing her best to veil her disappointment, Sassie managed a smile. "Yes'm."

"Why, you seem too young to have such a job."

"No'm, not really. I been cookin' all my life. My auntie wuz a cook…I learned from her." She helped herself to a sweet pickle, stabbing into the jar with a fork.

Etta crowed, "An' Sassie live dare too! At da Preacher's House!" She found it novel that someone so near to her own age lived all alone, and in a boardinghouse, no less.

With this information, in a tone of genuine concern, Auntie Beulah pressed further. "Have you no fam'ly, chile?"

Sassie took a sip of her sweet tea and nodded. "Oh, yes'm, I has a family." After the smallest pause, she explained. "When Mama died four years ago, some of her friends took me in. We's ain't blood kin, but we's close as any family I ever seen." In that they *cared* for each other.

RAMONA BRIDGES

After giving Sassie a pitying look, Beulah looked down the table toward Rosette and commented, "Why, you an' dis girl already have sum'thin' in common …all her peoples be dead too."

Rosette coughed disapprovingly. She knew the *family* Sassie spoke of was Claire Ellis and Addie Graham. *White folk.* Fixing Sassie with a snide look, she said, "So, I'z correct in assumin' den, yo' mama wuz white."

Hers was an expression one might wear upon discovering a wad of chicken manure smeared on the bottom of their shoe. And, had she been looking at Ezra, she would have seen that her husband was looking at her similarly, only with a mixture of humiliation and admonition added in—the way he looked sometimes when his bull-headed wife's deep-seated prejudice of white people reared its ugly head. Sassie saw this look and immediately sensed there was discord between them.

A dead hush fell around the table; Rosette's assumption was left hanging in the air. Sassie did not at first grasp the essence of what she said. Though she felt like all eyes were upon her, as she glanced around the table she saw that all eyes were in fact lowered. Not one person was looking at her. *Why?* It was like they were waiting for time to pass or waiting for something apocalyptic to happen.

As her thoughts tossed about, she looked around the table again at all their faces. Only this time, she actually *saw* their faces. That's when it finally dawned on her!

Sassie's cheek smarted like she'd been slapped; a shiver ran down her spine as the cold reality of it invaded her consciousness. She thought, *Why, here I sets—one li'l white dove in da midst of a whole covey of blackbirds…*

All her life Sassie had considered herself to be a Negro, was proud that her mama's blood ran through her veins. Regardless of this fact, though, she also knew she could almost pass as white. Yet still, in her heart of hearts, she *was* a Negro. *But I look white.* Now, seeing herself through Miz Quinn's eyes, and at the same time through the eyes of folks like Anna Bradley, the sad irony of what she glimpsed sawed at her nerves.

Obie slowly raised his eyes and looked at her, like a little boy with hurt feelings. His face bore apologetic and ashamed as the hardness in his mama's heart lay exposed before them; in particular, before the one he loved.

For Sassie, it was an epiphany. In that one moment, she learned two things: one, she loved Obie too much not to rescue him from passing on his mama's hate to another generation, and secondly, she was in for a fight. In the next moment, somewhere outside, a rooster commenced to crow shrilly. Upon hearing it, Sassie couldn't help thinking, *The battle cry.*

An embarrassed Auntie Beulah hastily went about trying to reset the course of things by asking, "Any yaw want mo' ham or some o' deez greens? Or iz we ready fo' sum'thin' sweet? Sassie...?"

"No, thank you, ma'am."

Emboldened by this flash of insight and fired with a new purpose, Sassie's young will rose within her. She straightened up in her chair and squared her shoulders. *Well, Miz Thang, so it's like that, is it?* She'd been brought up to show respect to old folks, but she hadn't ever run up on another black person like Rosette Quinn before.

Good manners blazed away, resentment rising from the ashes, Sassie was mad. Black, white, red, or purple, no human being should be made to feel inferior because of the ignorance of another. She raised her chin and leveled her gaze at Rosette, and this time what she was feeling just came right on out; she didn't even try to stop it.

"No, ma'am, Miz Quinn. My mama wuzn't white, she wuz black as you, only she jus' black on da outside...From what I sees, *you* iz black through an' through!"

❧

When Obie pulled onto Sparrow Street, Sassie jumped down from the wagon before the wheels creaked to a stop. "Sassie..." he pleaded.

47

Stomping off up the sidewalk, she hollered back over her shoulder with a warning. "Leave, Obie Quinn, befo' I kill you!"

Helpless to do otherwise and used to taking orders, Obie did as directed.

Sassie stormed up the stairs to her room. She snatched off her hat, and it went sailing. Stripping off her starched and ironed Sunday frock, she let it drop to the floor; she gave it a disgruntled kick. She then proceeded to fight her way into a simple, frill-free calico shift.

Wishing to forget the earlier events of the day, particularly the words she'd said to Rosette Quinn at the dinner table—even though she had been severely snubbed by her—Sassie couldn't stay inside. Minutes after changing her clothes she was venturing through the quarter along a narrow, dirt street lined with tenant shacks. Sassie loved to wander through this part of town. She, in fact, felt drawn here, maybe because it reminded her of the community where she grew up, in Collinsville.

On this fine, hot, summer day folks congregated in the shady retreats of their yards and porch swings, marking the passage of time at a whittler's pace, their lives growing fuller and sweeter as they shared and partook of the simple yet rich fare of time spent with family and friends. Sassie felt a profound envy for these people. A certain twinge of resentment went through her as she wondered if they even recognized and counted themselves blessed for the feast spread out before them.

The atmosphere was alive with the noises of children, fiddle-playing, booming laughter, clapping, and singing. The enticing aromas of barbeque and coffee wafted through the air. Taking in the scene surrounding her—hearing and smelling and feeling it all—brought a melancholy longing down upon her, making Sassie suddenly and acutely aware of the hunger that gnawed at her insides. Her craving, however, had nothing to do with food.

Ever since her mama had died, maybe even before, just as the Israelites had wandered through the desert in relentless search of the

Promised Land, Sassie herself had been uprooted from her home and sent out on a pilgrimage. All this time she had been searching, homesick for a place she hadn't belonged to in a long while, a place familiar to her heart, one that nurtured the soul. To be part of *this*, happening all around her, was what she was hungry for, what she longed for.

She thought, *An' if it wuzn't fo' Obie's mean-ol'-banny-hen of a mama…*

All of a sudden, Sassie stopped dead in her tracks.

Out of nowhere a huge yellow dog appeared and blocked her path. Caught off guard, she stood frozen as the mongrel bared its teeth and growled at her menacingly. Trying not to panic, without making any sudden moves, she backed away cautiously, her heart hammering in her throat. The dog slunk toward her slowly, snarling, crouched low to the ground, in position to attack.

Scared out of her wits, Sassie could almost feel its teeth sinking into her flesh as her back pressed against a rusty iron fence in front of a wall of overgrown privet hedge. There was nowhere for her to go. She stood petrified, not even breathing. Fear stirred in her stomach like a hive of angry bees, making her feel nauseous.

In the next instant, she heard a dull *thud* followed by a surprised yelp as the cur was struck between the eyes with a hard chunk of clay. Much to her relief, it quickly whirled around and scampered away with its tail between its haunches, retreating into an alley, howling pitifully.

Sassie let out a trembling sigh of relief. When she turned her eyes to see who had hurled the clod and saved her from being bitten, she encountered a most unusual-looking person. The light-skinned, wrinkled face was framed with a mass of long, twisted locks that went every which way but right and hung around the woman's stooped shoulders like ropes of gray wool. She looked a little crazed, but not in a way that scared Sassie. The splattered smock she was wearing gave her identity away—that and the clay-caked fingernails.

Sassie had heard Miz Ruthie talk about buying churns and crocks from the mute potter that lived on this street. Miz Ruthie claimed the woman possessed the power to charm birds right down out of the sky and that her mama had had the gift of prophecy, could predict a person's future by gazing into their coffee cup or reading the palm of their hand.

Growing up, Sassie had been spooked plenty by the superstitious tales of her auntie Dorrie and her mama, but now she tried to ignore such gossip. Anyway, she'd been taught not to believe in sorcery; Miz Claire and Miz Addie said that witchcraft was blasphemous, the way of the devil, not God's way. *However*, she did have to admit, the woman standing before her did look somewhat like a witch.

As her terror subsided and she recovered enough to speak, she exclaimed, "Praise God fo' yo' strong arm! Another minute, an' I might've been chewed to pieces!"

The woman was looking at Sassie with equal interest; her pale-green eyes scrutinized the girl's face. After a long moment, won to what she saw, she grinned toothlessly, unlatched the gate, and motioned for her to come in off the street.

Glad for the opportunity, in the unlikely event that the dog might return, Sassie proceeded through the gate.

Beyond the wrought-iron fence and ugly hedge, heavily laden branches of crepe myrtles bowed down to greet her; their spent blooms littered the walkway like pink confetti. A bed of verbena ignored its borders and spilled over onto the footpath; clove-scented dianthus spiced up the air. It was a delightful, pink paradise! *Sarah Beth would love it here!* she thought. As she followed the woman, a cat walked between them, and another peeked at her suspiciously from its hiding place under the house.

The woman motioned to the single stone step leading up to the doorway and waited for Sassie to sit down before she went into the house. While she was gone, Sassie looked about. In one corner of the backyard, under a ramshackle lean-to, was a potter's wheel, and nearby a primitive brick kiln. Earthen vessels of various sizes and shapes were strewn hither and yon. The potter's shed was engulfed by sweet-smelling honeysuckle, and her ears caught the humming of bees thereon. Sassie took a deep breath. Considering the day she'd had so far, she felt blessedly at peace here.

A few minutes later, the woman reappeared with two cups and handed one to Sassie before sitting down beside her.

"Thank you." Sassie raised the cup to her lips and sipped the calming mint tea.

It seemed awkward not to introduce herself, so she said, "My name's Sassie Boone…I cook an' stays at the Preacher's House over on Sparrow Street."

She couldn't explain it. Maybe it was the peaceful setting, or perhaps it was because the woman, like herself, was of mixed race; whatever the reason, Sassie sensed they shared a bond of some sort, and she felt comfortable and content sitting there next to her.

Next thing she knew, seized by a moment she'd not intended, she found herself pouring out her soul, telling all about how Rosette had treated her and what she'd said back. She went on about how wonderful the potatoes tasted and how the rooster had cried out a rebel yell. One thing led to another until, pretty soon, she'd just about narrated her whole life story. The woman listened intently while drinking her tea.

"I know it wuz wrong fo' me to talk back dat a-way, but I wuz so upset I couldn't see straight!" She wished the whole thing had never happened, but it had. And to make matters worse, before it was all over, she'd blamed everything on Obie. She sighed. "Po' Obie! An' po' Mistah Ezra. Work hard all day an' have to come home to *dat!*"

That made her companion grin.

Feeling a bit foolish for having gone on so to a perfect stranger, Sassie told her, "Law' knows I didn't mean to bother you with all my troubles, but Miz Ruthie all time be sayin' 'confession good fo' da soul'…I reckon she be right, 'cauze I sho' do feel better now." After all, it wasn't like she was going to tell anyone, she being a mute. The monologue finally ended with, "Law', *why* my po' mama had to die an' leave me here in dis mess all by myself—I'll never know!"

In the silence that followed, Sassie finished her tea. A few minutes later, earlier tensions all but forgotten, she stood up to leave and held her empty cup out toward the woman. "Well, I best git goin'. I sho' did enjoy da tea. An' much obliged again fo' scarin' off da dog."

The woman reached out and laid her hand on Sassie's abdomen then moved it upward and spread her fingers apart over her heart. She grinned up at Sassie like she knew a special secret.

Sassie didn't know what to make of the odd gesture. Without pondering it further, a minute later she waved good-bye and slipped through the gate.

In the fading light, the mute potter named Georgianne Knight watched Sassie walk away; her pale-green eyes held a look of age-old understanding, a look mixed of pity and sadness.

Keeping to the street to avoid the shadows, Sassie could feel the woman's gaze branding her back as she made her way toward home. Hard as it was not to, she didn't look back.

Yet the same could not be said of Georgianne. After her encounter with Sassie, it was only natural for her to look back. In her mind, she looked back to a time long past, to a place remembered—the place where her own life's story took origin, the place where she'd come from ...

In the spring of 1856, the sound of the slave trader's whip cracked menacingly close to the head of a young, beautiful, green-eyed mulatto as she reluctantly approached the steps of the auction platform.

Only moments before, she'd been forced by the auctioneer to lay the bundle she clutched to her bosom on the ground. The olive-skinned baby girl had immediately commenced to crying, suffering from the pain of cutting teeth.

Amidst the noise and commotion as the sale started, a dark-skinned Negro girl about the age of three toddled over and plopped down beside the bawling baby and patted her head, trying to comfort her.

A mere child herself, bitter anguish streamed down the mother's face as she faced the jeering crowd. She knew she and the child would soon be separated, sold away from each other.

Yet, because of the sympathies of an old plantation owner named John Knight, when the bidding was over, a family remained united. Because she now belonged to John Knight, the quadroon baby called Georgianne became known as Georgianne Knight…

A victim of despicable circumstance, Georgianne's mother had started having relations with men around the time she turned nine years old. By the time she was thirteen and pregnant with her first child, she had already grasped a certain knowledge of her plight in the world and understood the odds of survival were ranked against her. Clever and determined, she learned at a tender age how to maneuver effectively life's perilous current, using whatever wiles she could to better her advantages.

During the Civil War, she fell in cahoots with one of Old John's grandson's, Newt Knight. Newt made a name for himself as a notorious deserter of the Confederacy, and in her, he found a match for his own prowess. She became an accomplice to his cause, providing both aide and pleasurable entertainment to him and his band of outlaw followers.

Customary to that day, most men carried with them a hunting horn, usually made from the sawed-off horn of a steer. The horns were used as a means of communication, primarily for sending out distress calls. Newt and his fellow outliers created a code of signals so they could send messages to each other while hiding from the Army in the Leaf River swamps. Newt owned a unique horn of polished ebony, one whose music held a distinctive and mysterious tone said to possess a strange power.

Hand in hand with this colorful myth, Georgianne's mother was reputed to be a sorceress, one anointed with the gift of strange and supernatural powers. Rumors spread of her ability to cast evil spells and glimpse into the future by studying the lines that time etched into a person's palm. Pleased by this mystic perception, she always kept a variety of potions on hand and a pot of coffee on the coals of her hearth so she had a ready supply of grounds for those who regularly dropped in to have her predict their destiny.

In addition to being a fortune-teller, Georgianne's mother was also a prostitute.

Droves of men, mostly white men, rode over trails and traveled the beaten paths through the woods to her cabin, seeking her out for the purpose of satisfying their most primal appetites. Like hogs to slop. The house was nothing more than a brothel, a veritable cesspool of corruption and debauchery. It was in that such distressing place where Georgianne existed and was left to whatever fate befell her.

After the war, little seemed to change for them; they continued to live the same. There was a strong bond between Newt and his beautiful mulatto, and though freed, she chose to stay on at the Knight Plantation. Besides, there was no place else for her to go with her houseful of quadroon and octoroon offspring.

Of course, Newt's relationship with the brazen Negro harlot caused friction in his household. It tormented his white wife, especially every time another light-skinned baby appeared at her cabin in the woods. However, the witch held Newt under her spell, and malicious as she was, she savored the hold she had over him because it gave her an illusion of power and importance in an otherwise dire and miserable existence.

When word got out that Newt was cavorting with a Negro woman, he was the subject of much derision. Because he was declared guilty of mixing the blood of the races, he was banished from society. His whole family despised him; they became the laughing stock of the county, his white children were social outcasts, looked down upon and shunned simply because they were the children of the notorious Newt Knight.

Presently, Georgianne went inside, taking the teacups with her. She fixed herself a plate of crowder peas and cornbread and sat down at her kitchen table to eat. A soft rustling sound made her look toward the window. When the raven lit down on the sill, she smiled fondly and reached out to stroke her old friend's lustrous feathers. Then she crumbled some of her cornbread at his feet.

While she and the crow ate her supper, Georgianne chewed on the remembrance of Captain Knight and thought, *Dese ol' eyes o' mine sho' has seen some thangs…*

The echo of the black horn lay forever harbored somewhere deep in her soul, an echo which oftentimes still haunted her dreams.

Thinking back over it all, Obie had himself a time laughing.

During the ride back to the Preacher's House, Sassie had been beside herself, in a mortal tirade. Thoroughly put out with him and his mama, the whole way home she let it fly, relived every detail of the scenario with Rosette with a generous peppering of embellishments. Obie of course understood how Sassie felt. He'd grown up in the house with Rosette Quinn. Talk all day, Sassie couldn't tell him anything he didn't already know about the woman.

As they had ridden along, at first, Sassie vented her frustrations mostly into the air; however, inevitably, it wasn't long until she turned them on Obie. Even if he had braved enough to throw in some word of explanation or assurance—not that anything had come to mind that would make a difference—he couldn't have wedged a word in. So he just rode along quietly, justifying the situation in his own mind as best he could:

Best thang fo' Obie Quinn, jus' set here wif my mouth shut…she fo'ever mo' mad an' gone give me da devil no matter what I say…for not giving her some kind of warning about how his mama was.

Man! Dis don't make no kind o' sense! Jus' what I s'posed to say—say, "I'z gone take you by da house to meet my mama an' by da way, don't git too close 'cauze she nutty as a squirrel turd"? So he just sat helpless and let her babble on.

Then, as the recital grew lengthier, something unexpected happened.

The longer Obie listened to Sassie rant on and on about it all, the more ridiculous the whole thing started to sound until…*Law' help me, I jus' caint hold it in no mo'!* Obie couldn't stop himself. He burst out laughing.

By the look Sassie gave him, Obie knew he'd messed up. *She sho' nuf be cut'n da fool now!* But for some reason, that just set him to whooping louder. Unable to control himself, he could only hope that given time to cool off, she'd get into a better humor and forgive him. He had to admit, after her performance earlier today, he admired her spirit more than ever. His mama wasn't used to anybody throwing back on her! She'd gone stiff as a corpse—and the expression on her face! *Law', I thought my mama wuz gone fall out her chair an' hit da flo'!*

Right there in the middle of Sparrow Street, Obie had laughed so hard he became weak. Bent forward on the seat, doubled over, his whole body shook. After a few minutes, he straightened up and wiped the tears from his face and flipped the reins to make the horse pick up the pace. Off they went into a trot, but not to home. In hopes of salvaging what was left of the day, he had headed straight for his cousin's house.

He turned the wagon onto a trail where the sweet smell of green pine filled the air. Tying the reins to a bush, he took a shaded path through the woods well known to him. When he rounded the bend and came close to them, he inched along, barefooted, trying to make no noise. Zeke and Jasper were fishing for bream with cane poles and nightcrawlers from the leafy creekbank. Obie crept toward them, trying to sneak up and scare them, but when he stepped on a dry twig, Zeke turned his head, and Obie heard him say to Jasper, "I want you to look comin' yunder!"

With a flash of white teeth, Jasper hollered raucously, "Obie, you ol' son of a gun! We'z wonderin' where yo' black ass bin hidin'!"

The three of them sat quietly for half an hour watching the corks.

It was July, so it was hot. Jasper swatted at a horsefly that lit on his neck and said, "Let's git in da creek!"

A minute later, they'd shucked their clothes and jumped in, savoring the sudden cool on their bodies. For a while, they thrashed and wallowed, playing a game to see which one of them could hold his breath and stay under water the longest. Using their toes, they picked up rocks from the sandy bottom.

When they tired of that, they raced to the watermelon Zeke had buried earlier in the shallows next to a fallen log. Busting it open on the hard ground, they squatted on the bank and scooped out the red, sweet, juicy meat and ate with their hands. They made a contest out of how many seeds they could spit into the creek.

"Sho be good to have some salt," Jasper said. Obie and Zeke nodded agreeably. They swatted at the flies that attacked the sticky melon rind.

By the time they finished eating, their bodies had dried off, and they pulled their clothes back on.

While Jasper went to pick up their cane poles, Zeke asked Obie, "Hey, man, you want dis mess o' fish to take home wif you?" He held up seven bream, strung on a forked stick.

Obie shook his head. He rubbed his stomach and belched. "Naw, man. I'z too sorry to clean 'em. Give 'em to Auntie Beulah." She would be proud to have them; she dearly loved a fish.

They walked out of the darkening woods, and Obie left to go home.

Now in the late evening, he drove the wagon to the barn and un-hitched the horse. Across the way, he saw Ezra, moving unhurriedly through the rows of the field, making his thoughtful last inspec-tion of the day of the crops he so meticulously tended. Obie heard him mumbling, talking to the plants. He shook his head over it and thought, *Law' if Mama an' Daddy ain't bofe gone slap crazy!*

Coming up on the porch, a furtive glance through the window confirmed Obie's worst fear. He was sorry, but not surprised, to find his mama lying in wait for him in the front room. Whereas he may have been able to laugh about things earlier, presently he would rather her come at him wielding an axe than endure the wrath he knew was forthcoming, having suffered it often enough in the past. If only he could somehow turn his ears off.

She heard his steps on the porch and called his name. Filled with a sense of dread, Obie didn't answer immediately but paused and took a deep breath, mentally assembling his armor. He looked out across the fields. It was dusk-dark.

Entering the house, he went into the parlor to dutifully face his persecution. "You called me, Mama?"

Without preamble, she lit into him, her voice full of rage. "What in Jezus's name wuz you thankin', boy?"

There was no point in pretending he didn't know what or who she was talking about. He knew his mama's mind. Without an under-standing of why, he'd known from the start his affections for Sassie would run contrary to her principles. "I wuz thankin'—hopin'—you might act right fo' once." Apparently that was too much to hope for.

His frank answer surprised her. "How could you let yo'self? It a shame an' disgrace fo' you to parade around such a girl."

"Sassie's a nice girl." He said it softly.

"She a *white* girl! An' dat *white* fam'ly o' hers didn't teach her a thang 'bout how to talk to her elders!" She still couldn't believe the way that girl had sassed her!

"Her mama wuz colored; she can't help who her daddy wuz." There was no call for her to be looked down on for something that happened before she was even born. As for the sass, his mama had it coming.

Rosette asked curtly, "An' does she even know jus' who her daddy iz?"

When he didn't reply, she was mistakenly satisfied that her point was proved.

Obie sighed in exasperation, knowing it wouldn't have mattered if Abraham Lincoln had been Sassie's father. "Why do you hate white people, Mama?"

Rosette's voice was like a whiplash. "Boy, you best hush yo' sighin' an' listen to me! Dat girl don't b'long here! Jus' what do you thank would happen if you wuz fool e'nuf to marry her?" She knew. "She'll ruin yo' life, an' us too!" In the past, she had seen the pillory, the public scorn that happened in families who defiled themselves with mixed blood. "I'z tellin' you—don't you brang her here again…You stay away from her! You hear?"

Looking at Rosette sadly, Obie shook his head. She'd been bossing him around his whole life, and he'd put up with it out of respect, but not this time. She was wrong about this, and he was going to stand up for what was right, and stand up for Sassie.

He replied boldly, "No, Mama. I sorry you feel dat way, but I won't." She was his mama, but she did not own him. Sassie was an unexpected flower that had bloomed in his heart; she made him happy, and she was, by far, the sweetest thing that had ever happened to him.

Rosette looked at him sharply. She couldn't believe her own son dared to stand there and defy her in her own house. How could he betray his upbringing and persist in siding with this girl who one might just as well say was white?

Since verbal fire proved ineffective, the only weapon she had left was physical force. Rising from her chair, she flew at him, swinging wildly. Obie closed his eyes and held up his arms to ward off the blows as she beat him about his head and shoulders. "You do as I say!" she hollered.

Wishing he could make her see, he opened his mouth to say something then closed it. Out of a deep reverence for her, he would say no more. There was no need. She had already decided Sassie wasn't black enough for him, and there was no reasoning with her warped way of thinking. And no way of changing her mind.

Yet, even though he didn't understand why she felt as she did, he refused to be defeated by it. He turned and started from the room, leaving things to take their own directions, leaving his mama staring after him, stunned. "I love you, Mama," he said.

"Obie! You git back in here when I'z talkin'!"

Obie went out. Tears stung his eyes. A gentle breeze whispered across the darkening fields; a symphony of crickets played a forlorn melody to his soul. As he walked, he tried to wish away the prejudice so deeply ingrained in his mama's mind, hoping that somehow this blight that plagued them might be destroyed before it destroyed them.

What is it, he wondered, *that makes her hate so?*

Sometimes he feared her heartless. If only she was more like his daddy. The kindest, most mild-mannered of men, Ezra, thank God, wasn't anything like her. If not for him, Obie might have exiled himself from his parents' house long ago.

From the corner of the house, feeling his hurt, Ezra watched sadly as the silhouette of his son walked past a stand of sycamore trees into the night beyond. His heart went out to him.

Lost in his own thoughts, he stared into the darkness long after Obie faded from sight and the pale trunks of the sycamores shone white. Then he went in, and in the front room found Rosette with her head down, crying in despair.

Silently he prayed, *Dear Jezus! Deliver my fam'ly out o' dis valley o' tears an' trouble…*

Finishing up the supper dishes, Addie squeezed out the dishrag and was spreading it over the edge of the windowsill to dry when Hiram came in carrying two empty coffee cups.

"Is something wrong, Addie? You've been awful quiet this evenin'."

She shook her head. "No. I'm fine. Maybe just a little tired." *Tired of Wilkes.*

In truth, the hands on the clock were moving unmercifully slow. She didn't think it was ever going to be time to go to bed. Much to her chagrin, Wilkes had played the proverbial altar boy all day. Acting as if nothing had occurred, he went to church with them that morning—Addie couldn't remember two consecutive words of the sermon—and afterward he joined them for Sunday dinner. He even had the gall to pull out her chair for her.

While they ate, a master at spinning yarns, he entertained Emily and Samuel with funny stories and jokes. He'd tossed several games of horseshoes with them. He couldn't lavish enough compliments on her chicken and dumplings, no matter that every bite she swallowed wanted to lodge in her throat. The walls had pressed in around her and gave her a throbbing headache.

But still, she refused to give him the satisfaction of thinking he was handling her. Though aggravated past the point of feeling outdone, she yet summoned the will and had somehow made it through the day smiling. *Pretty much.* Right at that moment, Wilkes was out on the porch playing his harmonica, much to the delight of her children. *I suppose when he's done performing he'll go down to the creek and walk on water,* she thought sarcastically.

"Addie, did you hear what I said?" Hiram broke into her thoughts.

"I'm sorry…what?"

"I said supper was good. I enjoyed it." He refilled the coffee cups from the graniteware pot on the stove and leaned in to peck her cheek. "*And* I said that Wilkes just told me he needs to get back to his tobacco crop..." Something in his voice made her glance up at him. "*And* that he'll be leavin' here bright an' early tomorrow mornin'."

She heard him that time. Despite herself, she couldn't suppress a huge smile. Before she could say anything, Hiram started from the kitchen. "I'm goin' back out on the porch for a while. You comin'?"

By the amusement in his eyes, she knew he hadn't missed the look on her face; as far as she could tell, though, there wasn't a whole lot of regret on his either.

"I'll be out in a minute," she replied.

A mixture of relief and gladness swept through her. She felt like jumping for joy! She'd sleep better tonight just knowing Wilkes would be gone from there tomorrow!

Not surprisingly, it was then that she realized her headache was all of a sudden gone.

CHAPTER 5

"Withdraw thy foot from thy neighbor's house; lest he be weary of thee, and so hate thee." Proverbs 25:17

The next morning it was hardly light enough outside to make out the shapes of the woodshop and barn when, making as little noise as she could, Addie made coffee, biscuits, and fried eggs. The heartiest farewells having been exchanged the night before, she saw no need to wake Emily and Samuel.

After they ate breakfast, Hiram and his brother left the table and wandered out onto the porch, where they stood and talked quietly for several minutes. Using the excuse of not wishing to invade upon that private moment, Addie stayed inside and cleared the dishes. Then before it could look impolite, she too went out to see him off.

When she stepped out the door, Wilkes took her hand and kissed her lightly on the cheek. Her pulse jumping wildly in her wrists and with an awkward tightness in her chest, Addie smiled and accepted his appreciation graciously.

Wilkes turned and looked up into the trees, glanced back at the house, and gazed across the meadow thoughtfully. He gave Hiram a final firm handshake. Hiram slapped him on the back. Last good-byes said, Wilkes got on his horse, the saddle creaked with the shift of his weight, and the horse pranced a little as though impatient to be on its way.

As he rode off into the blush of dawn, a few of the guineas made a show of chasing after him with their wings hiked back. Addie shared their sentiment. She had never been so glad to see anyone leave. So thankful to finally be rid of him, she could have wept with relief. Within minutes, Wilkes had trotted his horse past the wood-shop and was headed off down the main road. The farther down the road he went, the happier she felt.

As they stood at the front gate watching Wilkes depart, she and Hiram did not speak. When the horse fianlly disappeared around the bend, wondering where his thoughts led, Addie asked, "Do you reckon he'll ever come back here to visit us again?"

Because he understood how glad Addie was that Wilkes had left, Hiram couldn't resist teasing her just a little. He stroked his beard and grew thoughtful, pretending to take a moment to consider the question. When he was ready, he drawled, "So long as the Good Lord keeps hearin' an' answerin' prayers, I reckon not."

He and Addie looked at each other quietly for a moment before simultaneously bursting out laughing. He caught her up and swung her around, her dress billowing about her as she giggled with pleasure.

Hallelujah and God be praised!

There was not a cloud in the sky. Under the gabled roof of the open-air cookhouse out behind the Preacher's House, Sassie was working at an old table, chopping a pile of okra. She was barefoot; she had a kerchief tied around her head and her sleeves were pushed up to her elbows. Though it was only nine o'clock in the morning, the bodice of her light cotton dress was already sticking to her skin and her

hairline was beaded with sweat from the heat of the wood-burning stove behind her. Atop the stove simmered a huge pot of jambalaya.

Sassie inherited her love of cooking from her late-great Auntie Dorrie. Born into slavery back in the middle 1800s, Dorrie grew up working in the kitchen of the big house on a sugarcane plantation located along the Louisiana bayous. Though her master's mind was set against the marrying of slaves, Dorrie's heart was bound to a man she called "husband," a slave named Abner, and they had two fine sons.

However, they would not see their sons grow up. When the youngest boy turned nine, both were sent to the auction house and sold away from the plantation, away from Dorrie, and away from Abner. Her children taken from her, something passed from Dorrie's soul, as though she had been beaten unmercifully and left for dead. Then a month later, one morning shortly after the work bell rang, Abner's mutilated body was discovered in a cane field—slain with a machete.

After the Civil War, Dorrie became known as a FPC—*free person of color*—and though she forced herself to focus on those living around her rather than on those she had lost, the rest of her days were marked by an abiding sense of the despair of not knowing what had become of her sons and of the senseless, brutal murder of her husband. Despite all this, she passed on to her descendents the one treasure no one could take from her: a proud heritage, one influenced by and seasoned well with a dash of the Creole culture she grew up in before and during the war.

Earlier, Sassie had stewed two chickens and pulled the meat from the bones. The stock was well-seasoned with filé ("fee-lay"), a spice made from the dried, crushed leaves of the sassafras tree. After blending a rue of browned flour into the zesty stock, along with the tender boiled chicken, to it she added a big bunch of chopped green onions, several bell peppers and chopped celery ribs, diced tomatoes, and several links of sausage, cut into pieces.

By combining imprecise pinches of this and handfuls of that, Sassie recreated her aunt's old recipe for jambalaya from memory. In a couple of hours, when it came time to serve the hungry patrons, the thick, savory dish would be ladled over a plate of steamed rice.

To Sassie it seemed befitting that the jambalaya, which had become her signature dish and a favored item on the menu at the Preacher's House, was flavored with the very spice she was named for.

Out of the corner of her eye, she spotted Obie as he eased around the side of the restaurant and started tiptoeing toward the cookhouse. For his benefit, she pretended not to notice him. She found it humorous how he loved to try and sneak up on folks—and how terrible he was at it. Built strong with a thick chest and muscular arms, Obie was sturdy as a mule and almost as graceful. Suppressing a giggle, Sassie kept her eyes on the task at hand and continued chopping okra, ignoring his bumbling approach.

Propped against a post, for a minute Obie watched her. There was mischief in his eyes when he whistled low and said, "Girl, you iz lookin' fine dis mawnin'."

Inwardly, Sassie allowed herself to smile at his boyish cockiness, yet she did her best to appear indifferent. Yesterday, she and Obie had fussed for the first time; he'd laughed at her when he should have taken her feelings seriously, and it just wouldn't do for her to let him off so easy. "You best git! Miz Ruthie sees you out here she gone skin us both alive!" she scolded.

Obie's voice betrayed his doubt. "I had me a long night worryin' over whether or not you wuz still mad."

She huffed. "Good! Dat jus' what you deserve! Suit me fine if you don't ever sleep another wink!" Finished with the okra, she scooped it up into a pan and turned away to set it down on a smaller table near the stove. During the last minutes of cooking she'd stir it into the bubbling, aromatic pot of jambalaya.

"So, iz you?" he asked. "Still mad?" He had to know if she was, or if she was just playing with him.

Sassie had to bite her lip to keep from smiling. She could never stay mad at Obie for long. "I surely am! You might have tol' me yo' mama wuz a terrible ol' woman who hates white folk fo' no other reason 'sept deys white!" Do him good to squirm a minute, work for her forgiveness.

Taking a chance, he mocked her teasingly, "All right den, if it'll make you happy. 'My mama's a terrible ol' woman who hates white folk fo' no other reason 'sept dey be white.' An' I'z sorry she wuz mean to you, an' I'z sorry I laughed at you." Reaching into his pocket, he stepped forward and neatly placed a lemon on the chopping block. *A peace offering.*

Glancing first at the lemon then up at his hopeful face, Sassie saw that look. The look he had for her that filled her with a sweet feeling, the one that wrapped around her and made her feel all fluttery and confused inside. Boyish cockiness mixed with something gentle. Their eyes met and held the secret that lay between them. The thought of it sent a delicious thrill through her body. She couldn't stop smiling.

Just then, a booming voice snapped them both to attention.

They spun around and came face-to-face with Miz Ruthie's disgruntled frown. "Jus' what y'all thank y'all doin' back in here?" Ruthie, the overseer of the kitchen, stood with hands on wide hips, an apron tied beneath her ample bosom, eyeing them suspiciously.

Not waiting for them to answer, she poked a finger at Obie accusingly. "Obie Quinn, you ain't got no biz'ness cornerin' up back here in dis kitchen, hinderin' dis po' girl from her work! Sweet thang ain't no mor'n a chile!" She shot a speculative glance at Sassie and snorted, "*Hmmph!*"

Looking back at Obie, she asked, "Well, iz I jus' gone haf to stand here all day an' wunder, or iz you gone tell me what you brung us dis mawnin'—asides fo' yo' big, wide eyes?"

Nervously twirling his black slouch hat, Obie cleared his throat and stammered, "Y-yes'um, Miz Ruthie, I mean n-no'um. Dey be three bushels o' purple hull peas an' a whole mess o' corn out yunder on da waggin."

"Den I su'gest you quit yo' gawkin' an' take yo' proud self out from back in here an' git to unloadin' da waggin!" Throwing her arms wide, she shooed him like she was shooing chickens. "Git!"

"Yes'um, Miz Ruthie!" He scurried away, almost tripping.

Sassie picked up a long wooden spoon and went to stir the pot of jambalaya, making herself look busy.

With Obie put to running, Ruthie turned on her, mainly for effect, since Sassie had never been one to shirk her duties, like some of the others. "An' as fo' you an' yo' twitchy-tailed self, all I gots to say iz leave da honey pot open an' flies sho' ain't gone light on salt!"

"Yes'um, Miz Ruthie," Sassie mumbled, her cheeks flaming.

Ruthie bustled out shaking her head, grumbling loud enough to be heard clear across the yard, "I sees nothin' but trouble in dat young buck's eyes! No, suh! Ain't no rest fo' da wicked!"

Wesley was cutting a leather strip to repair a harness when Algie Thomason, owner of a neighboring farm a couple of miles away, rolled to a clamoring stop.

"Howdy, Algie," Wesley greeted him casually. "How's the world treatin' you this fine day?"

Foregoing civilities, the man cocked his head back and proceeded to cuss a blue streak. "I ain't come here to press accusations," he thundered on, "but I've seen yer boy huntin' on my place, an' so long as he's totin' a gun, that's fine by me. But, this mornin' I came across my best dog caught up in a steel trap ...had to put him down!"

Wesley straightened up and raked his sleeve across his brow. "Now you just hold your horses, Algie. You've got high cause to cuss over your dog, but I know blamed well Jesse didn't have a hand in

any such doin'. I ain't never owned a steel trap an' ain't studyin' on buyin' one today!"

"Well, I'm out servin' a warnin'! Any sorry rascal I find settin' a trap on my property, I aim to bust his hide, so consider yerself warned!" Without anything else occupying his mind and having said what he'd come to say, he slapped his horse with the reins and left without another word.

When Wesley walked down to the woodshop in the afternoon, he asked Hiram, "Algie stop by here this mornin'?"

Hiram marked the measurements on a board before answering. "Daniel said he came by, shattered the peace. I's in town, though. Didn't see him."

"Well, sir, you can be sure, he dressed me down good," Wesley remarked. "A fit's on him about them traps somebody set out on his place."

Hiram nodded. "Rightly so."

"Don't make a lick o' sense why a feller would run traps this time-a year," Daniel pointed out. "Pelts wouldn't be worth a slug-nickel."

It was plain enough in all three of their minds who the trap-setting culprit was, but it was Hiram who nailed it squarely out loud.

"If Wilkes hadn't saddled up an' rode off from here when he did, another week I wouldn't've had a friend left in these parts."

Next morning after breakfast, Wesley carried a large trunk outside and subsequently hoisted it onto his wagon, the trunk filled to over-flowing with the belongings of his eldest daughter. Sarah Beth had finally managed to whittle down her father's reserves. Back and forth they'd argued: he thought she was too young to leave home; she contended he was too protective. She'd wept and declared, *promised*, that she would come home and spend every weekend with the family in the country. Of course, Wesley didn't believe that lie for a minute.

Nonetheless, after days of hearing this, after much deliberation and with a certain measure of misgivings, Wesley gave in to her exhaustive pleas and Travis's assurances and resignedly cut the apron strings.

And so, sixteen-year-old Sarah Beth Warren moved to town.

CHAPTER 6

"He hath made the earth by His power...He maketh lightning for the rain, He bringeth forth the wind out of His treasuries." Jeremiah 10:12, 13

Attributive to their combined wealth, Travis and Abigail's house was steeped in style and comfortable elegance. The long, columned porch led into a graceful foyer, where floors made of glowing heart pine spread forth like honey. Every room was splendidly furnished; soft, silk draperies covered the tall windows, chairs were upholstered in rich brocades and chintz, tables were adorned with vases of flowers and porcelain figurines.

French doors divided the main parlor from the dining room; a crystal chandelier sparkled above the table, and a luxurious rug lay underneath it. In the drawing room, a portrait of Abigail wearing an extravagant, green ball gown and cameo necklace hung over the fireplace. Most recently, the house had been equipped with a modern water closet, making the old outhouse in their backyard obsolete.

With its lofty ceiling and walls lavished with pink and green floral-striped wallpaper, the room Sarah Beth occupied was particularly charming. The mahogany bed had an arched canopy and was skirted with a pink dust ruffle, with downy bedcovers to match. There was a large wardrobe and a bureau with a mirror that tilted. A chaise lounge was fitted into a window niche, offering a cozy spot for reading or gazing out at the garden. Her every comfort had been seen to. When first shown the room, she had clapped her hands together like a delighted princess, unable to contain her pleasure. In that moment, it seemed to her that she had died and been born again.

The lace curtains billowed with a sudden breeze, the unexpected draft waking her. Languidly, Sarah Beth sat up in bed and stretched. Glancing toward the clock on the piecrust table beside the bed, it was yet too dark to make out the time. She took a deep, contented breath and gloried afresh in the sweet fragrance of her rich, new surroundings. She never had taken to country living, despised most everything about it. The smell of manure had always made her wish she were dead, as did the countrified way her mama could so casually scrape chicken muck off the soles of her shoes on the edge of the porch steps.

Just the thought of it now made her nose wrinkle disapprovingly. Thank goodness, though, she was free of all that now. For the first time in her life, she felt she was living the life intended for her, free from the wretched smell of cows and chickens, free from the infernal crowing of roosters, free, free, free. *This is where I belong,* she thought.

Reveling in her good fortune and newly gained independence, Sarah Beth fell back against the pillows. Smiling sleepily, she tucked the coverlet around herself and drifted back off to sleep, wishing in her heart that when she woke again it would be Saturday instead of Wednesday, so she could loll in bed until noon.

Day broke to a red sky and sticky heat. Masses of annoying black bugs clustered together and seemingly clung to the peculiar, oppressive air that promised rain.

Addie cracked an egg into a bowl and added a couple of scoops of flour. She stirred in enough buttermilk to make batter and started pouring rounds of it onto a hot, greased pan. In another cast-iron skillet, thick slices of bacon were frying.

Hiram stood out on the porch for a few minutes studying the darkening clouds. The sky was grey and almost still, the sort of unnatural stillness that usually preceded a strong thunderstorm. A lone meadowlark warbled, perched on a fence rail.

When he came inside, he remarked, "It looks like we might be in for a cloudburst directly." He reached into the cabinet for four plates and took the same number of forks from a drawer.

Addie turned the last griddlecake over to brown its other side. There was a stack of them, golden crisp around the edges. "We could sure use some rain," she replied. Hiram sat down at the table and she handed him a cup of coffee.

Thinking out loud, he said, "I'm hopin' to finish that table I've been workin' on for Travis. Daniel's tendin' some things around his place today."

"How much do you lack on it?" Addie put a dish of butter on the table.

"I figure three hours, more or less. I should be through with it by dinner," he answered.

She set the platter of griddlecakes on the table and walked to the back door to call Emily and Samuel in for breakfast.

Samuel came running from the henhouse. Emily followed, carrying an egg basket half full of eggs, swatting at the bugs flying around her face. She left the eggs on the top step.

"Here, let me wipe your grubby little mitts," Addie told Samuel. "How many eggs did you find this morning?"

Holding up all ten of his fingers, fat as sausages, he said, "I found this many. Two."

Emily came in and sat down at the table. "That's ten, silly goose. Mmm, my favorite, pancakes an' syrup."

Hiram was ready to eat. "Let's bow our heads so I can return thanks. I'm hungry as a bear ..."

After breakfast, Hiram gave Addie a peck on the cheek, tripped down the steps, and headed out across the yard toward the wood-shop. Noticing how the momentum of the wind was picking up, he glanced toward the sky. At the rate the clouds had begun rolling in from the southeast, he seriously doubted he'd get the table assembled before the rain set in.

A few minutes later, any thoughts of the approaching weather were left outside the door of the shop as he went inside, where the air was filled with the pleasant smells of his trade. He gathered up a plane, his handsaw, and a chisel and threw his heart and soul into his work.

Hiram meticulously measured and marked the board for the pin half of the dovetail joint then used a saw to notch the pins out. Next, he went to work with his chisel. The soft pine sliced like butter as he cut through it with sharp, precise strokes. A woodworker through and through, he loved everything about wood—the feel of it, the smell of it, the sound it made yielding to his tools.

Some time later, he set the tails of the table joint against the pins and slid them together, pleased with the fit and the sturdiness of the piece. He stepped back to admire his handiwork and smiled. Making furniture had never struck him as a laborsome business.

Suddenly, a gust of wind slammed the door shut. He thought about going to push it back open, but he was almost done here for the day. He picked up his tools and went about returning them to their proper shelves. Out in the barn, he heard a horse nickering, followed by the sharp sound of metal clanking together.

What is that noise? Something was hitting the roof. Instinctively, the skin on the back of Hiram's neck prickled as he went to investigate.

When he pushed the door open a blast of wind struck his face like a mighty fist. Hailstones fell like rain from the sky; chunks of ice the size of goose eggs covered the ground, explaining the strange battering sounds. Despite the dark clouds, the atmosphere had taken on an eerie, greenish-gray glow. When Hiram gazed out across the field, his heart lurched as his eyes met with a fearsome sight.

He broke into a run toward the house. Taking the front steps two at a time, he burst through the door, shouting the words to Addie, "Get Emily and Samuel into the cellar, now! Hurry!" To answer the panicked question on her face, he yelled, "A funnel cloud's headin' our way! Hurry! There's not much time!"

As he started back out, he called over his shoulder, "I'll be right back!"

Addie frantically scooped Samuel up and ran, carrying him around to the side of the house, right behind Emily, the wind whipping at their skirts. The sky turned ominous, almost black. Emily struggled against the force of the wind to lift the cellar door back. With it opened, they scrambled down the steps into the dark, musty space below. Samuel squirmed and stretched out his arms toward the dim shaft of light that poured in through the stairwell, making Addie regret she hadn't thought to grab a lantern. A moment later when Emily pulled the door shut, they were entombed in the moldy darkness.

Samuel whimpered, "I want my papa." The boy buried his face in his mother's chest.

Addie hugged him close and whispered soothingly, "Papa's coming." She said an earnest prayer that Hiram would return soon.

As Hiram raced toward the barnyard, hail pelted him, stinging his face like a swarm of yellow-jackets. Instinctive fear fretted the horses; in their growing agitation they nervously pranced back and forth along the fence, blowing and snorting. Hiram flung open the gate to let them run at will to seek shelter from the storm. Hooves pounding the ground, they took off at a dead run across the pasture in the lashing hail.

Lightening flashed. The wind grew stouter. It bent the trees and pushed against Hiram. He cast a fearful glance toward the tornado that was bearing down on them. It was powerful beyond comprehension. The fierceness of it scared him as he watched it descend from the sky and begin to devour everything in its path. He knew time was running out if he was going to make it back the house.

A sense of urgency coursed through his veins as he raced toward the cellar, trying to outrun the storm. When he got there his clothes were damp from being peppered by the hail, his chest was pounding. The door fell heavily behind him; he barred it securely and braced for the worst.

Addie's eyes had adjusted enough to the darkness to be completely unnerved by the confession of fear on her husband's face. She had never seen him look that scared.

"What about the cats, Mama?"

Addie hated to think of anything being caught out in such a storm, but she did her best to assure Emily. "The cats are smart; they'll find a place to hide." She was more concerned about Daniel and Amelia, Wesley and Laura. And she was especially uneasy about Claire and Stell. Would they make it to a safe place in time? Was there such a place? Claire was infinitely dear to her and had been for thirty years, dearer to her than Addie's own mother. She couldn't bear the thought of anything bad happening to her. She just couldn't. *Please Lord, keep her and Stell from harm…keep us all from harm…*

In an anxious voice, Emily persisted, "Mama, do you think this is a good hidin' place?" She had never been so frightened.

"Yes, honey, I know it is." However, inwardly, she harbored fear and doubt. She knew there was plenty cause for worry. Even so, she willed herself to stay calm for the sake of the children, knowing that they were terrified.

Aboveground the storm intensified. Wind whined in the eaves. Something hit the side of the house. Samuel started crying. Hiram

reached over and took the child from Addie. With his free arm, he drew her close and felt her trembling.

He tried not to give in to his worst fears of the danger they faced, but he couldn't help it. He had no control over what was happening. As they all stood huddled together, he prayed. He prayed the house wouldn't fall in and bury them alive. He prayed for the storm to pass on by and that his family and home would be spared. Looking around, he wondered if there was anything down there they could get under for more protection.

'...whoso putteth his trust in the Lord shall be safe...'

Hiram's faith in the Lord was strong. Suddenly reaffirmed by this promise from Him, near Addie's ear he said softly, "Don't be afraid...God is with us." He was confident God would protect them.

In an attempt to still Emily's apprehension, Hiram tried to make light of the situation by saying to her, "Maybe this wind will blow those pesterin' bugs a far piece off from here. That'd be a good thing, huh?"

Though engulfed with doubt, Emily nodded meekly; she felt safer just with Hiram's strong presence being there.

For what seemed an eternity, hell beat at the door of the cellar as the deafening storm raged aboveground. It sounded like a locomotive was rumbling toward them. The wind whipped across the roof and howled in the eaves, squalling like a baby.

They felt gusts hit against the house, heard the thuds of things being tossed about the yard. Addie envisioned a mess of broken eggs on the back porch from the basket the children had gathered that morning. Thunder rolled, lightening cracked and popped, and the ground vibrated. Jars of canned food lining the shelves around them rattled and clinked as the vibration ran through the beams and down into the foundation. Grit sifted in through a small crack in the cellar door. The minutes passed with a harrowing slowness.

"Mama!" Samuel cried out.

"I'm right here." Addie stroked his head reassuringly.

His fingers sought out her face and touched it searchingly in the dark, like a blind man reading.

Then all of a sudden, it sounded as though the storm had changed course. The roaring sound seemed to be moving away from them, weakening to a distant mumble. A hush fell as the wind first slackened, then seemed to lay. Hiram passed Samuel into Addie's arms and climbed the steps to unlatch the door. He pushed it open and peered out, not knowing what to expect to see. No telling what manner of destruction such a storm had left behind.

A drizzling rain had started. Broken tree limbs were lying everywhere. The woodshed was blown down, piles of wood were strewn. As they walked around and surveyed the damage, they found that part of the barn roof was gone. Miraculously, their house had withstood the mighty winds. Hiram breathed a prayer of relief and thanksgiving. He knew the twister hadn't arbitrarily spared them. God orchestrated that.

When Hiram whistled the horses came galloping toward the barn, followed by the mules, John and Molly. Cows bellowed in the distance. Hiram figured there was plenty of fence down; the stock was probably scattered to parts unknown. But at the time, none of that seemed important. He told Addie, "I'm goin' to hitch to the wagon. We need to go check on the others."

Wesley and Laura's home sustained no irreparable damage.

As soon as the winds subsided, they hastened up the lane to Stell's place. They discovered a rocking chair lying upside down in the yard several feet away from the house. On the end of the porch the roof sagged badly where one of the supporting posts had given way, but they were relieved to see the quaint little farmhouse itself was still standing. There was only minor damage that could easily be mended.

The front door stood wide open. Laura ran through the house, calling, "Mama! Aunt Claire!" There came no answer.

"They've got to be here somewhere," Wesley said.

Laura called out again, louder, her voice choked, fearing of the worst.

Wesley cocked his head and held up his hand to quiet Laura. He said, "Come on, I think I heard somethin'."

They ran outside and listened.

The muffled cries were coming from a long-abandoned storm shelter dug out of the red clay embankment at the edge of the woods. The structure had, for the most part, caved in decades before.

Together, the two rushed over. A tree had crashed down and was blocking the entranceway that looked similar to the portal of an old mine. Wesley jumped up on the tree. It lay almost flush with the door. He shouted through the small opening, "Are y'all hurt?"

Claire answered, "Nothin' but our feelings. We can't get out, and there's hardly enough room in here for Stell an' me, much less all these spiders that we're keepin' company!"

"Hang on while we figure out a way to get y'all out of there."

Just then, Hiram pulled the wagon to a halt in front of the house. Wesley hollered, "We need a hand over here!"

Hiram and Addie hurried over. "Is anyone hurt?"

Laura shook her head, "No. Just shook up a bit. As soon as we get Mama an' Claire out of there, we'll all be just fine."

Hiram regarded the situation before them. He looked at Wesley and asked, "How do you aim to get 'em out?"

Wesley scratched his head, deliberating. Taking into account the size of the oak, he said, "I could go get the crosscut, but that tree's so thick it'd take us an hour to saw through it once. Even then it'd be too heavy for us to move by ourselves."

Hiram nodded. He thought that idea sounded unseemly. He could just imagine Stell's patience wearing thin while they tried to cut them out.

Wesley snapped his fingers. He'd come up with a better idea. He told Hiram enthusiastically, "I've got a loggin' chain down in the barn. We'll tie to the tree an' let the horses …" His voice drifted off as Hiram turned and walked away.

It became clear to him the poor old ladies would be stuck in there till dark dependent on Wesley's pitiful way of thinking. He went back to the wagon, easy and unhurried, and came back with a hatchet.

"I say let's improvise and just hack the door down," he said.

Wesley cocked his head to one side and stared at his brother-in-law in awe. "Well, kiss my foot. Now why didn't I think of that?"

The rotten wood didn't stand up to a half dozen blows. A minute later, Claire emerged from the hole, her silver-gray hair matted with cobwebs. A disgruntled Stell followed, crawling forth on her hands and knees, proclaiming, "Praise be to the Lord God Almighty! Just when I feared He'd gone deaf, He heard my prayers an' sent y'all to deliver us from this unholy pit!" Her ruddy cheeks were streaked with dirt.

Relief swept through Addie as she hugged Claire. "Thank God! I was so worried." Claire motioned that she was fine, happy enough just to be alive.

The men helped Stell to her feet. "Mama, look at you! You're covered with dirt, head to toe!" Laura exclaimed.

Stell didn't like being fussed over. She horned coarsely, "For the love of Job! I've lived through the ten plagues of Egypt. Surely a little dirt won't kill me!"

They all turned to see their neighbor, Algie Thomason, galloping up on horseback. "Ever'body all right here?" he yelled.

Wesley answered, "We've had us a wind fierce enough to blow a three-hundred-pound hog into a milk jug, but the Good Lord watched over us—nary a hair out of place! What about y'all?"

"We've got thangs strowed here an' yunder, but the worst of it missed us. But you best git to Asher's place quick as you can! Him an' Anna an' the girl survived with li'l more'n a few scratches, but the storm got their place! I'm headed back there now to help out however I can!"

He said no more and kicked his horse to a trot down the lane. Wesley and Hiram sprang into action and ran toward the wagon. Addie turned to Claire, but before she could get the words out of her mouth, Claire told her and Laura, "Leave the young'uns…go on with the menfolk an' see about things. Me an' Stell can tend to this here!"

At the end of the carriageway they met up with Daniel, who had come to check on them all and to announce that they had made it through the storm practically unscathed. When they told him what Algie said about Asher's place, he charged off ahead of them on Gent to offer what assistance he could.

Following the course of destruction left in the wake of the tornado, rounding a long curve in the main road brought them to where an alley of trees had once lined the carriageway leading to Asher's house. Now it seemed like a corridor to hell. With the trees uprooted, they could see clear across the way, and having never seen anything to compare to the scene spread out before them, they were shocked at what their eyes beheld. They could only shake their heads in wonder as they gaped at a landscape transformed into desolation. Everything lay gnarled, broken, and ravaged.

All that was left of the house was its broad front porch; the barn and outbuildings stood no more. All that remained of the structures were piles of broken timbers and bricks. An oak that had once shaded the house lay halved, its trunk split down the center. Pieces of furniture, articles of clothing, and bed linens were scattered over several acres. The entire place lay in ruin, a wasteland.

They marveled at how anyone could survive a force so brutal as to cause such destruction, yet by some miracle—by the grace of God—amidst the devastation, there was Asher, meandering about in a kind of stupor, taking inventory of his livestock, most of which was dead.

Anna and Libby were pillaging through a mound of broken glass and debris, searching for buried treasure, hoping to uncover some promissory, any small personal belonging that might lend a sense of certainty or special memory of a day past. Anna tried to fit some pieces of china together but saw that it was useless. Addie and Laura saw that she cradled in her hands a single item—a floral teapot.

Seeing the wagon pull up, Libby started running toward them, wailing. Delicate- boned and petite, she had always appeared small for her age; however, now, as her frail, waif-like figure flew toward them with her damp hair plastered to her head, shoeless and dragging one of her dresses through the mud, the pitiful vision she painted was enough to sear the soul. Laura dropped to her knees on the wet ground and caught her niece in her arms.

Libby burst into confused tears. "My room's gone, Aunt Laura. An' so is my doll," she cried.

Laura cooed to her comfortingly, "Shh. Shh. We'll get you another doll, you hear?" After a moment, she stood up and took Libby by the hand and said, "Let's go see what we can do to help your mama."

They went to Anna.

She had not even noticed their arrival and continued, bent over, picking through the rubble. When they approached and called her name, she flinched as if they'd startled her, as if she had been sleeping. She turned and stared at them vacantly, unblinking, her face very still, void of any emotion. Shock had taken her beyond the traumatic ordeal they'd just lived through. Her sleeve was torn; there was an ugly gash on her arm.

As calmly as she could, Laura said, "Oh, Anna. We're so thankful y'all are alive …I'm so sorry about the house …We're here to help any way we can." She reached out and touched Anna's hand, but Anna simply stood there, staring past them as if in a trance, rain streaking down her face. Unable to understand what was happening, she pressed the coolness of the teapot to her cheek.

Addie and Laura stared at each other briefly.

Addie glanced around at the despairing sight and saw the monumental task that lay ahead. Remembering the terrible fire from four years back that destroyed her home and most of her possessions, her heart went out to Anna. From tragic experience, she knew all too well what she was feeling.

Addie wished she could make her see beyond all this. She wanted to tell Anna the most important thing was that her family was safe, that material belongings could be replaced, houses could be rebuilt. Yet, she chose not to. She knew, especially with so raw a wound, words brought little comfort. Nor could she offer any firm assurance of recovery. That is, except by the Father.

It looked like the rain was setting in; they were all becoming drenched. Addie addressed the situation practically. "It's going to be dark soon, and there's little we can do in this rain. We might as well head home, get Libby and Anna into some dry clothes, and see about that cut on her arm. We can all come back here first thing in the morning."

Anna's bottom lip began quivering as Laura put her arm around her and led her to the wagon.

It rained all that night.

While the breeze lifted the curtains away from the windows, Anna lay stiff as a corpse, listening to her husband's light snores and the rain falling outside. Tonight she found no comfort in these ordinarily soothing sounds, only despair and misery. An invasive emptiness penetrated her soul. Fear about what had happened and uneasiness about what else may yet happen rose in her throat, making it difficult for her to swallow or draw breath.

Haunted by the vision of the splintered remains of their house, in her mind she saw tattered bed sheets flapping like ghosts in the only tree left standing in the yard; the ground was covered with shattered china and glass; dead chickens and cows dotted the barnyard. Akin to the images in her head, Anna felt splintered, tattered, shattered, and lifeless. She wished she could get out of bed, run down the hall, out the back door, down the road, and never look back.

At last, surrendering to the emotional fatigue that seeped through every fiber of her being like stagnant pond water, she broke down and began to cry, making no sound.

When the night was spent and dawn broke fair, she had not even dozed.

At first light, the men set out for the long and busy day ahead. It would take several days of hard work to clear away the wreckage of the old house before Asher could begin to rebuild. They would pile and burn the refuse and stack that which might later prove useful; some things would get thrown into a gully in the woods. It made young Jesse feel grown to be included in the clean-up.

Anna could not be persuaded to go. Even so, Addie had not forgotten how the outpouring of goodness from others had sustained her through her worst storms, so she, accompanied by Claire, Stell, and Emily, went on without her to see what they might be able to salvage while Laura stayed home to fix them all dinner.

When the women arrived at the site, the shock of the destruction hit them anew. It was hard to know where to start; everything looked even more a mess after being rained on all night. The stench of decaying carcasses hung in the air.

Near to where the barn had been, a few forlorn cows and a mule had ambled up to the dilapidated corncrib and were munching on ears of dried corn still in the shucks. Chickens pecked in the mud; a rooster crowed.

"Just listen at that fool!" Stell said. "He just don't know how close he is to bein' plucked an' dropped in a pot."

With her usual brand of refinement, she went to Asher and said, "Son, there ain't no disputin' the devil's dealt you a sorry hand. This here's a dire turn of fortune an' you have indeed ended up on the wantin' end of the stick. But you bear in mind, I recall a time so poor we had to eat off of magnolia leaves, so thangs could be worse; the world will go on." With cause to wonder if those were the most consoling words she could rake together, one had but to know Stell to understand their meaningfulness.

An hour later, carrying a bundle of soggy clothes to the wagon, she said for the hundredth time, "This here's the worst I've ever seen."

No one could argue that point.

Throughout the morning, they recovered a variety of useful items and some that might again be made useful: utensils, pans, a footstool, a broom. Addie rolled a feather mattress over and uncovered a gallon of cane syrup and a small, framed picture of Libby, taken at school the year before. Claire found a couple of perfectly good chairs, not a mar to be found on them anywhere. Emily came running, carrying a basket. "Look what I found!" She presented half a dozen eggs.

Their efforts proceeded slowly; as the sun climbed, the heat began taking its toll on Stell and Claire. By ten-thirty, they looked like they were about to drop. Addie determined it was best she take them home. The last thing they needed was for them to have a heatstroke. Expecting them to protest, she crafted an excuse. "I could use a rest and a cool drink of water. Let's go home with what we have and get these clothes washed and hung out."

They agreed. Tired and dirty, they went back to Laura's.

Anna appeared to have just gotten out of bed; her hair was in wild disarray. She was sitting motionless in a chair by a window, staring out. So still was she, she appeared statue-like, like a troll posing for a portrait. She showed not one spark of interest in hearing about what they'd brought back on the wagon, nor did she make any move toward offering them assistance in unloading it.

When they headed outdoors to start the wash, Laura suggested, "Anna, wouldn't you like to come sit outside on the porch an' get some fresh air?"

Anna seemed to consider it a moment but then shook her head and turned her face back to the window. No, she didn't feel like it. The effort seemed too great. Anyway, what difference could fresh air make now? She could not imagine.

Two days later, from atop the woodshop where he was helping Hiram repair the roof, hearing the sound of horses' hooves Daniel lifted his head and looked down the road. He spied two men approaching on horseback, traveling at a fair gait. Still quite a ways off, he squinted in an effort to make out their features. As they came closer, he recognized Sheriff Wiggington, but the broad, burly man accompanying him was a stranger.

Gesturing with his hammer, he said, "Wonder who that is comin' this-a way with the sheriff."

Hiram paused and watched, and when the men veered off the road in their direction, he and Daniel made their way down the ladder.

"Mornin'," Hiram greeted them cordially.

Neither man dismounted. Sheriff Wiggington tipped his hat back and said, "Mornin', Hiram, Daniel. Glad to see y'all fared well." He glanced about. "It'd be fair to say we had ourselves one mother of a storm." He stopped there pretending he'd come to engage in general talk.

"This here's John Rutland, from over in the Sweetwater community. He come askin' for my help in tryin' to track down the whereabouts of a feller named Graham, an' since you're the only one I know of in these parts, I brought him here."

From beneath a shaggy set of brows, the man Rutland gave Hiram a thorough going-over. Shaking his head, he said, "Ain't him, but if it weren't for the beard, he could be kin."

The sheriff had figured as much. He'd had his own run-in with Wilkes. He told Hiram, "I'm thankin' he might have business with your brother, Hiram. He still around?"

Hiram took his time answering. "Why you askin'? He done somethin' wrong?"

Rutland shifted tensely in his saddle and bellowed, "He's a durn thief, is all!"

Hiram didn't take kindly to the tone the man directed at him. "What'd he steal?" he wanted to know.

Red-faced, the man answered, "He stole a roan gelding from my stables, an' I've come to reclaim it, that's what!"

Sheriff Wiggington intervened. "Seems your brother tried to buy a horse from Rutland here a week or so ago, only it weren't for sale. He says it's since went missin'. If we could talk to Wilkes, he might help clear the matter up."

"When did the horse go missin'?" Hiram asked.

Rutland replied hotly, "I turned him out Thursday mornin' with the rest of the herd; ain't seen hide nor hair of him since."

Hiram let the conversation rest a minute, speculatively, while he thought about what the man said. Then, "Wilkes ain't here. He left out first thing Monday mornin', headed back t'wards Virginia. That means he was a smart distance from here when you say your horse went missin'. Could be you've got some fence down from the storm like the rest of us. Could be that horse of yours might wander back up yet."

With his hands clenched, Rutland sputtered, "That all sounds mighty convenient now, don't it? Could be you've got your brother an' my horse hid out some'ers!"

"Careful, Rutland! There ain't no call for accusations!" the sheriff warned. "Throwin' off on Hiram here ain't gonna get you your horse back! I happen to know this man's worth his salt, an' if he says his brother ain't here, then his brother ain't here, an' that's good enough for me!"

The other grunted.

Hiram said it calmly, yet there was a certain power in his voice. "Mister, I hate you think my brother wronged you, but you have my word. He rode off from here Monday mornin' on the same sorrel mare he rode in on about a month ago."

For a long moment John Rutland stared intently at Hiram's face, evaluating the worth of his words, evaluating him. Hiram held him up to eye level, even though the man towered over him astride his horse. In the end, Rutland said, "I got no quarrel with you, but I know as well as I know my name somebody stole my horse, an' I got a strong suspicion it was that brother of yorn." Without further comment, he jerked the reins and urged his horse toward the road in a cloud of dust.

"Well, I reckon I've hindered you boys from your work long enough," the sheriff said in leaving.

When they had gone, Daniel, who had been listening with keen interest to every word, uttered, "That feller John Rutland give me the feelin' of a man I wouldn't want to go up against."

No scrapper by nature, and considering the man's size and attitude, Hiram felt inclined to agree. On the other hand, if warranted by necessity, he felt qualified to answer the call. As he climbed slowly back up the ladder, he drawled in response, "Son, in this life you have to take 'em as they come. If ol' whistlebritches John Rutland could play it, I 'spect I could dance to it."

While this made Daniel grin, as Hiram mulled over the encounter again in his mind, he was nagged by doubt, especially where the man's horse was concerned.

CHAPTER 7

"Oh that I had wings like a dove! For then would I fly away, and be at rest." Psalm 55: 6

Once uncovered and inspected, the foundation of the old house was found to be sturdy enough to rebuild upon; even so, with help, it would take Asher months to reconstruct their home. Wesley and Laura were glad to accommodate them for as long as was necessary; they had more than enough room, especially now that Sarah Beth had moved into town. And though she had never had the slightest understanding of her sister-in-law, Laura made every effort to make Anna feel at home.

With so much to do every day, since she was the one who spent the most time around Anna, it would be Laura more than anyone else who would notice the changes in her. Hence, she began to worry, especially about Anna's state of mind.

Asher religiously went about making things orderly again. Anna, on the other hand, took no part in the work and showed no inclination toward such. She seemed to have no desire to set foot upon the place again, not even when Laura tried to persuade her that they go there together to see what progress was being made. For the first couple of days after the storm, a flow of neighbors and church members came and went, bearing heart-felt encouragement and gifts of every kind. Clothing, foodstuff, quilts. Laura received them. Anna avoided them. She retreated, kept to her room, out of sight.

Another day went by and then another. Anna hardly spoke; conversation held no interest for her. She lay abed until noon, wouldn't eat, didn't seem to have the energy or care to even brush her hair. Her only solace came from isolating herself from the others. She just wanted to be left alone, locked away in her own world with her own miseries. She barely paid any attention to Libby. Laura saw Anna smile a little once or twice at something her daughter said, but thankfully for Libby, being around Jesse and Meggie seemed to make up for her mother's remoteness. Otherwise, the child may as well been nonexistent.

Thursday morning, Laura pressed her, "Anna, won't you please eat something?" Anna had not eaten since the storm; when water was offered she'd drink a swallow or two. And, it seemed everyone trying so hard to cheer her up only had the opposite effect on her, only upset her more. Each day she seemed unhappier than the last. As she grew increasingly despondent, she appeared content only in her seclusion.

On that very afternoon, she heard Laura and Addie whispering in the hallway and knew they were whispering about her.

Laura's nerves were starting to wear thin at playing the nice hostess. Once out of earshot of Anna, she told Addie, "I've just about had it up to *here*! While we're all workin' our behinds off, what I really feel like doing is marchin' in there, grabbin' her by the shoulders and shakin' some sense into her!"

She didn't want to argue with Laura, but Addie felt sympathetic toward Anna. She understood her pain and how awful it was to lose a home, to lose a life. She assured Laura, "We just have to keep praying for her. Encourage, not try to force her. It's only been a few days. Given time, she'll come around…you'll see."

Lo and behold, the following Saturday morning, the woman who had barely risen from a chair in over a week did indeed finally come around. She filled the claw-footed bathtub full of water and bathed, washed her hair, and donned a pretty, fresh frock. Overnight her eyes had lost their hollow look. Anna was like her old self again, only better.

She sat at the table and ate breakfast with the family, declaring, "I'm famished!" After drinking a glass full of milk, she filled it again to the brim and drained another. Her ravenous appetite and cheerful mood left everyone mystified.

Sometime later, Laura observed her pushing Libby in the swing that hung from a limb of the oak in the backyard; she even went with Asher to their place to see how he was getting on with the rebuilding of their house. She spoke to him warmly, graciously praising him for all his hard work. The transformation in her demeanor was nothing short of remarkable, more like miraculous, if not downright peculiar.

That night after supper, Anna yawned. A few minutes later, she yawned again and said, "I don't feel like I've slept in a week…I think I'll turn in early." She went over and kissed Libby on the top of her head. "Good night, all."

Anna went out of the room, Laura and Wesley gazing after her in stunned silence, convinced that she had finally gone mad, Asher smiling, immensely pleased and relieved, because he had gotten his wife back.

Hours later, Anna reached for her shawl and tiptoed out of the house into the silvery gleam of night. She kept to the road for about a mile and a half before turning onto a trail that led into the woods. The night was so clear, so starry.

She thought, *My mind is so clear…*

The creek beckoned her on. Feeling a burst of energy and filled with a sense of euphoria, she practically ran through the woods. When she got close enough, she could smell the water. She closed her eyes and listened. She heard breathing. The trees were breathing. The woods were alive!

I haven't felt this alive in days, she thought. No longer would she be trapped, battering around inside a cage. She was so happy she felt like she was soaring. She envisioned herself as a bird flying to freedom. *I'm going to sprout wings and fly off from here!*

When she came to the place she chose, she sat down on a soft carpet of moss and drew her knees up under her chin. She gazed out across the water, it catching the glow of the moon.

She was so happy to be alone, out of the house, away from everyone. She felt like an alien amongst them. As she sat there, even though she hadn't really been a devoted mother and wasn't bound by any strong attachment to Libby, for a moment she thought of her and was saddened. *She'll get on fine; Asher will see to it. Asher's a good man.* She knew he had done his best to be a good husband to her. *Yet, I don't love him.* Anna knew she could trust Laura to help him look after Libby. *Laura's always been kind to me, unlike Stell.* No, she definitely would not miss ornery old Stell.

She then fixed her thoughts on her unborn baby and tried to imagine what she, or he, might look like. *No doubt handsome, if it's a boy.* Asher had always wanted a son. *Every man wants a son…*

Anna looked up at the moon. She took off her shoes and arched her feet slowly. The sand caressed her toes, moonlight shimmered on the water, a chorus of frogs sang…

The voice inside her head assured her she was doing the right thing. She knew she could never be happy here again …*I will never be happy here again.*

She had long coveted an escape, and now it had come. An owl swooped down from its lofty perch ...*like a bird from prison bars has flown...*

The two farms that lay on either side of the creek were the one owned by Asher and Anna and that of the Thomason family. In the vague, predawn light, Algie followed a rutted path cut over time by his cows as they trekked methodically to and from the watering hole every day. He was on his way to open the gap at the creek-crossing to turn the lowing herd in to graze on the new grass in the upper field.

To Algie, this was the best part of the day. Carrying a leather strop used for prodding the slowest and laziest of the cows, he went along at a moderate pace, savoring the freshness of the morning air, slapping the strop against his thigh while he idly whistled a tune.

A half hour later, with the cows situated, he headed for home, veering off the path to walk along the creek. He knew Eunice would have breakfast ready, but he was coming up on a spot with a little sandbar where he'd fished a dark, bottomless hole with favorable luck for bream one day last week. He was planning to drop his line here again soon and just wanted to spend a minute scouting it out.

He abruptly stopped his whistling-slapping.

"What the ...?" He muttered to himself when a peculiar sight caught his eye. They were sitting on a patch of green moss at the edge of the sandbar. Squinting, he thought, *I must be goin' blind!* He started down the embankment to get a closer look, easing up on them as cautiously as he would a coiled-up cottonmouth.

His first thought was that maybe they'd been picked up, from Lord knows where, probably by the twister, and this is where they'd finally landed. But now, as he was bent over them, staring, he realized such a notion was pure whimsical. He thought, *Ain't no way in hell that happened.*

Considering how they were positioned, he realized they'd been placed there by someone, deliberately. Set side by side, perfectly aligned. Like someone just took them off, laid them down, and walked off. Scratching his head, Algie was puzzled: *Now who in tarnation had left a pair of woman's shoes here on the creek bank like that? And why?*

His eyes trailed downstream.

Suddenly Algie let out a choked scream and peed on himself! What he saw scared the living daylights out of him! It was a sight he would never forget. Unable to overcome the gruesomeness of it, he couldn't bring himself to do what he ought to do. Instead, he turned around and tore away like a bolt of lightening.

Coldness ran through him as he groped and stumbled up the sloping grade of the embankment, clawing like a madman trying to reach flat ground. Still, he couldn't stop himself from looking back at the grisly sight of her, afloat, her dress caught on a snag in the shallows, her hair fanned out in the current, her skin colorless and translucent.

Mentally, he covered his eyes. He wouldn't look at her again. *I ain't lookin'! I ain't lookin'!* Gulping for air, he took off across the field, shaking like a leaf, tripping over every obstacle in his way. Unembarrassed at his fear, he kept stumbling on toward the house, where he would tell Eunice the grievous news.

Anna Bradley had drowned herself in the creek.

Travis, Abigail, and Sarah Beth came out from town as soon as they received word of Anna's death. Compelled to see with their own eyes that she had indeed drowned, there was already a somber group of people standing around in Wesley's yard, mumbling speculation over what had taken place. The shock of her suicide was great, the suicide itself beyond reason.

After a brief examination of Anna's corpse, Travis went into the front parlor, where he found Asher standing, staring out the window. The man looked exhausted, disheveled, much older than his thirty-five years, as though he'd aged ten in the last night.

"I'm sorry, Asher," Travis said. "I know this is hard for you." Even for a doctor it seemed particularly difficult to find words for a death of this kind. "Can you tell me what happened?"

Asher had already told the sheriff all he knew, which was nothing, except that Anna had not been herself since the day of the storm, the day they lost their home.

He looked at Travis blankly. "I'd like to believe it was an accident, but deep down, I know…" He swallowed the words in midsentence as he thought about how Anna had always been afraid of the water. After a pause, he acknowledged, "She wouldn't've gone there otherwise, her not bein' able to swim."

What surer way to end it? Travis thought.

"How could she have done this? Why?" Asher asked. "An' why didn't I see it comin'? How could I have let this happen?"

What Asher was feeling was exactly what Travis expected. Asher was in a cluttered place, besieged by a barrage of emotions—grief, anger, confusion, guilt. He was being attacked from every side. Too, there was a certain shame in the manner of his wife's death, which signified, in his eyes, his failure as a husband. He felt responsible. These were all normal reactions to a loved one's suicide.

Asher looked over at him helplessly. "I promised her I'd build the house back." And since the day of the storm, he'd been working tirelessly at it, from sunup to sundown, trying to rebuild their home, with the hope of rebuilding their lives.

"This ain't your fault, Asher. The mind is fragile. An' ever'body don't handle things the same. The terror of livin' through the storm, losin' her home—it was just all too much for her to cope with." It was Travis's guess that Anna had been unhappy for a long time; these factors just finally pushed her over the edge; she broke down, saw suicide as her only escape from the storm that had most likely been raging inside her head for some time, years maybe, maybe all her life.

"I'll admit she'd been actin' poorly for the last few days. It was understandable after all that happened. But she seemed like she was startin' to get over it," Asher said. "Why, yesterday she seemed happy as a lark."

Travis nodded. "Because she'd come up with a plan." He knew when a mentally disturbed person showed improvement was usually when they were most dangerous to themselves. "In her mind, Anna had reached a resolution to her problems. She'd come up with a way to put an end to all her worries." The dread of facing another day had been too overpowering for her.

While Asher let this sink in for a few minutes, it got him to thinking. Anna had always been selfish, never one to spend her concerns and affections on others, with no exception for him. But being of enduring character, in it for better or for worse, he hadn't complained. He'd just made do, figuring he was probably better off than some, no worse off than others.

Not to say he and Anna argued. They didn't. They just didn't share much. Nor had she ever lost herself in Libby as one would expect a mother of an only child to do. The longer Asher thought about it, the clearer it got. Anna had simply found another way to leave Libby and him alone. For good.

Rubbing his temples, he looked at Travis and said a bit resentfully, "Well, she picked a fine time to end her worryin', us not even a roof over our heads." He sighed heavily. "Can't do much else about it now, I reckon, 'cept pick up an' go on."

Yet still. His thoughts flip-flopped. Even though theirs might not have been the most satisfying of arrangements, considering all, especially Anna's bleak upbringing, over the years Asher had always held a sort of compassionate protectiveness for her, had stood by her in a way that others could never understand. Presently, he thought about how little attention he'd paid her lately. He couldn't even remember what tenor of words passed between them last.

He turned back to stare out the window, retreating back into his private despair. Feeling lonely and sad, he only wished Anna were alive again.

Word of Anna's death spread through the community like wildfire. *Of course, she was crazy,* went the whispers.

Anna had indeed been a strange one. She had possessed no spirit of hospitality, had not been a pleasant woman to be around, not very lovable. Attributive to her audacious temperament and curdling disposition, she had a sparse number of friends, almost none of whom felt particularly close to her.

Outside of her relatives, there were few true mourners at her funeral the following day; yet attendance was large, not so much due to charitable feelings as curiosity, since none in the area could boast of ever having known a person who'd committed suicide before. Even Brother Higgins seemed at a loss in choosing adequate words to comfort the family members who stood around the grave like pillars of stone, their thoughts as bleak as the setting. They got through the burial with their minds adrift:

How could I have been so busy not to notice how distraught and sick my own wife was? Asher lamented. He would never forgive himself for that.

Exhausted, he found it hard to think straight. He'd lost track of time since the day of the storm. *Had that only been a week past? Only eight days ago we lost our home? And now Anna is gone? How is it possible for things to change so in such a short time?* Unable to make sense of it all, he swallowed hard against the tightness in his throat. Libby clutched his hand so tightly his fingers ached.

Laura struggled with the guilt that weighted her shoulders down like a heavy cloak. *I should have been more patient, more understanding…*

Addie mused sadly, *All Alfred put me through, I never thought of ending it all like this; I persevered for the sake of my children.* In truth, she had grown in her trials; when Alfred died she'd come to recognize the other side of loss and sorrow. Alfred's death had set her free in more ways than one.

Sly as a fox, sour as vinegar, temperamental, ill-bred Anna…throwed off her high horse an' laid low at last. Stell recalled there had been a time when she and Anna would dedicate half a day to thinking up slights to hurl against each other, one always trying to best their opponent. The memory filled her with a regret that surprised her. She dabbed her eyes with her handkerchief. *Oh, Anna, poor, foolish, temperamental Anna…*

Of course most disturbing of all, never would one of them forget the sight from the day before, of Libby lying on the porch, curled up in a fetal position beside Anna's wet corpse wrapped in sheet. The child refused to get up until the coffin was delivered from town.

At one point, she had taken the sheet off her face—"So Mama can breathe," she'd said. Nor would they forget the mournful sound of her crying, the mournful sound of a child lost. No one could protect her from the hurt of having to come to terms with the grim truth that her mother was dead.

"…thou return unto the ground, for out of it wast thou taken, for dust thou art, and unto dust shalt thou return…" The preacher's dry voice summoned them all back to the present. "Likewise, I say this to you, our sister, Anna Bradley, shall your dust return to the earth as it was, and your spirit shall return unto God who gave it. Amen."

Rituals serve a purpose, and well understood was the ritual of a bereaved family gathering around a table to share a delicious meal, it being a proven fact that good food could heal most any hurt. Adhering to this tradition, the ladies of the church had a feast worthy of celebration awaiting them when they returned to the house following the funeral. However, there was no gathering around a meal that day, nothing for them to celebrate. Instead, an impermeable chill seemed to descend upon the house.

Libby fell into an exhausted nap; Asher and Wesley went back to the cemetery to watch the filling in of the grave; Stell crept off up the lane and took to her bed. Claire, not wanting to wake her, spent the afternoon planting a patch of gourds and tending a flowerbed abloom with marigolds and zinnias. Laura sent Jesse and Meggie outside to play while she sat and worked silently at the embroidery on her lap.

That night at supper, Emily finally spoke the words she'd been saving all day. "That smart aleck Millie Stevens said the most hateful things to Libby today."

Wearing a concerned frown, Addie asked, "What did Millie say?"

"She said if Uncle Asher had prayed harder, their house wouldn't've been destroyed by the storm."

"Why, that seems a bit unfair," Addie replied. "You don't think that way too, do you?"

Emily shook her head and answered, "I guess not." She glanced at Hiram. "But when we were down in the cellar that day, you prayed, and the storm didn't hurt us."

Addie was quick to respond. "It pleases God when we ask Him to help us in times of trouble, and He no doubt answers prayers, but it's wrong for us to automatically look at every tragedy that comes along as punishment. Sometimes God uses storms in our lives to strengthen us, and bring us closer to Him."

She looked Emily full in the face. "The storm was indeed a terrible tragedy—sort of like when our old house burned down. Bad things happen, and when they do it's important for us to remember that God loves us. If we pray and put our trust in Him, He will never fail us."

For a moment, Emily pushed at her food with her fork thoughtfully.

"Millie said something else too," she said softly. "That God sends people who kill themselves straight to hell." Tears sprang to her eyes; she felt so sorry for Libby. "Is that true, Mama?"

When Addie hesitated, Hiram got up from the table and came back with his Bible.

"I think I can put our uncertainties to rest about that," he said.

He began reading from the book of Judges. "...And the woman bore a son, and called his name Samson, and the Lord blessed him."

He paraphrased the story in words that Emily could understand, telling her how Delilah consented to help the Philistines capture Samson by discovering the secret of his strength and how she had bound him up first with seven green twigs and then again with new ropes. Finally, the Philistines shaved off Samson's hair, causing the Lord to depart from him.

Hiram continued reading from the sixteenth chapter, "And Samson called unto the Lord and said, 'O Lord God, remember me, I pray thee'...and Samson took hold of the two middle pillars upon which the house stood...and Samson said, 'Let me die with the Philistines'...and the house fell..."

At the conclusion of the story, Emily was satisfied that God didn't forsake Samson, even though he took his own life. When she excused herself from the table and left out, Addie wondered aloud, "Well, we know Samson went to be with the Lord, but I'm curious, what do you suppose ever became of Delilah?"

Hiram met her question with a grin and twinkling eyes, his tone conspiratorial. "Lady, you bind me up with ropes, I'll do my best to satisfy your curiosity about that an' anything else you might want to know."

Addie could only smile at her wonderful, incorrigible husband.

CHAPTER 8

"Remember the days of old, consider the years of many generations." Deuteronomy 32: 7

After the preaching, as was common most of the children took in after one another, racing through the arched, iron entrance of the cemetery to run a zigzag course among the headstones. Anna's was the freshest mound, beneath a big sycamore tree that shaded one corner of the graveyard.

Lost in thought, Addie looked out across the way with unseeing eyes, not noticing that anyone had come to stand beside her until Claire joggled her attention with, "It's said that only us Southerners raise our young'uns amongst the dead."

Nothing struck either of them odd or disrespectable about hearing peals of laughter echoing across what to some might be considered a sorrowful and sacred place. Addie smiled and replied, "*Actually,* I think the saying goes 'only Southerners *live* amongst the dead'."

Regardless of how stated, the gist of the adage was true. Like a creek bank in summertime or the courthouse square, not only did children play in cemeteries, men met up there to smoke before going inside the church to worship, and women wandered about the plots, touching a headstone here and there, and gossiped. Even young lovers were known to stroll through them into the night.

"I was just like them when I was little…could hardly wait for the preacher to hush so I could go outside and run through the Eminence graveyard. What the fascination is, I don't know."

Claire offered profoundly, "One thing for sure, they won't offend a soul out there." Her thoughts were far from morbid when she added, "An' since we're on the subject, when I pass from this world, don't y'all plant me here. Take me back to Collinsville an' bury me at Eminence beside my Luke."

Addie refused to entertain the thought of Claire dying at all. She dismissed the subject by making light. "I'll tell you when you can die, not an hour before."

What Addie said next was the last thing Claire expected. "Claire, what would you say if I told you I've been thinking of telling Sassie that Alfred was her father?" She had been standing in a pool of uncertainty over the matter ever since Sassie told her of the cold reception served her by Rosette Quinn. *Miz Addie, I jus' wish I wuz either white or colored…I don't b'long nowhere…*Only a handful of people had certain knowledge of her paternity, and two of them were dead.

Taken back, Claire didn't hesitate in letting her disapproval be known. "I'd say that was a far cry from the best idea you've ever had!"

Addie fixed her mouth to answer, but Claire stopped her short. "Trust me, child, you'll be sorry. I done seen enough livin' to know— no good ever comes from diggin' up old graves!"

With that, she turned and walked on ahead to Wesley's buggy, her skirts swishing, leaving Addie calling after her.

"Claire! Whatever do you mean? Claire!"

"Lord, much obliged for this fine day an' the fellowship an' sermon You bestowed on us this mornin'. Be with Preacher Higgins as he shepherds us; help us apply Your Word to our lives daily. Bless this food, use it to strengthen our bodies..."

No sooner than *Amen* passed over Wesley's lips did the prayerful lull erupt into deafening clatter of plates and silverware as bowls of food began passage around the table.

Laura was the first one to say, "As much as I'll miss Brother McElreath, I for one enjoyed listenin' to a new preacher for a change. And, his wife seems really nice; I loved that dress she was wearin'."

Amid an almost unanimous bobbing of heads, Stell heaped a mound of mashed potatoes onto her plate and snorted. "Well, *I* for one am totin' a cussin' for ol' Preacher McElreath! Weren't no sense in him quittin' us in midstream! After we'd put up with him this long, you'd a-thought he'd a-stayed the duration!"

Laura marveled. "I swanee, Mama! The poor creature is old as dirt, purely gone to seed! He's earned a rest!"

"He can rest when he dies, like the rest of us," Stell scoffed. "An' as for him bein' old, same could be said of ol' Claire settin' here, gray as a coon, but she still puts forth the effort to put one foot before the other." Dipping from a bowl of butterbeans, she took her time about dredging through the pot-liquor to scoop out the big hunk of salt pork used for seasoning before passing the dish on around the table.

Without appearing to pay any attention to the slight, Claire leisurely drizzled a spoonful of creamy chicken gravy over her potatoes. Of course, her marked pause was deliberate, she taking her lead from Stell. Then pretending to speak to no one in particular, she bleated musically, "Ol' girl's all in a tizzy. Got a bee up her nose 'cause she couldn't set an' snore like a bear through the sermon today like she would ordinarily. New preacher-man hindered her *much-needed* beauty rest."

This caused tittering around the table because everyone knew what Claire said was true. Stell was faithful to nod off during the

service, but this new Reverend Higgins was somewhat of a shouter, occasionally emphasizing his words by pounding a fist down on the pulpit in such a way that anyone would have had to be dead to sleep through it.

"Shame, I say! A soul ort'n't be mocked for reverencin' the Lord with his eyes closed, 'specially in the church-house!" Stell declared firmly. "Matter a fact, it says that in the Bible in Isaiah: 'Now therefore be ye not mockers …'"

With challenging eyes, she said, "An' as for *your* new preacher—as if it weren't bad enough him a-hollerin' an' carryin' on so—I pray to God we don't damn the day, but listenin' to his jabberin' gave me a notion we might've welcomed us a *Yankee* into the fold!" She spat the word *Yankee* from her mouth like it tasted of bitterweed. "For all we know, he could be some thievin' scalawag from some'ers way up north. Come to think of it, he don't look like nobody I ever set eyes on, an' I ain't never heard the name 'Higgins' mentioned in these parts before he rid into town!"

"Well, he can certainly quote the Scripture," Claire said placidly.

"Same can be said of the Devil," Stell reminded her stoically.

Defending her fortress, Claire replied, "Why, yes. I do believe you just proved that with your recitation from the Book of Isaiah." She took a satisfying bite of cucumber and tomato salad, tossed with vinegar and a pinch of sugar.

Wesley's face was suffused with incredulity as he stared across the table and watched the two as if they were crazy. Shaking his head, he chewed his food in silence. On the one hand, Stell's tireless ability to find fault with everything and everybody in the world never ceased to amaze him. On the other, watching the interaction between her and Claire always rendered more entertaining than a scripted play.

"I do declare, Mama! If you're not pure ridiculous, Moses didn't part the Red Sea! The man's given name is *Jefferson Davis* Higgins. I'd wager there's not a whole lot of Yankees walkin' around with a name like that!" Laura cried.

Claire passed a platter piled high with golden fried chicken to Stell with, "I'll have you know, you insensible old fool, once upon a time, I had a friend who was a Yankee. As fine a feller as you'd ever want to meet."

"Blasphemy!" Stell cried indignantly, spearing a pulley bone. "Take me to the mangy dog so's I can cut out his gizzard an' put him out o' his misery!"

Claire kept up the exchange for amusement's sake. "You've long outlived any such opportunity. Dear ol' soul's long-time dead. More'n thirty, forty years now."

Hopes dashed, Stell insisted, "At least impart his name."

For a moment, Claire's eyes lay fixed on Stell's sagging jowls as a name flitted forth.

Samuel.

With a shake of head, she sighed and said, "When you get as old and gray as a coon as I am, the mind hides things. I can't seem to remember now..."

Her plate now laden with food, Stell raised her fork triumphantly and prepared to dig in. "A-ha! Just as I figured! Another one of your far-flung tales, made up just to bait my appetite! Now hush up an' let me eat!"

That night, a slender coil of black smoke rose from the globe of an oil lamp burning on Claire's desk. Outside her window, an owl hooted softly.

Unable to concentrate, she sighed and closed her book. Ordinarily not one to worry over much, her earlier conversation with Addie out by the cemetery weighed upon her mind as heavy as a tombstone. She hadn't meant to bite her head off, but Addie'd caught her off guard when she brought it up about disclosing the fact of Alfred being Sassie's father. Such a truth! Was it really necessary?

Knowing full well scandals are sometimes forgiven—even forgotten—with the passing of time, still her conscious wavered. *Tell me again, Luke, that what we did was right.* It had seemed so, way back then, but at this particular moment, it waxed troublesome. Tonight the past echoed back to her like the haunting call of that old hoot owl.

Though it all happened decades ago, she remembered it vividly, like it was yesterday. They'd soldiered up into the yard, heavy-footed like walking dead—Luke and Samuel—gaunt and weary, home from the war.

Claire would never forget Luke's first words to her upon arriving home. He said, "Wife, I've been to and come back from a place I hope not to revisit."

As he and Samuel had marched through the mire and ashes of a war-ravaged land, they considered themselves fortunate to be among the blessed few who had managed to keep body and soul together, for they'd seen so many others fall by the wayside, so many others buried far from their homes.

Circumstance often overlooks misfortune, and during such a time as it was, with every folk preoccupied with change and hardship of his own, nothing needed to be explained to anyone. Samuel Warren, who came to them a stranger, was generally accepted by the community as who he claimed to be—a wayfaring soldier, wounded in the fighting at Vicksburg and befriended by Luke on the long march home. A Rebel who was never again to return to his home state of Alabama, once his heart was smitten and then saved by Rachel—and hers by him.

Fact was, Samuel's past and the man he had once been had both been lost, given up to the war. That Samuel Warren simply ceased to be, any evidence of him brushed away as easily as he'd brushed the hair out of his eyes the moment he met Rachel. No one needed to know, cared to know, or ever knew he was actually a Union Army deserter—a lonely, war-sick soul who slipped away into a night that reeked of blood and gunpowder and the decay of mankind, seeking refuge. That was when he met Luke, and good friends they became; their bond of friendship and love transcended any differences that may have been.

Continuing on the trail of ghosts, Claire conjured up the name Dalton Davis. *Now there's a scoundrel if there ever was one!* Lordy, she thought she'd buried that man's identity along with his bones! Just this very day, had she not told Addie, *"I'm not one to favor diggin' up old graves"?* And here she sat with a shovel in her hands!

Claire shook her head at the memory of Dalton. She recalled how back in 1863, he'd up and run off to join a band of renegades, Confederate deserters led by a cold-blooded murderer by the name of Newt Knight. Their headquarters and hideout was known as the Devil's Den, a cave located underneath the perilous bluffs along the Leaf River. During this time, the county of Jones seceded from the state of Mississippi, declaring itself the "Free State of Jones."

It was a well-known fact that Newt had kinfolks around Collinsville who took occasion to help the cunning fugitive hide from the law, but as far as she could recollect, Claire had only laid eyes on the man but once, years back.

Sitting astride his horse, he had struck her as being a madman. An imposing figure of arrogance with unruly, jet black hair and beard and a crooked nose, he had unforgettable eyes—clear gray and cold as steel. And he had an exceedingly extraordinary habit. He unconsciously moved his lips as he thought, making ugly faces somewhat in the manner as a child might while pantomiming before a mirror. Perhaps most notable of all, looped around his neck on a fine leather string, he wore his legendary black hunting horn.

To some, nothing worse could be said of a man than accuse him of taking part in the mixing of whites and coloreds. Newt Knight was reputed for doing such. Because of this, he and his children were disgraced and banished from society, he disowned by his family and disassociated by any friends he'd once had. He did, in fact, prove

himself to be a madman, indeed, one snowy Christmas Day when he forced two of his white children to intermarry with those of a Negro harlot living on the old Knight Plantation.

Eventually, Dalton Davis was captured by the cavalry and hanged to death over in the community of Cracker's Neck, along with two other men, for their involvement in a raid on army stores for arms and supplies.

Dalton Davis. *Rachel's first husband.* He was one reason Rachel had years later so despised Addie's husband, Alfred Coulter, for the two men had been cast from the very same, sorry mold.

Had Wesley and Addie ever known these things, it would have gone a ways in explaining to them why their mother all but lost what was left of her mind after their little sister Rebekah fell on a jar and tragically bled to death, for Rebekah was the only child produced of the great love between Samuel and Rachel.

When Dalton abandoned Rachel, Wesley had barely been three years old; Addie, a babe. Samuel Warren loved and raised Rachel and Dalton's two children as his own. The collective identity he assumed seemed such a plausible and uncomplicated solution... Samuel needed credible cause for tenure. Wesley and Addie needed a father. They were too young to know the difference.

Samuel, the gentle, beloved father of Addie. No finer man, no.

Only the four of them had known, and they made a pact never to tell. Luke, Claire, Samuel, and Rachel. Now Claire was the sole guardian of an elaborate secret contrived of friendship and ideals nigh forty years before. Once, and only once, she lapsed clumsily, almost letting the truth slip out while recounting to Addie the story about when Rachel, pregnant, took a trip to New Orleans with her uncle. Luckily, she'd caught herself just in time and managed to smooth over the blunder with a well-meaning lie.

All thought out, Claire rubbed her tired eyes, her mind once again certain. After all this time, truth of the matter was surely barren of purpose.

As nighttime sometimes will, the night suddenly played fanciful, making Claire imagine she felt Luke's breath move across her face. The sensation of it stirred some longlost ache within her. After all this time, she still missed him terribly. Yearning to capture and preserve the sweet sustenance of her beloved husband's spirit against her skin, indulging the fantasy, Claire pressed a hand to her warm cheek in an attempt to hold him there, lest the feeling flee.

Alas, too soon the magic did indeed pass away; the sweetness inevitably escaped her. Once her sensibility was restored, Claire whispered, *Yes, Luke, we were right all along...I stand steadfast on our promise.* To unearth the past now would be pointless, even hurtful.

She extinguished the wick of the oil lamp; the faint glow in the room died, and Claire was again alone. From a small pouch on her bureau, she stuffed Luke's old pipe, tamping the sweet-smelling tobacco down hard with her thumb, and went out on the porch to smoke.

CHAPTER 9

"Fear thou not, for I am with thee..." Isaiah 41:10

With all the pots and pans cleaned and put away, Sassie dragged herself wearily up the stairs to her room. Drained from work, drained from the heat, and drained from worry, she fell on her bed, exhausted.

With her face pressed against the quilt her mama had pieced together years before, for a moment Sassie stared at the wall and willed her mind to drift back, trying to pretend she was a little girl again. Oh, how she wished she could turn back the clock and have her mama here with her now! Surely she would understand what she was feeling; she had probably gone through some of the very same feelings herself. No doubt there were times she'd felt just this isolated and unhappy.

Of late, Sassie's sleep had come erratically, some nights not at all. She'd lie awake half the night, then, come midmorning, be plagued with drowsiness. Tired and unable to concentrate, she became clumsy, constantly dropping pans or utensils. Just this very morning, she'd carelessly scorched her fingers on the stove.

Within the last week, a couple of times she'd grown queasy and faint while cooking. Not one to be sickly before, at first she laid it off on the insufferable, Mississippi heat. It was probably that, she reasoned.

Sassie's mind was in turmoil. Scorched fingers were the least of her worries. *I'z bein' punished fo' my sin,* she thought. How could she have let such a thing happen? In her naïveté, she'd failed to consider the possibility of this. After all, she and Obie had lain together only a few times. At first, she'd cringed away from the truth and blamed the symptoms on everything else. Her long hours in the cookhouse, the heat, most of all the infamous Quinn Sunday dinner and disastrous run-in with Obie's mama, they all had taken their toll on her, sapped her energy.

But now she knew better.

When she hadn't come sick at her normal time, she finally had to face the indisputable truth of it. Ill luck prevailing, she realized she'd been burned by the first fires of passion in more ways than one. Her sin had found her out, her chickens had come home to roost. There was no doubt in Sassie's mind; she was expecting.

A tear crept down her cheek. She felt strange and scared and all alone. All alone, that was, except for the baby inside her that was due sometime in the spring. Her hand drifted across her belly in the same manner old Georgianne's had that day. *A baby!* How on earth was she going to be able to work and tend to a baby? She didn't have the slightest idea. Cook with a baby on her hip?

She wondered how Obie was going to react when she told him that evening. What if he ran out on her? Sorrowfully, she wondered, *What if he don't really love me like he promised?* What if his promises turned out to be nothing more than what Miz Ruthie called "bed promises"? Fear and uncertainty gripped her heart.

And what about Miz Quinn? She'd no doubt be to bury! Filled with a growing sense of desperation, Sassie drew her knees up and, for an endless time, sobbed quietly into her pillow.

The heat of the day filled the room, making her drowsy.

A light rapping on the door woke her. When she opened her eyes she was surprised to realize the day had faded; the room had grown dim. That told her she'd been sleeping for several hours. Dizzy for a moment when she arose, she walked over to the door and opened it. Obie was standing there in the hallway.

"Iz somethin' wrong?" They were supposed to meet; he'd been waiting for her outside for half an hour.

Sassie looked up at him and started crying. "Obie, dey's somethin' I haf to tell you."

One look at her swollen eyes made something dreadful and cold shoot through Obie's body. *Dis iz 'bout Mama,* he thought. *Sassie ain't gone see me no mo' 'cauze o' Mama...*

Sassie was saying something, but he was listening to his own thoughts. His heart hurt; he felt like his knees would give way. He wanted to grab her hands and say, "Don't do dis, I love you..."

Finally, as though drifting toward him through a fog, he heard Sassie rambling on. "...an' somehow Miz Georgianne *knew...* Dat's why she laid her hand on my belly an' my heart dat day! Oh, Lawd...I *tol'* you we didn't quit doin' wrong we'uz bofe gone go to hell!"

Obie stared at her in confusion."Girl, what *iz* you talkin' 'bout?" he asked.

Tears streaming down her face, Sassie said, "Obie Quinn, ain't you bin lis'nin' to a word I jus' said? I said I'z gone have a baby!"

Obie stood stock-still as the words echoed across his brain. Nothing showed on his face. When it became possible again for him to think, instantly and with a sense of doom, he thought of his mama. He knew her mind on this. This would bring shame to her—and condemnation to him and to Sassie.

Slowly, a sense of reason seeped into his mind. It was too late to worry about his mama's pride now. What was done was done, and it was his doing. He wouldn't let Sassie be blamed and persecuted, wouldn't allow her to be hurt anymore. He had to take responsibility. He had to take care of Sassie, had to take care of their baby. No— not *had to*. He *wanted* to.

Obie looked at Sassie's face and suddenly all his fears dissolved. All he wanted was to take her in his arms and hold her for the rest of his life. He wanted to see her smile for the rest of his life.

He lowered his gaze to her stomach, his eyes and heart full of wonder. The baby inside her was his own flesh and blood. *Dis baby is us, me an' Sassie*...He felt an odd stirring in the deepest part of him. For a few moments, he was lost to the awe of it all.

Sassie stood there, waiting, her heart pounding. Seeing his eyes travel to her stomach, in a trembling voice, she asked, "What iz you thankin', Obie?"

His face broke into a big grin. "I'z thankin' I love you...an' I love our baby. An' I'z thankin' we needs to git married as soon as possible!"

Sassie's heart nearly broke with relief; she felt a release, a soaring of soul she had never experienced before in her life. Obie joined in as her tears turned to laughter, and their laughter turned into sweet, happy tears.

A sash of clouds surrounded the moon, making it barely light enough to see. The doors of the central hall were thrown open wide in hopes that a cooling breeze might find its way in.

Libby woke with a start, instantly aware of some indistinguishable sound.

She lay on her side in the darkness, straining her ears. What had awoken her? Across the bed from her, Meggie slept soundly, her breaths coming soft and regular.

Libby stared at the window. In the vague, shadowy light, she saw the curtains move. There was an eeriness about the room that seemed to enfold her; the room itself seemed...watchful.

Despite the warmth of the night, she could not suppress a shiver of apprehension. Her breathing changed. Her face itched, but she dared not scratch it. She slipped her hand under the pillow; her fingers gripped the coolness underneath tensely. Instinctively, she knew there was someone else in the room besides her and Meggie. And whoever they were, they seemed close.

Libby heard, *felt*, something move behind her. She felt a faint flutter of air from whatever had moved touch the skin on the back of her neck. A rope of fear bound her to the bed, silent and still. If she remained very still, perhaps they would go away and she would be all right.

Then all of a sudden, she realized her foolishness. It dawned on her that it was probably Jesse. Always up to some kind of mischief, he had probably snuck in there to play a trick on her. Jesse, surely. She let out a long, trembling sigh of relief.

After one last brief hesitation, to prove to herself there was nothing to be afraid of, that there was no such thing as ghosts, she turned over slowly in expectation of seeing her cousin's snaggle-tooth grin and of telling him how mean he was.

When Libby rolled over, what she saw in the vague, shadowy light made her lose control of her bladder and wet the bed.

CHAPTER 10

"And above all things have fervent love for one another; for
love shall cover a multitude of sins." 1 Peter 4:8

Addie had said, "I'm sure you're bound to have wondered why
Sassie's skin is lighter than most other Negroes."

Of course Emily knew Sassie was half white, but she'd waited,
wondering more why the subject was being brought up out of the
clear blue.

As they sat together in the swing at the end of the porch, as
briefly as she could, Addie told Emily, "Sassie is your half sister…
You had the same pa."

Emily was old enough to understand the implications and embarrassed enough by them not to interrupt and ask a bunch of questions. It was very hard—surprising and a bit revolting—for her to
conceive the notion of her father having relations with a Negro
woman. What on God's green earth would make him do such a
thing? The thought surely took away any of the romantic fancy of
her girlhood sentimentalities of him. And, since she and Sassie were
very close in age, this obviously meant he had been disloyal to her

mama when he committed adultery with Creenie Boone. Emily was mature enough to understand this no doubt caused Addie to feel unhappy.

Yet, because Addie had never taught her to feel a certain way about black people, she didn't fully disapprove of claiming Sassie as her flesh-and-blood sister. Anyway, for the past four years they'd practically lived alongside each other as equals. Maybe she felt a little shocked by the revelation at first, but after that first shock subsided, she realized she was not even surprised. To her, it seemed she and Sassie had always been kin.

She remembered the first day they met. From the very beginning there had never been any shyness, only contentment, between them. Their sitting together on the steps of the mercantile while savoring the sweet coolness of peppermint sticks had felt as natural as breathing; their acceptance of each other had been instantaneous and unconditional.

She remembered them looking through old schoolbooks in the back room at Claire's old house and how they'd giggled as she tried to teach Sassie how to write her name. And how they'd cried together when Sassie moved to Golden Meadow after her mama died, their bond tempered by the mutual experience of losing a parent.

One born with an ease for adapting, Emily quickly settled the matter in her mind. Before Sassie had moved into the boardinghouse a few months back, the two of them had shared almost everything, even the same family, so this new knowledge was merely a confirmation of an affinity well-founded. When Addie finished talking, Emily said thoughtfully, "Sassie's been my sister long before now."

She would not ponder it further.

Addie had started down a path she must follow to the end. Later that afternoon, she entered the woodshop and said to Daniel, "Good, you're still here. There's something I need to talk to you about."

Daniel's face was quizzical as he looked at her. "What's wrong, Mama?" With that much concern in her eyes, he figured it couldn't be good.

Addie and Daniel had always had a sound relationship, one that had never required them to stand on ceremony with each other. Even so, Addie dreaded telling him about Sassie; more specifically, she dreaded the anticipated outcome of telling him.

She started with, "I've just come from telling Emily what I'm about to tell you; I thought it best I told you and her separately."

Daniel's eyes never left her face. Something in her voice held him captive.

"As you know, I don't care to bring up the past where Alfred is concerned, but something happened…about sixteen years ago. Under normal circumstance, I never would have felt it necessary for you and Emily to know, for I believe there's certain things better left unsaid…" Her voice trailed off.

There was a short pause before she continued. "However, I feel it's important to Sassie…important that she knows who her father was." In which case telling them became inevitable.

Daniel felt his heart catch. Instinctively, he tried to brace himself for whatever was coming next.

Realizing she was beating around the bush, Addie forged ahead to the heart of the matter. "Daniel, there's no delicate way for me to say this, so I'll just come right out and say it. Sassie is your half sister."

A deathly quiet settled in the woodshop.

Distrustful of his own ears, at long last Daniel asked, "Is this some kind of a joke?"

Addie shook her head and replied sympathetically, "I wish it were as simple as that, but unfortunately, what I'm telling you is no joke. It's true, Daniel. Sassie is your sister."

In answer to the disbelief crossing his features, she started trying to explain. "The night before Creenie died, she told me Alfred ran her down in the woods and raped her when she wasn't much older than Emily is now." Because of what Alfred had done to Amelia, she knew this detail would strike home hard with him, yet she felt it essential that he know.

Daniel's face clouded up; his hazel eyes were blazing. His emotions ran rampant as his mind drummed with the information. The smoldering hatred he had for Alfred sparked anew; Addie could almost feel the heat of it coming through the pores of his skin.

Addie continued to speak, but Daniel no longer heard what she was saying. In the picture in his mind, he was fifteen years old again, standing frozen at the edge of a field, watching in horror as Amelia struggled to free herself from his pa, *trying in vain to save herself from being raped by his pa.* The awful image both sickened and enraged him.

At that moment, he well understood how people could commit murder, and said so. Jaws clenched in anger, he fumed, "What I wouldn't give for that sorry devil to rise from the ashes one more time so I could run a pitchfork through him!"

Knowing it would be feeble consolation, Addie ventured softly, "This all happened a long time ago, when you were very young, and—"

Daniel interrupted her with a cynical half laugh. "Good gosh a-mighty, Mama. I can't remember ever feelin' young!"

Even though her son was only nineteen, it saddened her to know he meant this.

Bemused, he shook his head and mumbled, "Just wait'll folks catch wind of this; they'll no doubt talk it into the ground."

A brow lifted. Addie looked at him coolly, now interrupting him. "Since when do you give regard to the peddled opinions of tongue-waggers?" Without waiting for him to answer, she continued. "If it's *talk* that's worrying you, you can rest assured that on any given day of the week the town gossips generally spare more energy spreading lies than truth; therefore, you needn't worry overmuch!"

Daniel was no more concerned about busybodies than the man in the moon; he just couldn't seem to come up with words to match his thoughts on the matter, at least none appropriate enough say out loud.

Proving that the bearer of bad news is often blamed for it, Addie became the target for his anger and frustration. He lashed out at her heatedly, "You kept the truth about this hid for over three years 'cause, in your own words, 'they's certain things better left unsaid.' So why now, pray tell, have you just up an' took it on yourself to set the world out of kilter?" Given his druthers, he would rather have stayed ignorant of the whole sordid affair.

Addie did not miss the accusation in his voice. "Son, I know you're upset—"

The look he gave her was incredulous. "Upset? Yes, ma'am, I'd say that's a pretty fair assessment of how I'm feelin' right about now. Indeed I am upset." From there, he went into a sarcastic rant. "Dear Lord in Heaven, will wonders never cease? I do have to hand it to that no-'count, good-for-nothin' pa of mine, though. For a man dead three years, he still throws a wicked right hook!" Daniel had not forgotten the strength of his father's fists, nor the sting of his horsewhip.

"...But *never*, by hell, did I think I'd live to see the day when I could say I had myself a Negro sister! Of course, I do suppose stranger things have happened!" And, right at that moment, one came to mind. "Like how you could just make that black bastard of his a welcome member of our family!"

Whether he meant it or not, that was the wrong thing for him to say.

Addie had heard enough. Her eyes stung with outrage and pity at the hardness of his words. She loved her son and understood the reasons behind his attitude, but she also loved Sassie and wasn't about to stand there and let her be maligned and trampled on for something that wasn't her fault.

She interceded sharply, "And you can be sure that *precious girl* will *always* be a welcome member of our family, and nothing will ever change that!"

Daniel snapped back defiantly, "And I'm sure you'll pardon me if I don't feel the same! Just what was it you were hopin' for, Mama? That we'd all just kiss an' hug an' have a big, happy family reunion?"

Of course Addie was wise enough to know that feelings of kinship could not be forced. She took a deep breath to regain her composure. Striving for a calmer tone, she said, "You know, Daniel, I love you, and I didn't come here to fight with you, but it is really disappointing to me how you can feel so embittered toward Sassie. She's as much an innocent in this as Amelia was, and as sweet, little Rachel." With that, she turned to leave, realizing she had trespassed, precariously so, upon a place held hallowed in Daniel's heart. A place she hadn't intended to go.

Staring after her, Daniel sighed, regretful of their quarrel. "Mama, wait."

Addie stopped.

"I'm just sayin'…surely you can understand…this sorta thing's just fixin' to take some gettin' used to, is all."

God had sent down a tiny beam of hope. Addie went back and put her arms around her son and hugged him hard. She could feel his unhappiness. She kissed his cheek and whispered, "You know, you don't have to go on hating him forever." She figured, *In for a penny, in for a pound…*

He smiled at her almost solemnly and said, "Hate's all he ever gave me, Mama." He looked so childlike it made her want to cry.

Daniel had taken the news just as Addie expected he would, given its basis. She left knowing he was upset, and for that, she was sorry. However, his were not the only feelings deserving of consideration in the matter.

She was trusting that Amelia might be the one to lift him up and ease his distress.

Daniel and Amelia had loved each other since childhood. At eight years old, they had become inseparable, two people sharing one heart, neither one whole without the other. Amelia was pleasing in every way, sensible, and almost always cheerful. This was particularly amazing when one considered the dire poverty and drunkenness that bore her and the abuse she had suffered.

Nonetheless, with willful determination, she had endured and emerged. While Daniel's unfailing love for his sweetheart may have physically rescued her from a dreadful situation, Amelia knew it was the grace of God that ultimately saved her. It was He who lifted her up out of sin, He who established her heart and gave her peace, He who sustained her.

Going to the door, she looked out. Daniel was sitting with his back to her, gazing out across the yard with quiet intensity, his legs dangling off the end of the porch. Beside him lay Ben, sprawled flat on his belly with his head on Daniel's lap. The scene looked so peaceful, intimate almost, that at first she felt hesitant to intrude upon it, afraid that she might spoil it.

Amelia knew Daniel, was very perceptive of his moods. It was clear to her something was bothering him. Despite his efforts to act normal, all through supper he'd been preoccupied, seemed cast down and worried about something, like he couldn't wait for the meal to be over so he'd have an excuse to get off to himself. Shutting the screen door quietly behind her, she went over and settled herself beside him on the porch, letting her feet dangle beside his.

She'd let Daniel tell her whatever it was in his own time. Night falling, she looked out past the yard and toward the barn. The place stood gray in the dusk. Somewhere down the road, they heard a dog bark.

Daniel rubbed his dog's head. "Ben's gettin' old," he remarked contemplatively. White hairs were beginning to show in the copper fur about Ben's eyes and muzzle.

Amelia smiled and replied, "I still remember the day you got him. Ben was such a cute puppy, big clumsy feet, ears draggin' the ground."

Even though there was no one else around to hear, Daniel dropped his voice to barely above a whisper. "You wanna hear a downright sick'nin' story?" Not waiting for her to answer, he said, "Today I found out—as impossible as it seems—all this time, I've had a sister I didn't know nothin' about."

"What?" Amelia couldn't even to begin to imagine where the conversation was leading.

With a deep seriousness, Daniel began relating to her the staggering story Addie had told him earlier that day, including her view of the situation, and his differing one.

Amelia stared at him, speechless, not sure she was hearing him right. But the intensity of his expression said she was. She sat there thinking about it, her mind jumping from one point to another as she began connecting the many dots. *Alfred. Creenie. Sassie. Rachel.* It was a difficult puzzle to assemble. She didn't say it out loud but thought inwardly, *Dear God. That makes Sassie and Rachel half-sisters!* What a thought.

Faced with the choice, as a matter of sanity and survival, Amelia had stopped looking back a long time ago. God had let her bury the past and overcome it. By and by, He had even let her forgive. Even so, hearing about what had happened to Creenie Boone now caused her thoughts to flash back. In her mind, she could almost visualize the savage rape as it occurred. Her eyes glistened with pity for this woman she had never met.

Amelia remembered how tainted she had felt after what happened to her, how afraid and ashamed she had been when she realized she was pregnant. She had wanted to stay in hiding the rest of her life, conceal her disgrace from the world. However, all her worrying had proved needless; if the circumstance of her daughter's conception and birth had ever been a mystery to anyone, it was a mystery not pondered, for as impossible as it seemed, Daniel, knowing everything, had married her and took Rachel into his heart. He accepted the joy of her and made her his own. And so had Addie. Appropriately, the child was the namesake of Addie's mother and Daniel's grandmother.

"Maybe I'm wrong, but I can't bring myself to think of that girl as my sister," he said solemnly. "Not that I have anything against her personally, I hardly know the girl. An' it ain't so much on account of her bein' colored, either. It's on account of her bein' *his*." And yet, he had never thought of Rachel in that way, as Alfred's. Rachel was a part of Amelia, and because he loved Amelia with his whole heart, loving Rachel had come naturally to him. But somehow, this seemed different.

Amelia knew there was more to Daniel than that. Much more than even he knew. Though she understood what he was feeling at the moment, this was far from the worst thing either of them had weathered. She had no doubt, as impossible as it seemed to him right now, that with prayer, they could all very well inherit a blessing through this.

She looked over at him then. What she saw was a robustly handsome man, dark- eyed, with thick, black hair and a lean, muscular build. She felt incredibly lucky to have him and the incredible love that flowed between them. She reached over and ran her hand down the back of his neck. "You need a haircut," she whispered. She found his free hand and held it.

Automatically, Daniel's fingers closed around hers. Bringing her hand to his mouth, he rubbed her knuckles gently across his lips. He looked over at her and sighed deeply. "Sometimes I wish we were eight years old again."

Amelia made no comment on his wish, though she knew Daniel through and through and could almost imagine where his thoughts tread. Because of his father, he had suffered as much, maybe even more, as she had. Alfred had committed a multitude of sins that had affected and complicated the lives of so many. Why must he be the common thread that wove them all together? The look on her husband's face pierced her heart. He looked so vulnerable that all she wanted to do was take him in her arms and hold him.

She looked up to the darkening indigo sky. A sprinkling of stars suddenly reminded her of another such night years ago, when she and Daniel had lain on a quilt underneath a similar starlit sky. It suddenly occurred to her it was the great force of their love for each other, the enduring love they'd carried in their hearts for eleven years that was the one constant element of their lives. *Love* was the common thread that wove them all together. Not Alfred.

With the coming of night, a warm seductiveness settled over the place. Lightening bugs winked and darted about. Across the way, a whippoorwill called out softly. Her skirt brushed against Daniel's pant leg; the heat of his skin melded with hers through the fabric of their clothing.

Though Amelia was filled with a sharp, sensual yearning for him, what she was offering was more than physical; she knew it was Daniel's heart more than anything else that needed the soothing balm of her love tonight. Determined not to let their problems rob them of this beautiful night together, she murmured, "Rachel and Carson are fast asleep…let's go to bed. You might think I'm crazy, but I promise none of this will seem so bad in the mornin'."

Grinning boyishly, Daniel stood up and grasped her hands and pulled her to her feet. He slid his arms around her, and they held each other close. "Do you have any idea how much I love you, Amelia?"

She smiled at him and nodded.

As they started inside the house, Daniel bent down and kissed the top of Ben's head. Trying to keep the pride out of his voice, he said, "Sleep tight, ol' boy."

The next morning, heavy dew covered the grass. Daniel's boots were damp when he entered the woodshop.

Neither he nor Hiram spoke a greeting, but neither minded. This was not uncommon for them. It was their way. Sometimes they might work side by side for an hour without verbally acknowledging each other, quietly laboring in a companionable way, communicating simply by transference of thought. Though not his true father, Daniel worshipped Hiram.

It was several minutes before Daniel spoke, and when he did, he did so without elaboration. He said, "I reckon you know about what happened."

Hiram knew. Daniel knew he knew.

Moving about unhurriedly, gathering his tools in preparation for work, Hiram nodded slightly. Giving little in the way of response, he said, "Addie made mention of it." No use in saying more. He figured the more they talked about it, the redder Daniel's ears would get. And too, he knew anything he said would more than likely come across sounding lean, set against how Daniel felt.

Keeping his comments uncluttered, Hiram said, "Son, my best advice to you is to spend some time on your knees with Jesus. Give this battle over to the Lord." He knew Daniel was wrestling. He had bound himself to something that was hindering him from reaching out for what God had in store. *Hate's a grievous yoke,* Hiram thought. This he knew from personal experience. He had been there himself.

He also knew this was a wrestling match Daniel was destined to lose if he was ever to be at peace in his soul, for to prevail with God is to yield to Him.

But Daniel would have to come to this in his own time.

Daniel looked away, feeling a little uncomfortable, not with Hiram but himself. Then after a long, thoughtful moment, as though once again seeing it all fresh, he sighed and said, "I swear, I ain't never seen the likes of my pa. He was undoubtedly the sorriest man ever created."

Giving relief to the seriousness of the situation, Hiram replied dryly, "Contrariwise, it's my contention the Devil made a lot of sorry fools just like him."

The following day, Hiram received a letter from Wilkes. It was a short one, post-marked Richmond, Virginia. He wrote to say he had made it home, uneventfully, and to emphasize again what a fine time he had during his visit to Mississippi, the "hospitality state," he called it. He went on to brag about how tall and full-leafed his tobacco plants were standing and what a bountiful crop he and his partner were anticipating in the fall.

Hiram was pleased. He was pleased to hear that his younger brother was back in Virginia and, considering how his presence had upset the normal order of their lives while he was here, he would be even more pleased if Wilkes would stay there for good.

CHAPTER 11

Addie began gingerly, "Sassie, there's something I need to talk to you about."

Sassie's stomach flipped. Her first thought was, *Miz Addie knows I'z pregnant!* But how? She was looking at Addie as seriously as Addie was speaking to her.

As it turned out, what Addie had come to say was nothing she could ever had expected.

"I know who your father was, and I think it's time you knew too."

With the missing piece of her life's puzzle finally revealed to her, Sassie flinched with the shock of it. Her mind raced. She heard perfectly well what Addie said, but she couldn't yet fit it all together. *How could this be?* A dozen questions flew through her mind. She could not think straight.

Her breathing came quickly as she voiced the question. "You mean ...So, he was Daniel an' Emily's daddy an' mine too?"

Addie nodded as Sassie stared at her in confusion and disbelief. She told her gently, "Daniel is your half-brother; Emily and you are half-sisters."

It was early afternoon; Sassie was done with work for the day. She and Addie were sitting side by side on her bed.

Sassie pondered the particulars aloud. "I jus' don't see how that could be. Me an' Emily are 'bout the same age …an' he wuz married to you!"

Addie said, "Sassie, you know I wouldn't lie to you …I promise, Alfred Coulter was your daddy."

As her thoughts flew ahead, Sassie cried angrily, "Then that means Mama …but she said she wuz yo' friend! She said she loved you! So how could she …?" Her voice faltered.

Understanding what she was thinking, Addie took both Sassie's hands in hers and shook them to emphasize her point. "No, no, no! You listen to me. Your mama didn't do anything wrong! Creenie *was* my friend, and I loved her …very much. Alfred was a horrible, mean man." She went on, trying to explain, "When Creenie wasn't much older than you are now, Alfred forced himself on her and raped her. What happened wasn't your mama's fault."

As Sassie heard and absorbed the information, the images it brought to mind were almost more than she could bear. She loved her mama and couldn't stand to think how terrible it must have been for her to be raped. And, this too explained why she had always sidestepped any questions concerning the identity of her father. All Sassie had known was that he was white.

After another long moment of consideration, Sassie was hit by yet another revelation, one that made her even sadder. She drew her hands away from Addie's. "She couldn't have wanted me den—not after what he did to her," she whispered. Without making a sound, she began to cry.

"No, Sassie, that's not true! I want you to put those thoughts out of your mind this instant! Creenie wanted you very much!" Addie said it almost scoldingly. Then, softer, "You are her daughter, and you were the world to her. Of course she didn't want things to happen the way they did, but the day she told me about it, she made it plain that even though she was sorry about the rape, she had never once regretted *you*."

Addie ran her hand over the quilt covering the bed. Tears gathered in the corners of her own eyes as she remembered how Creenie had told her about the rape the day before she died. "I'll never forget…She said you'd always been her shining star."

Sassie's tears would not stop. She sniffed. "So, ever'body knows… the truth about me?"

Addie shook her head. "Not everyone. Only Claire and me and Travis. I told Hiram before we were married, and now Daniel and Emily know."

"Emily feels like my sister."

Addie recalled Emily had remarked similarly when given the news. She put her arm around Sassie. "I don't think you know how precious you are to us. I think of you almost as my own daughter; Claire does too." She rocked Sassie lightly and stroked her hair.

For a few minutes, they sat without talking.

Nothing alerted Addie that another confession was forthcoming.

Sassie had been worrying for days, wondering how to tell Addie and Claire she was pregnant. She was scared to death and ashamed of what she had done. She'd give anything not to have to tell them, for them not to know, but she knew she wouldn't be able to hide her secret much longer. She swallowed hard, trying to summon up her nerve. Against Addie's chest, she confided in a small voice, "Miz Addie, I'z gone have a baby."

Sassie! Pregnant! Addie was thunderstruck. She hardly knew what to say, didn't trust herself to speak. Yet no matter what she was feeling, she knew it was important that she try to sound calm. *Now I know what seemed different about her at the party*, she thought. When she found her voice, although she tried not to stammer, she asked, "A-are you sure? You've ...missed?"

Sassie nodded. She tried to speak but couldn't. The humiliation of it all burned within her soul.

Sensitive to Sassie's need to be comforted, Addie pulled her closer.

Sassie sank into her chest and burst into another fit of weeping, "I'z sorry, Miz Addie! Please don't be mad!" She was beside herself, so sorry for what she had done. Miz Addie and Miz Claire were such good and respectable people. They'd always been so good to her; they brought her up right, had taught her right from wrong. She had known better, and now she had disgraced them both. She could only imagine their disappointment in her.

Addie kissed her forehead and soothed, "Oh, honey, I'm not mad ...shhh ...things will be all right." Seeing how the girl was so distraught, Addie was willing to leave it at that. She'd never been one to cast blame or judgment on someone just to see them hurt more. Not to say that right about then she wasn't leaning strongly toward wringing both Sassie's and Obie's necks! Yet calling to mind the teachings of Paul ...*bear ye one another's burdens, and so fulfill the law of Christ...*, clearer thinking allowed her to be more practical about it. *For who am I to judge*, she thought. *They need helping now, lifting up, not chastising. Let God be the judge, let them see the beauty of Jesus in me...*

In a way, Addie sort of blamed herself. She had known Sassie and Obie were courting. Maybe if she had been more straightforward with her about the power of lust and what the Scripture says about remaining pure until marriage, maybe then they wouldn't be in this predicament. She sighed regretfully. Then, on second thought, she decided things could be much worse. *At least this child wasn't conceived of rape or infidelity...*

Stroking Sassie's tear-splotched face, she questioned tenderly, "Does Obie know?"

"Y-yes'm." Sassie had the hiccups from crying.

"What are his intentions?"

"H-he says he l-loves me an' that we'll git m-married soon as he f-figures out 'bout w-where we gone st-stay." They needed to find their own place to live, but Obie didn't have money to pay for it.

Inwardly, Addie breathed a sigh of relief. She thought, *Even though they're starting out wrong, at least if they get married, the baby will be legitimate.*

Sassie, however, saw their situation as far more distressing and complicated. "Obie's mama gone disown him fo' sure now!" she sobbed. "To her, blood means ever'thang. *Negro* blood, dat is. I'z too white fo' her eyes; an' that's sum'thin' I won't ever be free from!"

Addie took a moment to weigh the statement in her mind. She knew that Rosette Quinn's lack of acceptance had hurt Sassie deeply. Yet still, Addie had seen the sun rise and set on more than her share of troubles, and as she reflected on the possibilities, it came to her that perhaps this didn't have to be an entirely bad thing.

Babies had been known to unlock hearts and bridge gaps deemed otherwise irreparable; they sometimes had a way of bringing—and keeping—families together. She hoped it would be so in this case, for Sassie and Obie's sake.

Unable to give advice based on indefinite hopes and possibilities, she replied, "You and Obie do not need his mama's permission to marry. And, regardless of what she says, you are a beautiful person inside and out, one who deserves every happiness in this world."

Calling to memory a passage of scripture from Galatians, she quoted, "'There is neither Jew not Greek, there is neither bond nor free, there is neither male nor female; for ye are all one in Christ Jesus.' So just you remember, by the grace of God, the color of your skin will only enslave you if you let it."

The words flowed into Sassie in the form of compassion and understanding, flooding her with a calm assurance. With her tears finally subsided, she said, "Miz Addie, I hope I can be as good a mama to dis baby as you an' Miz Claire bin to me since Mama died."

"Oh, sweet girl, I have no doubt you will." Addie rubbed her hand across the quilt they were sitting on. It was one Creenie had pieced together some years before. With a smile of fond remembrance, she said, "This baby's gonna be *your* shining star."

A half hour later, Addie slapped the horse lightly with the reins, and off she headed toward home. Indeed! Just to think! A short while ago, when she was making her way into town to tell Sassie that Alfred was her father, certainly she never expected any such things as a wedding and a baby to be occupying her mind when she parted!

She didn't know whether to scream or cry.

Later that night, when Samuel had fallen to sleep and Addie went outside, the heaviness of the air enveloped her in a sultry embrace. Dressed only in her undergarments, her skin was damp with perspiration. Carrying with her a towel and a clean nightgown, she ducked under the clothesline and walked across the backyard, stopping near the well to open the valve of an elevated cistern, which allowed water to run down a wooden sluice into the bathing enclosure. While the cistern ordinarily caught rainwater, that morning Addie had drawn enough water from the well so that she might enjoy a bath this evening. The water had warmed during the day in the unrelenting heat.

Stepping into the privacy of the enclosure, Addie lit a single candle and set it on a low footstool beside the clawfooted tub, along with a bar of lavender-scented soap. She piled her hair up, stripped, and eased herself down into the water. Sighing deeply, she relaxed and leaned back against the rim of the tub, luxuriating in the refreshing feel of it.

For several moments, she gazed up through the vine-laced arbor that covered the bathing enclosure into the starlit sky. The yard and surrounding woods were cast in a faint blue light; she could smell

the sweet scent of gardenias from a nearby shrub. From somewhere, a bobwhite called. June bugs sang. Addie closed her eyes and gave the stress of the day over to the fragrance and music of the night.

Several minutes later, startled by the sudden tinkling of a wind chime, she opened her eyes. Hiram was standing there, twirling a gardenia in his hand, taking in the scene appreciatively. It was a sight he would never tire of. Addie could not have guessed how irresistibly beautiful she looked to him in the soft glow of candlelight, nor the depth of his love and desire for her. He was held for a moment in the spell of it.

"What a fetching sight you make, sweet," he murmured huskily.

As he moved forward and leaned over the tub, Addie replied weakly, "Today when I was in town, I bought a new nightgown..."

With a one-sided grin, Hiram bent closer and traced the curve of her face lightly with the gardenia. Chuckling softly, he said, "Show it to me tomorrow."

CHAPTER 12

"Yet setteth He the poor on high from affliction, and maketh their families like a flock." Psalm 107: 41

Summer's youthful bloom long faded, the season had ceased to enchant. They were four weeks into a draught. The ground was baked; trees and foliage drooped wearily under a heavy coat of dust. Temperatures soared; the days were overly warm, even for this time of summer. Claire came down the hall into the parlor, dabbing at the perspiration on her neck with a handkerchief.

"I tell you, it's hotter than the soles of Jezebel's feet!" she exclaimed. "I have purely worked up a lather wrestlin' into this dress!"

Stell sat fanning. Not in the best disposition, she replied, "Now you see why I've a mind not to go." She said it like her mind was undecided, but her mind was made up. She was not going.

More to herself than to Claire, she grumbled, "Day like today, ever' pesterin' gnat in the state of Mississippi'll show up, an' I don't feel up to fightin' 'em off." She closed her eyes and added, "I'm studyin' hard on stayin' home an' prayin' for rain."

This got Claire's goat. Making no attempt to mask neither her annoyance nor amusement with her, she stared at Stell long and hard before saying huffily, "Sassie will be disappointed if you don't go."

Without opening her eyes, Stell's response was dry and philosophical. "Poor soul will learn soon enough life's tamped with disappointment." Drawing a little strength from Claire's irritation with her, she added, "I 'spect if you don't go rubbin' it under her nose, she won't even miss me."

Shortly thereafter, Addie made the circle around the oak tree at the end of the lane, and they swapped happy salutations as Claire walked toward the carriage. Emily moved over to make room for her on the seat. Climbing in, before Addie had opportunity to ask, Claire charged, "Hit the grit! This heat's got Ol' Stell off her feed! She's solemnly sworn not to stir 'til it turns off cold enough to keep a corpse fresh!"

Hot as it was, Addie didn't begrudge anyone for wanting to stay home. Under any other circumstance, she might be tempted to do the same. When she'd asked Hiram if he planned to go with them, he'd simply groaned at the prospect of putting on a suit. So instead, he and Daniel had taken the children to cool off in the creek. She laughed and politely defended Stell's choice. "Before the day's out, I might wish I'd been as prudent, but right now, I wouldn't miss this wedding for all the tea in China!"

She made a clucking sound to the horse and off they went, carriage wheels spinning speedily toward Mt. Zion Church.

Mt. Zion Baptist Church sat perched atop a small hill against a background of hardwoods and magnolias. The whitewashed clapboard structure was flanked on either side by lavender-colored Rose of Sharon; hydrangeas abloom with voluptuous clusters of blue flowers adorned its front. The setting, so picturesque, could well have been a beautiful painting. Contrary to expectation, despite the oppressive heat a crowd of people assembled in their Sunday best to witness the marriage of Obie Quinn and Sassie Boone, and to wish them well.

Sassie's dress, a gift from Travis and Abigail, was simple yet deserving of compliment—ivory satin with an overlay of ivory lace. When the time came, Etta crowned the beaming bride, affixing a woven tiara of tiny wildflowers upon her head.

The week before, Sassie had asked Travis to give her away and when the pianist struck the chords of the wedding march, they started down the aisle, she clutching his arm, her stomach full of butterflies.

Addie's heart caught at the sight of them.

Imagining her thoughts, Claire leaned over and whispered, "I'd give anything if Creenie was here to see this." Addie turned her head and saw the tears on Claire's face. Feeling her own eyes fill, she reached for Claire's hand and squeezed it briefly.

In contrast, Rosette sat beside Ezra stiff as a salt cake, her head held rigid, eyes straight ahead.

After kissing Sassie's cheek, Travis gave her hand over to Obie and took his seat on the pew next to Abigail. The church choir began humming softly as the preacher took his place behind the altar. Spoken in a spirited lilt and characteristic dialect, the recitation of the marriage vows rose and fell in poetic idiom:

"Obie, do you promise you's gwine love Sassie, comfort her, honor an' keep her, in sickness an' in health, fo' better an' fo' worse, so long as you bofe shall live?"

"Yessuh. I do," Obie spoke the words gently, promising himself to Sassie; her heart heard, knowing his love was true.

"Sassie, do you promise you's gwine love Obie, comfort him, honor an' keep him, in sickness an' in health, fo' better an' fo' worse, so long as you bofe shall live?"

"I promise," she squeaked excitedly, her face shining with happiness.

When the preacher asked for the ring, Obie slipped it on Sassie's finger.

"Deeze promises made, in accordance wif da Lawd God Almighty an' da laws o' da state o' Miss'sippi, I do pronounce yaw husband an' wife."

Just as Obie and Sassie turned to face the congregation, Zeke and Jasper raced up the aisle with a broomstick and held it low to the floor just in front of them. The newlyweds linked their arms and jumped high over the broomstick together, laughing like hyenas, causing the crowd to burst into applause, rejoicing with them in their marriage. Proceeding from the church, once outside the couple was showered with handfuls of downy rose petals and flowery congratulations.

Behind the church, two long tables weighted down with the wedding feast were draped with tablecloths, and several little girls danced around a smaller refreshment table, waving palmetto fronds to discourage the flies from lighting on the wedding cake and swimming in the punch.

Almost immediately, a stringed quartet of banjos and fiddles began playing. Children jounced and jigged and screamed with excitement as the whole party joined in a circle around Obie and Sassie and clapped their hands in time to the music, watching the newlywed couple dance the first dance.

Given a certain zeal for life and a natural gift of charm, even in such a complex assemblage, within minutes Travis had captured the affections of the crowd. He stepped forward into the circle and bowed before Sassie, whereupon charm and youthfulness had the next dance. In succession, Ezra danced with Sassie, Travis partnered with Claire, and Emily with Obie, while the others paired themselves off as they would.

Addie and Abigail disengaged from the circle of clapping hands and dancing feet and backed a short distance away. The air was stifling, making it near impossible to breathe. Abigail opened her parasol and blotted her neck with a delicate lace handkerchief. "How they can dance around like a bunch of wild Indians is beyond me! I am duly perishing in this heat. Would you just look—my feet are swelled a sight!"

Addie nodded sympathetically. "I know exactly what you mean. When I get home, I'll have to pry these shoes off with a chisel!"

"Well, I have to say, it *was* a sweet ceremony, and I am ever so relieved the preacher omitted that 'speak now or forever hold your peace' part," Abigail pointed out.

"Mm," Addie agreed. "It would have made quite a spectacle—me having to throw a rope around Obie's mama and wrestle her to the ground."

Abigail glanced around and asked, "Refresh my memory, would you. Which one of those ladies is his mother?"

Her eyes followed Addie's to a group of women sitting in the shade of a live oak, fanning, their chairs drawn together in a semicircle. With a straight face, Addie whispered, "I just told you, practically. She's the one with the cloven hooves."

Abigail burst into a fit of laughter, glad to have Addie as a friend.

There was a break in the music, and Travis and Claire made their way toward them. In high spirits, Claire exclaimed merrily, "I dearly love a weddin'!"

Addie immediately thought of Stell, who in contrast would have been solemn as a crow and completely miserable had she come, particularly since in the last week, on a passing whim, she had up and declared herself against dancing.

Travis's coat was slung over his arm, his vest was unbuttoned, and his shirt lay open at the collar. With his face and hair dripping sweat, he crowed to Abigail, "I bet you're impressed to see your old man still has the vigor to cut a rug like that!"

Abigail fluffed his hair and gibed good naturedly, "Not nearly as impressed as I'll be if you still have the vigor to cut your own meat come suppertime." She adored Travis but knew from living with him, all that dancing was for the crowd's benefit.

Whether he would admit it or not, at fifty-eight, his "rug-cutting" days were coming fewer and further between. "Let's go home. I'm about to fall out from this heat."

"Very well then, my sultry goddess, we'll go home." With twinkling rancor, Travis slipped his arm about her waist and put his lips close to her ear and murmured, "I know it drives you mad to see me this sweaty."

"Oh, stop slobbering on me." Abigail giggled and slapped at his hands. He was still vigorous enough, for fifty-eight.

They quickly said their farewells to everyone and drifted down the hill toward their carriage.

Claire admitted to Addie, "I am a little tired, so I'll be ready to go whenever you are."

Seeing Addie motion to Emily, Sassie realized they were about to leave and came over. Before she could protest their departure, Addie reached out and touched her cheek and said, "Look at you, married and so beautiful—and the wedding, so beautiful. We'll come visit you in a week or so, when y'all get settled." As a wedding gift, she and Claire paid the first year's rent on a tiny, shotgun shanty in the quarter and gave them some linens, quilts, a set of dishes, and a few pots and pans. The few furnishings Obie and Sassie had accumulated were by no means fancy and a bit worn-out but would do very well to set up housekeeping.

Addie put her arms around Sassie and held her for a long minute. "Go now, and enjoy Obie and your guests." Moments later, they waved a final good-bye as Sassie skipped back over to rejoin the others.

When the three of them were alone again, Addie turned to Claire and Emily. "Has Mrs. Quinn so much as uttered a gracious word to either of you all afternoon?" she asked.

Emily shook her head. Claire replied, "Nary one." Most everyone else had taken pause to introduce themselves, but Rosette had scrupulously avoided them. Reading Addie's expression, Claire asked warily, "Oh dear, what are you thinkin'?"

"Well, I don't know about you," she answered, "but I can't leave here with a clear conscious without going over and properly introducing myself." She tilted her head slightly toward the women sitting beneath the tree.

Claire sighed nervously. "Oh, please now. Let's not make a scene and rain on Sassie's special day."

"I wouldn't dream of it," Addie replied. "No denying, every amicable word will undoubtedly stick in my craw, but like you always say, 'sowing the seeds of kindness is never out of season.' Come. I give you my word—I promise to sow kindly." She couldn't stand it. She squared her shoulders, pasted a smile on her face, and started briskly out across the yard, accompanied by Emily, with Claire following less enthusiastically, a bit reluctantly even, a few steps behind.

Conversation between the Negro women dwindled then died dead away as Addie, Claire, and Emily approached. Once in the midst of them, Addie said, "Good afternoon, ladies. I'm Addie Graham, and this is Claire Ellis and my daughter, Emily Coulter."

She turned to Rosette, bringing her eyes to rest upon the woman's face. "Before we left, we just wanted to come over and say what a lovely wedding it was and tell you how pleased we are to welcome Obie into our family."

Making little effort to conceal her disapproval of them, Rosette smiled humorlessly and nodded curtly, not a trace of hospitality in her.

The preacher's wife, however, leaned forward a little in her chair and returned the courtesy, responding warmly, "Why, it so nice to make yo' acquaintance. Sassie seem like such a sweet chile."

"Indeed she is," Addie replied.

"If yaw don't mind my axin', how it be she come to live wif yaw?"

The question only stoked Addie's pleasure. She had not forgotten the trap Rosette Quinn snapped on Sassie a few weeks back at Sunday dinner. "Not at all, I would be more than happy to explain that to you," she said. And, without a qualm, she did:

"You might say Sassie is mine and Claire's daughter, though obviously we didn't bear her in the traditional way. Her mother, Creenie Boone, God rest her soul, was a dear friend of ours, and my late husband, Alfred Coulter, was Sassie's father."

Eyebrows went up as she pointed to Emily. "That makes Sassie my son's and daughter's half-sister, they of course now being Obie's half brother- and sister-in-law."

As the women thought about all this, their faces showed confusion.

Addie pressed her hands together and concluded, "Well now, it's been nice meeting you all. We must try and get together again real soon."

With a round of similar sentiments being expressed, Rosette kept her pose. While Addie itched to go over and give her a good slap, she instead rose and met the challenge with what was left of her manners and, in leaving, made herself smile sweetly at her. As they headed down the hill to the carriage to go home, no other word was spoken, but Emily glanced over at her mama in admiration.

Once out of earshot, Addie said, "There now. Let the old cow chew on that cud awhile!"

Later, as night settled in and they sat on the porch indulging their vices, Claire recounted every detail of the wedding to Stell, who savored every syllable. When she got to the part about Addie and Rosette, Stell intermittently reached over and grabbed Claire's arm, interrupting her to make her stop talking so she could laugh without missing a single word.

When Claire was finished, Stell said, "I'm so glad I didn't go! Otherwise, I'd a-deprived myself from hearin' you tell about it!"

Claire sucked on Luke's pipe and let out a pungent wreath of smoke. Lightening flickered incandescently across the distant fields, followed by a roll of thunder that sounded like horses' hooves rumbling across the earth toward them.

The wind changed and carried the smell of approaching rain.

CHAPTER 13

"Take fast hold of instruction; let her not go: keep her, for she is thy life." Proverbs 4:13

"M-i-crooked-letter, crooked-letter-i, crooked-letter, crooked-letter-i, humpback, humpback-i!"

Come the middle of September, with the harvest in and the busiest pickling and preserving season past, school took back in. While the older pupils worked quietly on multiplication tables, Bernice Crowley smiled as she stood looking through the window observing the class being conducted out-of-doors under a big oak tree. It delighted her to see young minds learning, and the children seemed to respond more eagerly to a younger teacher. *Indisputably*, Bernice thought, *Emily Coulter has a wonderful gift.*

Emily was only five or six years old when her probing blue eyes discovered the power of books. Merely cracking open the pages sparked a fascination in her mind comparable to none other. A voracious reader inquisitve to all genres of literature, Emily pryed into the writings of Twain and Bronte', Dickens and Keats. As a little girl she had spent countless hours in her make-believe classroom in the hayloft of their barn playing school-mistress to an assembly of feline scholars. The loft had been her private haven. For as long as she could remember, it had been the desire of her heart—her *calling*, actually—to someday become a real schoolteacher.

Now at last, in a way, her dream was coming true.

The ever-growing population of Oakdale had caused a significant increase in student enrollment, in turn causing the small schoolhouse to become severely cramped. In addition to there being a shortage of space and desks, this year the children were being forced to share books as well. All that, and taking into account the diversity of the students' ages, Bernice had quickly realized there was little hope of her taking a strong part in any individual instruction of the pupils. So, after careful thought and with Emily's parents' approval, she had enlisted Emily to help instruct the beginners an hour or two every day in reading, writing, and spelling, so long as it didn't interfere with her own lessons. Of course it didn't, as Emily was already as proficient as Bernice in those subjects. Thus far, the arrangement was working out satisfactorily, except on rainy days.

Presently, Emily was taking a circle of nine pupils through a spelling lesson. As they chanted and clapped their hands in rhythm to a silly rhyme, they were having so much fun they didn't even realize that they were learning. To keep them from becoming bored, she frequently took her group on nature walks, sometimes making them lie in the grass and spell out cloud formations–embodying the elements of God's creation into her lesson plans.

No, I've no doubt that Emily will someday make a fine teacher. As Bernice turned away from the window, she thought how she might have envied Emily's youthful zeal for the profession had she not been looking forward to retiring in a few years. The prospect of which bode all the more well in the next moment when a spitball launched by Wiley Parker flew past her shoulder and hit the blackboard behind her desk.

What, retire and give all this up?

Wherever would she find solace? she wondered.

The bank in Oakdale was one of five such establishments owned by Abigail's father, a lawyer and prominent businessman, until his death in the year 1890. Now it—as well as his holdings in Tennessee—belonged to Abigail and her brother, Jonathan.

Handsome and rich, thirty-two-year-old Jonathan Langford was extremely self-assured and self-confident, in some folks' opinion, dauntingly so. He set great store on personal cleanliness, in fact prided himself on clean fingernails, in that he made his living by using his mind, not by dirtying his hands. Presently, it was well past noon, and he was working in the back room he used as an office when he was in town, he having returned to Oakdale on the coach from Memphis the previous day.

When he heard the door of the bank open, followed by the musical lilt of a female voice, his curiosity stirred. A man to entertain any and all opportunities presented him, he put aside the documents he had been poring over carefully for the past hour and rose, grateful for this temporary diversion from the tedium of bookkeeping.

Sarah Beth was in high spirits, squeaking like a delighted child. "Oooooh, Aunt Abigail! Just wait 'til you see what I just bought at Suzanne's Dress Shop!"

Completely mindless to interrupting Abigail's busy schedule with such frivolity, she gaily set about posing, giggling at herself as she lifted and turned her head, proudly showing off a stylish, plumed hat.

With a half smile playing about his lips, Jonathan stood deeply engrossed, watching the display covertly from the door of his office. Sarah Beth was wearing a lavender dress that accentuated her trim waist and dark eyes perfectly. The sun streaming through the window outlined her profile in a radiance, the effect of which brightened the dull, stuffy atmosphere of the bank considerably. One could

only marvel at the appearance she made, the excellence of her figure, the beauty of her features.

Finally, he went forward, clearing his throat sharply to gain their attention. When Abigail's green eyes met her brother's, she saw his brow rise inquisitively.

"Why, Jonathan! I don't believe you've met Travis's new assistant and our houseguest, Miss Sarah Beth Warren. Sarah Beth, this is my brother, Jonathan."

Jonathan stooped to pick up a feather from the floor, shed from the plumage that adorned her hat. "Why, would you look at this," he said. "'Tis no doubt fallen from an angel's wing."

Sarah Beth gave him a quick once-over. Realizing she was obligated to say something, she lifted her nose primly and murmured the briefest of acknowledgements.

"Pleased to make your acquaintance, I'm sure," she said coolly. With poised aloofness, she turned her attention once again to her pretty new hat, dismissing him as if he were invisible.

One whose face was trained to never give away his inner thoughts, Jonathan bowed stiffly in salute to her echoing indifference of him, his eyes lit with amusement. *Very well then, little Miss Prim and Proper.*

Abigail stared at them, somewhat dubious, trying to understand the true nature of their exchange and could not. On any other occasion, Sarah Beth would have carried on a flirtation with a stickhorse, so naturally she was left wondering why she so conspicuously, if not rudely, disregarded her handsome, eligible brother, a man in control of a bank, in a position of power and distinction second to none, except maybe for Travis. What, pray, was she missing here?

Before she could ponder it further, through the window, she saw Travis walking up the columned boardwalk toward the door of his practice. Sarah Beth saw him at the same moment, and seeming to be herself again, she exclaimed lively, "I better get back; Uncle Travis might have something he needs me to do." Bidding a hasty farewell, she bustled out the door in a flurry of petticoats.

As soon as she left, Jonathan ambled over to the window and watched leisurely as she crossed the street, appreciative of the graceful swing of her hips and the way her dress swirled about her. "Glory, glory," he muttered under his breath. Over his shoulder, he mused, "Why, Abigail, it seems you've been holdin' out on me."

Abigail came to stand beside him at the window. First noting the feather in his hand and then seeing where his gaze followed, she replied, "That girl's flighty as a hummingbird. Besides, she's not but sixteen years old—half your age."

Jonathan looked at her doubtingly. "Say again?"

Abigail nodded to indicate what she said was true. "Not that she appeared the least bit interested, but trust me—you would be making a big mistake with that one. To begin with, unlike you, her daddy knows which end of a hoe cuts; he'd have your head on a platter."

Jonathan grimaced and rubbed his neck in a way Abigail presumed meaningful until he said jestingly, "Sounds like a fairly reasonable old chap to me. Perhaps you could arrange for me to meet him one day, in say five, six years." When she didn't smile at his humor, he turned from the window and said, "So kind of you to watch out for my welfare, dear sister. Now if you will excuse me, I shall return to my remote little corner of the world and finish goin' over the Brady accounts."

"Sounds positively riveting," she replied absently.

It was ten minutes later when Abigail looked out and saw Sarah Beth and Travis climb up in his rig. When he flicked the reins and the horse pitched forward, for a fleeting moment, she wondered where they might be off to.

"I beg you to pull over!"

In the fading haze of twilight, Sarah Beth was on the seat beside Travis, sobbing spasmodically. As soon as he brought the buggy to a stop, she bailed out rather ungracefully. Leaning against the wheel, she felt like she was going to vomit again, or better still, maybe she would faint dead away and be freed of her misery.

"How *could* you, Uncle Travis! You're just plain *awful*." she cried. How could he be so casual?

Travis sat in the driver's seat holding the reins, staring straight ahead, totally confounded by the girl's reaction. He'd honestly believed she would enjoy it, count it as a learning experience, like he had intended it. Instead, his plan had somehow gone completely haywire. *Taught me a lesson I won't soon forget, though,* he thought wryly. Admittedly, he had made a foolish mistake in assuming from her full-blown physical maturity that she was ripe and ready for such an experience. *Ass-u-me*—he'd heard the expression all his life.

Noticing her dress was soiled, Sarah Beth beat at her skirt and railed disgustedly, "Just look at me! This used to be my favorite dress!"

Now she swore to throw it out and never wear it again, certain the very sight of it would conjure up bad memories of the ordeal she'd been through that day. If God were merciful, maybe she would just forget the whole, horrific mess like it never even happened. And to think, just a few hours ago she was having the time of her life, trying on hats.

The thought sent her into a fresh burst of tears. "I'll surely scream in my sleep tonight! I still don't know why you made me go, Uncle Travis!" The entire experience had traumatized her, left her nerves completely unsettled. She was no longer the same person she'd been in the hat shop that morning, no longer innocent, no longer a girl.

Travis fought the impulse to hop down and shake her. He was near drunk with fatigue, and she was ridiculously overreacting, being totally absurd.

Knowing his words would be ineffectual at this point, he muttered dourly, "Well I don't know, Sarah Beth. Could be I was thinkin' you might be of some comfort to Isabelle, you bein' female an' this bein' her first baby an' all; or maybe I was thinkin' you might possibly be of some help to me, at least give the baby his first bath. Heck, call me an old fool, but I probably even thought you might actually get some sort of glory out of witnessin' the miracle of birth."

He sure never thought she'd take to her heels and light out like a scalded dog, though she was about as much use as one when the time came. In the course of his career, he'd attended many births, but hands down, this one took the cake!

Seeing Travis was outdone with her, Sarah Beth turned defensive. "I'd rather die than see another baby born! I thought babies were supposed to be beautiful, but after all...all *that*, all poor Isabelle had to show for it was a scrawny little red and wrinkled-up thing that looked like a skint rabbit!"

Tired and aggravated as he was, Travis couldn't help smiling. "Oh, for Job's sake, stop your bawlin' an' let's go home. Abigail's probably wonderin' what's happened to us!" The day was near gone and he longed to get home to a nice bath and a tall glass of bourbon—not necessarily in that order.

Nausea subsided, Sarah Beth took the hand he offered and climbed back up into the buggy, saying, "Poor Mama! After she had me, what on earth possessed her to want two more?"

Giving her a sidelong look, Travis replied dryly, "I do wonder."

CHAPTER 14

Regardless of the date on the calendar, each year Hiram and Addie celebrated the anniversary of their wedding on the first Saturday in October, for this was the day on which they were married.

On this, their third anniversary, Addie awoke to the sweet sound of her father Samuel's old fiddle. She rolled over in the bed and smiled up at Hiram sleepily. He was so handsome she couldn't take her eyes off his face. For a few minutes, she watched him, listening with pleasure as he played. Her very soul tingled with delight as his love for her swirled softly about the room, the stirring serenade weaving a tantalizing spell around them.

When the melody ended, Hiram took the fiddle from under his chin and drew near. Time seemingly stood still as he bent down and pressed a possessive kiss upon Addie's lips. She melted, the kiss leaving her feeling warm and giddy.

"Happy anniversary, sweet," he whispered, his voice thick, husky. All the desire and passion they felt for each other was reflected in his eyes.

Though married previously for a number of years, until Addie married Hiram, she had never tasted the full measure of intimacy with a man. Alfred had never "rendered unto her due benevolence" as commanded by the Lord; therefore, he never treated her as a true wife, nor to the rightful affections owed one. Instead, he had used her selfishly for his own pleasure. Subjected to his demoralizing pawing, Addie had been coldly unmoved and unsated, left completely ignorant of passion's joy as God so commissioned.

With Hiram, however, such could not be said. With him, she at last had discovered all that which had eluded her before. Oh, how he spoiled and pampered her! He approached romance as an art and was a master in his own right. Addie thrilled to his caresses; their lovemaking was bold and fevered, all-consuming, and mutually satisfying.

Presently, a roguish grin spread across his features as the sheet began to slip away from her as he pulled at it slowly, uncovering her. His eyes were like a pair hot coals; his gaze devoured her.

While all logical thinking fled, somehow she managed to say, "Happy anniversary, my dear husband…"

Later, while Addie fried bacon and turned flapjacks, Hiram went out to the meadow and returned with a mixed bouquet of yellow daisies and purple asters. When they'd eaten breakfast, he extended a hand toward her and said, "Come. Walk with me. I've asked Emily to tend to Samuel for a while."

Addie smiled at him warmly and took his hand. A few minutes later, they stepped out the back door.

Content to be together, for a while all else was forgotten as they enjoyed the splendor of the clear, bright morning. As they walked along hand in hand, they stopped to admire a popcorn tree set ablaze by the season, its leaves glowing ember-red. They passed a persimmon tree laden with tart, orange fruit—not to be ripe for picking until after the first heavy frost. Goldenrod and joe-pye were blooming.

They had walked this path a hundred times over. Addie knew their stroll would eventually lead them to a particular landmark: the mighty white oak that stood alone on a gentle slope overlooking their property. At the base of the slope lay a partial, centuries-old fence made of piled fieldstones.

Over the past three years, they had come to the spot countless times, sometimes together, sometimes in solitude. The tree had become their special place. Like the great oaks of Mamre of biblical times—the grove of oak trees where Abraham took up residence in the land of Canaan—Hiram and Addie had come to look upon this tree as their tree of promise.

On the day before their wedding, the oak had showered them with a gentle cascade of falling leaves while they picnicked beneath its branches and spoke in whispers of their hopes and dreams for the future. Since that day, it had sheltered some of their most intimate moments, overheard their deepest secrets, and echoed many of their prayers.

The tree had stood by Hiram as joy flooded his heart the day Addie brought him here to tell him they were to have a child…and again several months later when Samuel was delivered. Hiram had come and knelt in the leaves in humble awe of the miraculous gift to give thanks to and praise to the Lord for his son.

The tree had also stood in silent counsel when life's inevitable storms arose, offering a restful cove in times of strife, a place of quiet comfort for the weary soul. An ally, supporter, and sympathizer, the stately oak had seen them through times happy and sad, likened to an old and trusted friend.

As they approached the tree with fingers interlaced, Addie immediately noticed something was different about it. It appeared as though a large patch of the bark had been scraped away from the trunk. Teased by the mystery of it, she let go of Hiram's hand and hurried up the slope for a closer look. When she drew nigh and saw what he'd done, a sweet, romantic gladness washed over her. He was

forever surprising her. Her heart beat faster, and tears blurred her vision as she read the words from the book of Samuel: "And they two made a covenant before the Lord..."

The intricate carving had been rubbed with stain to accentuate the script; the surface of the wood canvas was lightly sanded and polished to a fine luster. Below the verse, Hiram had etched two ornate hearts, one slightly intertwined with the other, and therein their names were engraved. It was an eloquent expression of the sentiment he held for her, that one which was carved upon his own heart.

Hiram came up quietly to stand behind her as she reached out and lightly touched the beautiful work of art. Loose tendrils of her hair fell down her back and moved in the gentle breeze.

In speechless wonderment, Addie turned and gazed into his eyes. Love hung in the air between them. Hiram smiled at her tenderly, knowing she was pleased with his gift.

Banked fires are nonetheless fires.

Evening's fading light found Travis wandering leisurely past a line of storefronts, enjoying his last cigar of the day. When he came to the end of the clay street where the town trailed off, he wove through a stand of oaks and came to a place he ended up at sometimes, a place where he could think whatever was on his mind and feel whatever was in his heart.

Past the brick entrance of Oakdale Cemetery, his eyes skipped along the rows of tombstones stretching out before him. One, the one that drew him there most often, might as well have been painted red, it stood out so. For a moment, he stood quietly looking around, absorbing the serene atmosphere, thinking how a setting of such stillness and beauty hardly seemed an appropriate resting place for a devil so mean as Alfred Coulter.

Invariably, being there at Alfred's grave took Travis's thoughts back to a day particularly tamped in his mind. Travis knew the memory would never leave him. Sometimes he even wondered if it might be his last one, the memory he would carry with him into death.

God, he prayed not.

While Travis would admit he had never felt called to the priesthood, neither had he ever been one to seek out trouble. Most certainly, he'd never wanted any part of killing. As a doctor, he knew life was precious and fragile and shouldn't be wasted. Alfred had wasted his. Three years ago, he had tracked Daniel and Amelia down and come there specifically with killing on his mind.

In the face of death, Travis had been forced to make a decision. After carefully weighing the situation, he had settled on saving lives, decided that Alfred was too insane and too dangerous to go on living. Seeing no other reform, he'd aimed his rifle ...

Travis didn't trouble himself greatly over the happening, healed by the belief it was something that occurred as it had to. He'd done what he had done because it needed doing. Not to say the event didn't carry with it a credible degree of regret, yet in his opinion, he would have been less than a man had he not taken the action he did to save Daniel and Amelia. *And Addie.*

Held private, inside him, Travis was in love with Addie. Unbeknownst to anyone else, she had been his heart's desire for twelve years, since shortly after the death of his first wife, Caroline.

There had been a time, during the briefest window of hope right before Addie moved to Golden Meadow, when Travis revealed himself to her. With the wish that his love might be sufficient enough for the both of them, he played his wildcard and proposed marriage. Though deeply touched, Addie rejected his proposal. The love she felt for him was not romantic.

Travis had long ago accepted that he could not have Addie. Addie was in love with Hiram. She married Hiram; it was he who held her heart. Though disappointed, Travis was not unhappy. He

was not awkward in Addie's presence, nor was he jealous of Hiram. In fact, their friendship was sustenance to his spirit.

A man needful of female companionship and with true love beyond his grasp, Travis worked around his disappointment and married Abigail, and they were a well-matched set. Together they had created a delicate balance of admiration and adoration. He admired her; she adored him. Now, it was only sometimes, when he was alone, in this place where he came to purge his soul, that Travis allowed himself to sorrow in his heart for the love he had not been able to bring to fruition.

Presently, he raised his cigar to his lips. When he drew on it, he discovered it had burned out. He dropped it on the ground and, purely out of habit, crushed the stub under his boot.

Growing chilled, Travis made his way home in the dark.

CHAPTER 15

"Remember the words of the Lord Jesus, how He said, It is more blessed to give than to receive." Acts 20: 35

It was the following Saturday that Hiram and Emily celebrated her birthday with their annual father-daughter date, and as always, they went to the Preacher's House for dinner. Since the day they first met, there had been the purest of affections between them, as though they had been part of the same life from the very beginning. Seeing them together and seeing their closeness made people smile.

Because of the commencement of the county's traditional cane-grinding and syrup-making, there was a big crowd both in town and at the Preacher's House that day. While they enjoyed their food, Emily chattered incessantly about the children at the school and of her deepest dream of becoming a schoolteacher. At certain times when Hiram listened to Emily, though he considered himself to be a reasonably well-read man, her expression of knowledge and under-standing of the world and its people was such that it made even him feel amazed and inept.

Taking note of the birthstone ring she'd outgrown and now wore on a chain around her neck, he said, "Maybe when we leave here we can go to the jeweler and buy you a new ring."

Emily touched the ring, remembering how Hiram had slipped it on her finger and "proposed" to her on bended knee three years before, just prior to marrying her mama. In her eyes, no other one could ever replace its meaningfulness.

"Thank you, but this one's fine," she replied cheerfully.

"Perhaps a bracelet, then," he suggested.

Considering this for a moment, she seemed tempted, but actually, she had her eyes on something else. Looking through the window, she was so anxious she could hardly sit still.

When they were done eating, Sassie came from the kitchen, bringing Emily's birthday cake. It was her favorite—a moist, buttery cake with hard chocolate icing. Sassie walked it out slowly, deliberately, so the candles would stay lit. There was fourteen plus "one to grow on."

When Emily made a wish and blew them out, all the patrons applauded and sang "Happy Birthday," and she was delighted. It was a perfect birthday.

As soon as she and Hiram left the restaurant, she pulled him across the street toward a sign that read, "Free Pups." The young man greeted them and drew forth a puppy from over the side of the wagon. Handing it to Emily, he said, "He's the only one left."

"Hey, boy." She took him and stroked him behind his ears. The puppy licked her face, making her giggle.

Hiram understood now, sort of.

"You'd rather have that puppy instead of a new ring?" he asked.

Nodding, Emily lifted her enormous, blue eyes to him imploringly. "He's so cute. Pretty please, can I have him—to give to Samuel?" She felt so bad that her little brother had cried after her and Hiram, realizing he couldn't go with them. "Not this time," Addie had said. "This is Emily's day."

Now Hiram understood. He looked the puppy over. It was part collie, black and white, with pretty markings. He smiled and scratched the puppy's chin. It was a fat, little fellow. Samuel would have a fit over him.

"All right, Emily," he said.

"Thank you!" She hugged him, and the puppy.

The puppy seemed content to be tucked under Emily's arm as she and Hiram walked through town toward the jewelry store, Hiram intent on buying his daughter a bracelet for her birthday.

Later, back at home as the day was coming to an end, the whole family stood watching as Samuel rolled around on the ground euphorically with his new puppy.

Emily said, "Y'all look like a couple of roly-polys," to which everyone broke out laughing.

"You're going to have to come up with a name for him," Addie said.

Samuel looked up at her, grinning ear-to-ear. "Poly," he said. "Poly." He repeated it several more times until the name stuck.

So, Poly it was.

Hermit. Shrew. Witch. Gypsy. Root doctor. Since folks really didn't know anything about Georgianne Knight except that she looked different and didn't speak, that made her a preordained target for much speculation, ridicule, and gossip. Given her unkempt, crone-like appearance, most believed she was mentally deranged; some even feared her. Therefore, people generally kept their distance and ignored her. Georgianne was left to herself.

The whispers and stares and rejection didn't bother Georgianne; she learned early on in life not to rely on people. She knew her true self and was happy, and happiest when left alone. She found pleasure in observation. She tasted, touched, smelled. She earned enough throwing clay to feed and clothe herself. She had her garden and her cats. What else was required?

Georgianne hadn't had a friend in a long time. But now that had changed.

At the end of a workday, two weeks after she and Obie had married and moved to the quarter, Sassie stopped by, swinging a lidded basket. Inside was what was left of a chocolate pie after everybody was served at the Preacher's House, she said, and hot as it was, it wouldn't be fit to eat after it sat out all night. Was she hungry? Georgianne was.

Since then, Sassie's visits had become regular, and Georgianne found herself looking forward to them. She hadn't realized she was hungry for some sort of human contact until Sassie reached out to her; but in truth, she liked the girl's company.

There was no shyness in Sassie; her youth and spunkiness, her funny jibber-jabber, all cheered Georgianne. She liked hearing about Sassie's job and family, about her mama and her Auntie Dorrie, and how it was that she came to live in Oakdale. Moreover, Georgianne just liked Sassie. She'd come into her life unexpectedly and lit upon her heart like a bright, chirping bird.

Sassie didn't come every day and never stayed long, usually just long enough for them to sit together and enjoy whatever sweet she brought with her. Today, it was peach pie. She told Georgianne about Emily's birthday and about how the chocolate cake had been devoured, not a crumb of it left.

Georgianne led them indoors to the small, cramped kitchen. Ordinarily, it smelled of coffee and old grease, but as soon as they entered, Sassie noticed a nice, sweet scent on the air. Looking around for the source, she discovered several large bunches of herbs—sage, basil, bee balm, and mint—drying above the window. She smiled, knowing how some of the townspeople would swear that Georgianne intended to use them to brew potions.

Motioning for Sassie to sit down at the kitchen table, Georgianne made her close her eyes before disappearing into the adjoining room. A moment later she returned, carrying a piece of stoneware. The salt-glaze dish was round and shallow, only about three inches deep, and cobalt blue. Georgianne had turned and fired it especially for Sassie. It was truly a gesture of her deep fondness for her, and Georgianne's eyes danced as she placed it into Sassie's hands.

Sassie opened her eyes and gasped. As she looked at it admiringly, she cried, "Oh my gosh…it's so beautiful…Miz Georgianne!… Did you make dis fo' me?"

Georgianne nodded, satisfied and happy to see how thrilled Sassie was with the gift.

Sassie was overjoyed. She cradled the dish in her hands lovingly. "Oh, thank you, Miz Georgianne! I love it! I promise to cherish it forever!" Except for her mama's quilt, it was the most special possession she had. She could hardly wait to show it to Obie.

CHAPTER 16

"God is our refuge and strength, a very present help in trouble." Psalm 46: 1

A mockingbird chased a red-tailed hawk against a cornflower-blue sky that lay empty of clouds. Columns of sunlight poured through a sprawl of barren branches. The pine-scented woods were still.

As Emily and Jesse crunched along, Jesse randomly kicked at mounds of dry, fallen leaves, sending them flying. The damp soil underneath smelled of earthy richness and sweet decay. Their cheeks were flushed from being out in the cool autumn air. Besides the squirrels they'd killed, they'd also picked up a bag full of chestnuts. Ben, too up in years to care about treeing squirrels, trotted along with them, as close as their shadows. The younger, more inquisitive hound, Tracker, caught scent of some critter and took off into a blackberry thicket.

"Tween us, we got 'leven squirrels." Thinking ahead to supper, Jesse calculated aloud, "That makes 'leven backs an' forty legs."

Emily snickered. Teasing her cousin good-naturedly, she corrected him, "Unless some of these are three-legged, you can't count worth spit. If we've got eleven squirrels, all together that's *forty-four* legs!"

Jesse grinned. "The way you add 'em up sounds even better." He could taste them already, fried and tender. "Huntin' sure makes me hungry."

"Everything makes you hungry," she replied.

Soon they came to where the creek made a sudden bend. Walking along and talking, they almost didn't notice that a large tree, one probably laid down by the bad storm back in the summer, now bridged the entire breadth of the stream.

Jesse propped his gun against a sturdy sapling and hurriedly shucked his shoes and socks. Sliding down the steep embankment, he called over his shoulder, "What cha waitin' on? Come on, let's cross over to the other side! Last one there's a rotten egg!" He spit off to the side in a show of bravery.

The prospect of falling into the cold water didn't tempt Emily. She hollered, "You'll be sorry when you fall in an' freeze to death!"

She stood with a hand on her hip as Jesse ignored the warning and climbed over a mangle of up-turned roots and proceeded to scale the log, agile as a coon.

About midway across the log, one of his feet slipped. Emily in-haled sharply as Jesse toppled forward then backward, teetering pre-cariously at a lofty height above the dark, frigid water. For a minute, Jesse held his breath and struggled to steady himself.

Hearing nothing but the beating of his own heart, he focused on the colorful leaves that floated beneath him in the rippling cur-rent. His eyes followed them as they continued on a course around the soapstone bend before drifting out of sight. Moments later, he regained his balance, and with both arms raised, he glided, catlike, across the remaining distance.

Emily sighed with relief as Jesse dismounted—a champion, full of glory—into a tangle of dead branches on the opposite bank.

Her relief was, however, short-lived, for an instant later Jesse gripped his leg and screamed out in agony.

Bewildered, Emily watched as he sank to the ground. "Jesse! What's the matter?" she yelled. But he just kept screaming, and she couldn't see him for the fallen tree. Dropping her gun and the sack of squirrels, fear compelled her to brave crossing the log to investigate. When she got to where Jesse lay, a dreadful sight presented itself. He was holding his leg and had a terrible look on his face.

At a glance, not knowing what else to do, she told him, "Jesse, I've got to go for help…I promise to be back soon…"

Though she felt bad about leaving him there alone, she set out running for home. The sound of his cries followed her until they died out in the distance, but the weight of his pleading eyes stayed with her all the way. A couple of times, she stumbled and almost fell as she ran frantically through a thick growth of laurels. She kept on running until she thought her trembling legs might give out and refuse to carry her one step further.

By the time she reached the gap at the old cotton shack that Jesse and Wiley used as a fort, the shadows of late afternoon painted the field. From here, she caught sight of the house. Chest pounding wildly, she stopped a few seconds to catch her wind.

True to her promise, shouting to the top of her lungs, she set out again, sprinting breathlessly toward home…toward help for Jesse.

Before the hour was out, Wesley and Hiram had run back through the woods with Emily to where Jesse lay, pale as milk and shivering.

When the ferocious jaws of the steel trap snapped around Jesse's ankle, its rusty teeth pierced through his tender flesh and embedded to the bone. By this time, the blood from the puncture wounds had clotted; his skin was bruised and swelled up a sight.

When Wesley dropped to his knees and pried open the trap, Jesse let out an ear-piercing scream. Freeing the ankle set off a new wave of excruciating pain. It felt like hot blades were pressing into his skin; the scorching pain wrapped around his entire lower leg.

"Freezin' to death," Jesse said in a trembling voice, his teeth clicking.

For a minute, Wesley was like a man gone mad. Bent on fury, with one strong tug he yanked the stake from the ground and, with a mighty curse slung the trap in a high arc, into the deep, dark water. It sunk straight to the bottom. With his jaw firmly clenched, he looked at Hiram and swore angrily, "That brother of yours would profit to stay out of Mississippi! Wilkes shows his face 'round here again—I aim to blow a hole through his guts big enough to drive a yearlin' through!" He meant every word.

While Emily gathered up her cousin's shoes and socks, their guns, and the burlap sack of squirrels, the men set out for home carrying Jesse, using a quilt as a makeshift gurney.

About halfway there, Hiram finally commented, "That'd be a frightful big hole."

Jesse's sleep was laudanum-induced.

His leg was propped up on a pillow as Travis worked slowly and methodically, cleaning his wounds by lamplight. Even in his unconscious state, Jesse moaned as Travis probed into the swollen flesh to wash out each small particle of rust and dirt. He was aware that what he was doing was inflicting pain upon the boy, but all he was concerned with at the moment was getting him well again.

Behind him, Wesley paced the length of the room while Laura was bent over Jesse, brushing his hair from his forehead, mothering him. They looked on anxiously and silently and let Travis do his work.

When he was satisfied the wounds were effectively cleaned, Travis set the basin of soapy water on a stool and motioned to Sarah

Beth. She hurried to remove the pan and handed him a clean towel and a bottle of antiseptic.

Jesse grimaced and twisted in agony at the first touch of the stinging medicine. Travis knew it burnt like wildfire, but it didn't matter; he continued to dab on some more.

It strained them all to see Jesse hurting. While Wesley paced, tears gathered in Laura's eyes and blurred her vision as she stroked her son's brow and tried to soothe him.

When Travis was done with his salve and bandages, he removed his spectacles and sat down on the stool beside the bed. Wiping his hands on a towel, he said, "Well, we've done what we can for now."

Wesley looked at him and asked hopefully, "Is Jesse gonna be all right?"

From across the bed, Travis read Sarah Beth's thoughts as her eyes met his. Looking at Wesley's knitted eyebrows, he said, "Oh, sure. He'll be fine. That ankle's gonna be sore as a rizen for a few days. Luckily, it's not broken, and Jesse's young an' strong, rough as a cob. He'll be swingin' cats again in no time."

Whereas he knew with an injury involving a rusty object, such as the trap Jesse stepped in, one ran a risk of contracting tetanus, he didn't see the need to worry Wesley and Laura needlessly.

Listening to Travis's assuring words, they gained confidence, and at least now Jesse did seem to be resting peacefully.

Pushing himself up from the stool, Travis pulled the covers over Jesse and said, "There's nothing else we can do tonight. Y'all might as well just go on home an' let me—"

Just as he figured, his suggestion proved futile. That was already decided. Wesley and Laura were shaking their heads. "We're stayin'," Laura said. "I want to be here when he wakes up."

Scratching his chin, Travis nodded and said, "I had a feelin' that's what you would say." With a hint of joviality, he added, "Well then, while the boy's sleepin', let's at least let my capable nurse here watch the patient long enough for us to go see if Abigail's learned how to make a pot of coffee since I saw her last."

Under present circumstance, his attempt at humor was lost on them, but they accepted his offer, since Sarah Beth promised not to leave Jesse's side.

As soon as Travis and her parents left out, half remembering something Travis had told her a few days ago, Sarah Beth whirled around and went into the adjoining room. Quickly searching the shelves, she took down a heavy medical book and began flipping through the pages. It only took a minute for her to locate what she so desperately sought.

Her eyes scanned the information: *Tetanus...the first sign is stiffness of the jaw and esophageal muscles...jaws become fixed...lockjaw... pain is persistent and great...the disease is usually, but not always, fatal...*

As she poured over the facts, the words that jumped off the pages filled her mind with fear. When she had finished reading, she returned the book and tiptoed in to stand by Jesse's bed.

Living and growing up in the same house with him, up until now she had regarded him as older siblings generally did regard a child his age. Normally, she had thought herself to be superior to him and had bossed him around, quarreled with him over the pettiest of things. She would have been just as content to ignore his presence completely and probably would have if he hadn't pestered and teased her so relentlessly.

In her eyes, Jesse had always been such a nuisance, forever spying on her, flinging frogs and worms on her. Once he'd even chased after her with a snake! What an aggravating little creature! One who most of the time smelled of wet dogs with a mingling of dirt and sweat.

But that was the past.

Whereas ordinarily Sarah Beth's heart held no home for certain feelings, as she stared down at Jesse now, something stirred within her, something unfamiliar and unexpected, something she hardly recognized. That was her little brother lying there, her *only* brother, and she realized she had taken him for granted. Even more surprisingly, she realized she cherished him beyond words, wet-dog smell and all. He may have been a pestering weasel before, but now all of a sudden he just looked small and helpless. What if…? The possibility was unsettling. Tears slid from the corners of her eyes as she reached out and touched Jesse's arm with tenderness.

Not one to pray often—since God seldom granted her requests, thankless and selfish as they were—she prayed now, hoping He was listening. *God, please heal my little brother. Please don't let him die…*

Cumbered with this unwieldy regard for someone's fate other than her own, Sarah Beth sank wearily into a chair to keep vigil over Jesse.

All the while, God kept vigil over them both.

When Jesse turned his head on the pillow and opened his eyes, it was still dark. He licked his lips and smacked. His mouth was dry as cotton.

It took him a minute to get his bearings in the dim room. He was having trouble remembering what he was doing there in Travis's office.

Seeing a water pitcher and cup on the nightstand, he tried to sit up to reach for them. In that moment, his memory came rushing back to him abruptly. Moving his leg drew an immediate reaction from him as an intensely excruciating pain made him fall back on the pillow. His ankle hurt something awful! It felt so heavy he wondered if he was tied to the bed. Right then and there, he figured he wouldn't ever be able to run or hunt again. His life might as well be over. He was an invalid.

Not wanting to wake Sarah Beth and look like a crybaby, Jesse squeezed his eyes shut tightly, willing the pain to go away. He found as long as he lay still, the pain was somewhat bearable.

Soon, he again dozed off, and for a while longer, slept.

For the first couple of days after the accident, Jesse was dependent on his family for everything, and they obliged him in every sense. They fetched and catered his every comfort, waited on him hand and foot. No sooner did he grunt would they trip over each other to fluff his pillows or prop his leg more comfortably on a cushioned footstool. Food was shoved at him like at a hog being fattened for the slaughter.

But Jesse soon learned even basking in hog-heaven had its disadvantages.

Whereas to begin with all the special treatment and petting made him feel pampered and important, once he started feeling better he discovered being fussed over constantly got old and annoying in a hurry.

Not only that, but he was also bored out of his mind. He was supplied with a pile of books, yet he didn't really enjoy reading. Reading was for sissies. He grew tired of whittling, tired of playing checkers, tired of eating, tired of lying around the house doing nothing.

Travis had said he needed to stay off his leg until it was healed. There was no sign of infection in the wounds that wreathed his ankle, and by the fourth day, the swelling was almost gone. The pain in his lower leg wasn't completely gone, but bearable enough. At least he could now wiggle his toes without cringing. As far as Jesse was concerned, he was healed enough. He was ready to get up and move around.

Taking up the crutches, at first he wobbled and almost fell. And they made his armpits sore. But after a few more tries, once he got the hang of balancing his weight and learning to use his lower body in a swinging motion, he found, triumphantly, he could go almost anywhere he'd gone before. It was the happiest day of his infirmity.

Thursday, after the midday meal, Jesse took his crutches and went out the side door to walk about the yard. Tracker wagged his tail at the sight of him, and Jesse held out his hand and called, "Come here, boy."

That day, in Jesse's mind, Jesse was turkey-hunting. He asked Tracker, "How much you bet me this time next week I'll be off these crutches an' me an' you will be huntin' for real? I wager you a hundred dollars." Though it sounded a bit extravagant, he figured it was a safe bet to make with a dog.

Soon boy and dog had set off in a footrace along the carriageway. It felt good to be outside. It was almost November; the air was fresh and dry. Right before the two of them reached the end where the carriageway joined the main road, Tracker detoured and trotted off into the brush.

And so, not having noticed anyone approaching, Jesse was met with the unexpected appearance of a stranger on horseback, one inquiring about Amelia.

CHAPTER 17

"Pursue peace with all men...lest any root of bitterness springing up trouble you, and thereby many be defiled."
Hebrews 12: 14, 15

They made a sorry-looking pair—the thin, bony woman and the thin, bony horse.

With a grimacing smile, she asked, "Where's yer ma?" as she looked around, casually appraising the place.

Rachel edged away from her warily. Turning, with the quickness of youth she took off running to the back of the house, where Amelia was doing the wash. Grabbing a tight handful of her mama's skirt, she gave a determined tug. "Mama, Mama." When Amelia glanced down at her, Rachel raised a finger and pointed. As if passing on a secret, her voice softly announced, "There's someone there."

Amelia looked closely at her daughter's serious face. In that moment, an old wave of apprehension rose within her. Her mind involuntarily leapt back three years to another such fall afternoon, when Alfred had reappeared to terrorize her. She propped the washboard against the side of the pan of sudsy water and laid the bar of lye soap on the table.

Touching Rachel's shoulder gently, Amelia urged her toward the back kitchen door. "Run along inside an' stay with your brother." She'd put Carson down for his nap a while ago.

Rachel obeyed.

Drying her hands on the front of her dress, Amelia proceeded cautiously toward the front of the house. A few moments later, she rounded the corner, thereupon confronting the visitor and a half-starved horse. Though forbiddingly gaunt, the woman wore a clean blue cotton dress, and her faded-brown hair was pulled back neatly away from her creased face. Seeing her, Amelia was struck dumb with disbelief. Her breath stolen away, she could but stand and wait.

Not yet sure how she would be received, the woman also waited, diffidently, without looking directly into Amelia's eyes. Looking fixedly at the ground, she seemed to be sorting through her thoughts.

The silence between them lengthened as Amelia stood staring at the downtrodden woman before her, the neglectful, abusive drunkard of a mother who had abandoned her years before. Bonnie Riley was the epitome of white trash. She had provided Amelia with so little, had barely seen to her, even when she was a baby. Amelia had all but forgotten about her except in her prayers, and now she had somehow happened back up. To be face to face with her again after all this time was completely unsettling.

And yet...

Taken on appearances, Amelia mistook Bonnie's reticence for regret and shame, surmising that deep inside, she must be sorrowing for the wasted years and the love she'd not been able to give. Making excuse, she thought, *That was the fault of the liquor.* She could almost feel Bonnie's misery and pain and was filled with compassion for her.

She thought, *All Mama needs is the Lord*...After all, had God not kept His promises to her, took her in and tended her, healed her when she herself was downcast and broken? ' *...For Jesus Christ maketh thee whole...* '

An unbidden love welled up within Amelia, making her realize she still loved her mama, regardless of the past. In that instant, all those things that had seemed so significant to her at one time didn't seem important at all anymore. The fact that she was here now...

Amelia's heart decided quickly. While words failed her, tears came falling.

Little above a whisper, she managed to say, "Oh, Mama!"

Without further delay, she went to and held her mother tightly while Bonnie gave herself up and wept in relief.

They'd talked away the afternoon, and now she'd left Bonnie inside the house playing with Rachel and Carson while she went out by the road to wait for Daniel. Amelia paced nervously. She dreaded telling him. Used to things being easy and playful between them, she had no idea how this might turn out. One thing she knew for sure: Daniel wouldn't be as happy as she was that Bonnie had shown up on their doorstep after all these years.

As Daniel walked toward her from the road, with a concerned look, he asked, "What's wrong? You look—"

"I was waitin' out here to talk to you." Slipping her hand under his arm, Amelia took a deep breath and blurted out, "I have the most incredible news, Daniel! Mama's here...an' she'll be stayin' with us for a while—"

Daniel stepped back and stared at his wife dumbly, like a mule staring at a new gate.

"What?"

Amelia's eyes shone. "I know it's hard to believe, but it's true! Mama's here, inside the house." Seeing a frown cross Daniel's face, she rushed on, "Aunt Jenny told her all about us gettin' married an' about Rachel an' Carson..."

Daniel exploded. "You tellin' me, here she's been gone close to ten years, never paid you a lick of attention before she run off, and now—Boy-hidey, she's got some nerve, showin' up here after everthing!"

He raked his fingers through his hair and muttered, "What give her the notion to come here, I wonder?" He was no fool. Bonnie wanted something.

Amelia interrupted, shaking her head. "She's changed, Daniel… Wait 'til you see how good she is with the children. I stalled her horse an' gave him a bucket of grain—he's so poor you could pitch a straw through him."

Daniel didn't care how good Bonnie *seemed* to be with the children or how skinny her horse was. "I don't see how—sorry as her an' Pete treated you, after all that happened—how could you just welcome her back in with open arms?"

Amelia's eyes flashed with angry tears. "And I don't see how—after all that happened—you can't just forgive and go on, especially if I can!"

There was a brief, silent standoff.

Daniel didn't like it when they quarreled. His tone softened at her tears. "Amelia, I just don't—"

Amelia pleaded with him, "Daniel, I'm tellin' you, Mama's different now. And, she didn't say it, but she looks like she's been sick. She came here near starved. She has nowhere else to go." She omitted the part about her mama eating all but the backs of two fried chickens and a pint of huckleberry jam with a half pone of cornbread.

"Please, can't you try and understand? I've never had a mother; this is my chance. Don't you see? God's givin' me this chance to finally love my mother…can't we just see if there's a way for us all to get along?"

As Daniel stood there listening to Amelia's pleas, he could call together no good reason to try and understand anything when it came to Pete and Bonnie Riley. However, against his better judgment, he put Amelia's feelings before his own and reluctantly gave in.

"I can't honestly say I believe God had a hand in her comin' here," he said, "unless He intends it as some sort of gruelin' test, but if you want her here, I reckon ain't no harm in her *visitin'* for a while."

Amelia hugged him in a burst of happiness. "Oh, thank you, Daniel! You'll see! Everything's gonna work out fine!"

Bonnie had watched the exchange from inside the house and now walked out on the porch. Amelia went inside, leaving the two of them alone to talk.

"Howdy-do, Daniel. Been a while. Last I laid eyes on you, you wuz just a boy in knee-britches."

There they were, adversary to adversary. Daniel regarded her for a few moments without speaking a word. He didn't feel the least bit like being neighborly to her. Finally, he simply said, "Well, I see you found us."

"Jenny told me where Amelia was." Bowing her head, she said meekly, "Jus' so's you know, I'm eat up with regret over the way I raised Amelia. I know I didn't do right by her, an' I know I ain't de- servin', but if she's willin' to give me a chance, I aim to try an' make amends."

What she said sparked a new fire in Daniel's mind, for in his mind still lived an image of Amelia as a dirty, hungry, unloved little girl, an image that to this day still tugged at his heart.

"'Didn't *do right* by her,' you say?" He huffed incredulously. "God have mercy, woman! You no more raised Amelia than I can raise the dead! You paid less a mind to her than I would a jaybird!"

Bonnie shrank a little inside and inwardly cursed Daniel, but she figured she better keep her mouth shut. She hadn't come this far only to mess in her nest now. She'd come there looking for three meals a day and a roof over her head, and she'd found it. She had nothing, was destitute. From the looks of things, they had plenty. Like it or not, Daniel could go to hell, for she wasn't leaving.

After a lengthy pause, Daniel sighed and said, "Amelia means the world to me, always has. For a reason I can't guess, she's got a tender spot in her heart for you and is glad you're here, though I can't say the same." He looked off a minute, fixing his words with his thoughts, his jaw set.

Harsh as it seemed, he just could not bring himself to meet her as Amelia had. His gut told him Bonnie was still sly as moonshine and he didn't intend to be her dunce. If circumstances had been different…But them being what they were, he told her plain, "I love Amelia, and this is our home. The day you hurt my family or bring whiskey into our house, I'll thank you to hit the grit an' drag on back to wherever it is you came from."

Having spoke his piece, such that it was, Daniel went inside the house, leaving Bonnie standing out on the porch alone. Before, she had been set on telling him how she'd been sober a good, long while—almost a year—but now she figured that bit of trivia would most likely whistle past his ears like the wind, so she saved her breath. She thought maybe, given time, she might be able to prove herself to him. She shrugged. *Or maybe not.*

For *time* was another thing she didn't have.

The following morning, no sooner than the sun had risen, Daniel set out walking with his thoughts, thinking about how he had every earthly cause to despise Alfred Coulter.

Like all boys, when Daniel was young, he craved his father's attention. He would've been content for him to do any one of the many ordinary things most fathers did with their sons, like take him fishing or hunting, shoot marbles, or throw washers with him.

Instead, Alfred had made up his own games, usually by finding fault with Daniel and provoking him to anger; then he'd use brutality to settle it, triggering more anger.

How many nights as a boy had he covered his face and wept as he lay in his bed, sorrowing with what was in his heart, knowing for certain his father didn't love him, but not knowing the reason

why. He never understood why his pa never did come to him, why he never gave him so much as a pat on the back or impart a single, kind word. Daniel had been carrying the memory of how that felt all through his life, a feeling others could never know.

Of course, one sure thing Alfred—and Pete and Bonnie Riley—had loved was moonshine. *A sorry lot,* Daniel told himself, kicking a rock.

Ever a violent man, Alfred had an uncommon meanness about him. What he'd done to Amelia, though, was the worst. Daniel's spine still turned to ice when he thought about it. Just as his father never did come to him, he would never forget, nor ever forgive, the evil he'd done.

Daniel knew he was blessed. He and Amelia had a happy life. They'd held on tight to each other's hearts from the time they were eight years old to this very day. She'd been his playmate, his friend, and his love right from the start. Now they had Rachel and Carson. And he loved his job in the woodshop, and he loved and respected Hiram.

Even so, while Daniel knew the world to be a fine place, and it was not in his nature to sit around and brood over the past, Bonnie's coming here had churned up all these bad things in his mind, had defiled his private thoughts.

Sick of it all, he opened the door and went in.

Hiram and Addie were sitting down to breakfast.

Addie exclaimed, "Good gracious, you're stirring early! Have you had anything to eat yet?" Not waiting for him to answer, she got up from the table and returned with a plate for him. Daniel took off his hat and turned a cane-bottomed chair backward and straddled it.

Void of preamble, he said, "If I was to give y'all a hundred guesses, you'd never guess who's turned up out of the blue an' slept in my house last night."

They looked at him expectantly, waiting for him to name the person.

"Bonnie Riley." He poked a hole in a biscuit and filled it with apple butter.

Hiram didn't know Bonnie Riley from Adam's house cat, so he had no comment and continued to eat. Addie, however, was astonished. Amazement registered on her face. "Well, I'll be."

Before she could ask any of the questions running through her mind, Daniel elaborated, "Beat's all I've ever seen. Amelia's brought forth the fatted calf!"

Sensing his agitation, Addie said, "Maybe Bonnie's changed… People do, you know." She got up and went to the jelly cupboard for a jar of fig preserves.

Daniel groaned. "Not you too! That's what Amelia says."

"What do *you* say?" Addie asked.

"I say her word's not worth a chaw of tobaccer," was his answer. "I figure she's come lookin' for a handout."

"How does she look?"

"Poorly. Her face is showin' a whole mess of winters…she's about as big around as my little finger."

"What on earth has she been doing all these years? Where's she been living?"

"I don't know. On top of Fool's Hill, I'd reckon."

Daniel sighed in exasperation. "Mama, to tell you the truth, I can't say. I couldn't think of much to say to the woman." He took a big bite out of his biscuit. When he'd swallowed, he muttered, red in the face, "And may I ask…since when does anybody give a hoot about what Bonnie-ne'r-been-worth-a-cuss-Riley's been doin' all these years? I swear to God, it is irksome to know I'm the only one who seems to take into account her sorriness. I guess the whole world's forgot how she just up an' run off an' left her own daughter to root-hog-or-die. Far as I'm concerned, her an' Pete *still* ought-a be strung up for the way they did!"

Hiram and Addie exchanged a look. Addie knew her son; she could read him like a book. Yes, it was true Bonnie and Pete neglected and mistreated Amelia; however, she knew there was more to what was really bothering Daniel this morning than Pete and Bonnie Riley. She knew the underlying cause for his tone had to do with his pa. *All roads led back to Alfred.* In a way, Daniel was imprisoned, was still allowing himself to be held hostage by the past.

Daniel did have a lot to live with. Alfred had done especially hard by him from the day he was born, but ultimately, Alfred had raped Amelia, and for that, in Daniel's eyes, dying hadn't been punishment enough for him.

Deep inside, a familiar whisper of remorse needled Addie. She felt she'd failed Daniel. Sometimes she felt it was her fault, that she was somehow to blame for not being able to shield her son and his heart from his father's brutal ways. Of course in reality, she knew she could no more have protected Daniel from Alfred than she could have protected her own mother from him. Or Creenie. Or Amelia. Or even herself. If only she could take his burden onto her own shoulders, she would. But she couldn't.

Addie reined her thoughts back in, steering them clear of all that. Even though she understood what he was feeling, the last thing Daniel needed was her pity and another excuse not to release himself from his silent hell.

How she wished he would let go of the hate in his heart! She knew from experience it was best not to hole up with one's bitterness. It wouldn't help matters to say what she was thinking, though.

Once before, when she'd tried to talk to Daniel about what the Bible had to say about harboring bitterness, he'd made his feelings sharply understood and walked away from her. It tore at her heart, but she had not broached the subject with him again. All she could do was continue to pray about it.

Daniel looked over at Addie and stopped chewing because she was looking at him so intently. There was a powerful bond between them, and as she gazed deeply into his eyes, she saw clean down to his soul. With an encouraging smile, she reached out and gently smoothed one of his sideburns with her fingers. She said softly, "I worry about you sometimes."

Daniel gulped down the last of his coffee and swallowed any sign of his anger with it. He jumped up, almost knocking his chair over, and gave her a big laugh and a big hug to go with it. "Mama, I'll tell you like you're always tellin' me—worryin's like a rockin' chair. It gives you something to do but doesn't get you anywhere!"

He grabbed his hat and followed Hiram out the door.

Addie called after them, "I'll get by in a day or so to say howdy to Bonnie!" *Once the smoke has cleared...*

Bonnie had been sick a long time, over a year.

At first, when she started waking up in the morning as exhausted as when she went to bed at night, she merely laid it off on getting old. After all, she was coming up on forty, and by that age death had already carried her own ma off. It was not until Bonnie was brought down with a cough and persistent fever that she felt bad enough to start admitting there might be something else more serious the matter with her. Even then, she'd put off consulting a doctor until she started coughing up blood.

Looking at her gravely, the first thing the doctor said after he had examined her was, "Prepare to meet thy God!" He was old, and having already attended more than his fill of dyings that year—a year epidemic with both yellow fever and consumption—his bedside manner was charitably lacking, to say the least.

After that initial, tactless spiritual advisory, he did go on to prescribe a regimen that might would help: cold baths, eating a rich diet, drinking sassafras tea, and taking in plenty of sun. Typical of Bonnie, who had always viewed both religion and logic in a dim light, she instead went home and rendered herself unconscious with whiskey, fully expecting, that night, to pass from her affliction and this world into her coming world, wherever that may have been.

That was last November.

In the weeks that followed, her condition worsened. The consumption drew her strength away; not a day passed without her running a fever. Her lungs hurt. Sometimes the congestion in her chest got so bad it became a struggle to breathe, especially at night; the besieging cough deprived her of sleep. Bonnie suffered terribly through the cold, damp months of winter, insofar that there were times she would simply lie and concentrate upon dying, earnestly wishing that death would come and release her.

Death, however, proved fickle.

Her symptoms gradually improved, and Bonnie began to recover. The cough and fever slowly diminished then eventually ceased altogether. Though left weak and plagued by chronic tiredness, in March, when the sap rose, Bonnie likewise rose from her sickbed, astonishing the old doctor, who had given her up for dead some months before.

And now, November had come again.

Presently, as Travis stared at Bonnie across his desk, his spectacles riding low on his nose, one word came to mind. *Cadaver.* How she had managed to stay above ground this long defied everything he knew about both medicine and the human anatomy. He could hear her chest wheezing, and the whites of her eyes were as yellow as corn. There was no need for a medical degree to determine her liver was shot.

Travis didn't believe in lying to a patient. He said, "Well, Bonnie, based on my examination an' everything you've told me, I'd have to say you're eat up with consumption of the lungs an' the ill effects of over-imbibin'. Of course, I 'spect you already knew this."

His candor brought a wry smile to her face. "You still the same ol' Doc Hughes. Never was very confidence-inspirin', was you?" she jeered. "I reckon you'll be expectin' double the pay for all this sweet talk."

Travis had about as little patience as most doctors do and let the sarcasm bounce off his ears. He leaned back in his chair and regarded her somewhat sympathetically, lightly tapping his spectacles against his thigh, thinking. After a minute, he offered as a matter of fact, "Folks have been known to survive consumption."

Barring a miracle of divine proportions, though, he ardently doubted Bonnie would be one of them. He knew there was really nothing he could do other than keep her comfortable, maybe ease her passing when the time came.

As if reading his mind, Bonnie said, "I didn't come here aimin' to git healed. I know my time's short. I only came 'cause Amelia wouldn't hear it no other way." Amelia had become alarmed when she saw her cough up blood that morning and insisted on her being examined by Travis.

Travis waited to see what else she might say.

Bonnie looked away from his face, then down at her hands, laying clenched on her lap. "I'll thank you for not lettin' on to my girl that I'm a-dyin'."

Saturday afternoon Addie went to see Bonnie. Upon arriving, she found the woman sitting alone, just beyond the shade of a mature magnolia in the side yard near the well. She was sprawled out in a rocker with her eyes closed; Addie watched her for a minute from where she stood before going forward.

Though Daniel had warned her, Addie was aghast at the sight of her. Bonnie was nothing but skin and bones. Her face was hollow-cheeked, her skin sallow and sickly-looking. Her legs were stretched out in front of her with the tail of her dress hiked up to her knees, her lower limbs bared to the sun. They were as orange and scaly as a chicken's.

"Hello, Bonnie!" Addie called in greeting.

Bonnie opened her eyes and saw Addie approaching. "Why, bless me if this ain't old home week!" she cackled. "First I'uz reunited with my girl, then I seen ol' Doc Hughes, an' now here comes my old neighbor walkin' up!"

Addie smiled at her politely. When she went to pull up a straight chair to sit down, Bonnie said, "You mightn't want to set so close, in case I'uz to go to coughin'."

There was no sign of Amelia and the children, so Addie asked about them.

"Boy's nappin'," Bonnie replied, "an' Amelia's got the gal helpin' her with some apple tarts." She shook her head and laughed, "That Amelia's a dotin' fool when it comes to them young'uns. Daniel too!"

Remembering Bonnie's paltry brand of mothering, Addie made herself smile. "Yes, Amelia is a good little mother, and you might say we're all fools about Rachel and Carson. Amelia works hard at keeping their home up, too." She truly was passionate and energetic, finding an interest in cooking and sewing as well as in tending a flower garden.

Gazing about the place, Bonnie agreed crassly. "Fittin' for the Queen of Sheba."

It was a mild day. Addie undid her sunbonnet and laid it in her lap. For the next half hour the two women engaged in light talk, with Addie doing most of the talking.

"What's become of Pete?" she finally asked. "Do you know if he's still living?"

Bonnie responded drily, "Yep, that ol' coot's still alive, ignorant as ever. I wuz countin' on livin' long enough to see him buried, but I reckon he's gone show me yet." Feeling her own death coming, she told Addie, "Come spring, I'll be pushin' up daisies." She said it matter-of-factly, without self-pity.

Addie paused only briefly. "Whatever ails you, Bonnie?"

"Pus, corruption, an' corn liquor—accord'n' to the Doc."

Addie hoped her smile presented sympathetic. She took a moment to consider, then took the next step boldly. "Well, I suppose sooner or later we all must face physical death, however in John 3:16 Jesus promises that 'whosoever believeth in Him shall not perish, but have everlasting life'."

Bonnie scoffed at her. "That's a right pretty notion, but as you might imagine, I never fell in high favor with the Almighty." She had lived her entire life on an unchartered course, unanchored and adrift.

"No matter," Addie persisted gently. "If we confess our sins, the Lord is faithful and just to forgive us our sins; the Bible says if we confess and repent, He will cleanse us from all unrighteousness." Her heart was fixed, established firmly in the Lord, and regardless of Bonnie's mocking expression, she felt compelled to witness to her.

Bonnie sighed indifferently. "The Lord knows all about me an' the thangs I've done. Don't make no sense to make Him suffer through my tellin' it ag'in." She had held on to her sin too long, her heart was hardened, her conscious sealed. Bonnie had quenched the Spirit. Sadly, for her, it was too late. Her soul belonged to the Devil.

Addie felt a pang of pity for her, and her unconcern.

Seeing Addie's rueful expression, Bonnie yawned loudly and closed her eyes. Wanting to be shed of the subject, she said, "Anyways, I'm too wore out right now to think beyond the grave."

There was no point in Addie pressing her further, not at this time. She had presented an idea and it had been rejected and she knew it. Before she surrendered complete defeat, though, she said encouragingly, "I'll be praying for you, Bonnie." She sniffed the air. "Mmm. I smell cinnamon. I believe I'll go inside and see how those tarts are coming along." So saying, she rose from her chair.

As she walked towards the kitchen door, she heard Bonnie mumble irritably, "Go on, an' pray if you've a mind to. But ain't no amount-a prayin' gone snatch me from the flames at this late date."

183

CHAPTER 18

"Be merciful unto me O God, be merciful unto me...until these calamities be over-past." Psalms 57:1

Near the end of November, weather came right for the first hog-killing of winter. So, on Tuesday before Thanksgiving, according to the plan everyone agreed upon, two were slaughtered and dressed at Hiram and Addie's place.

School having been dismissed primarily for this purpose but also for the holiday, Emily was put in charge of keeping the younger children occupied and out of the way so that the work might proceed more smoothly. It wouldn't be until the end of the day that links of sausage, slabs of bacon, and hams would be hanging in the smokehouse to cure.

Herded into the kitchen, Samuel, Meggie, Libby, Rachel, and Carson eagerly gathered around the table, where Emily supervised them as they measured out cupfuls of flour and sugar and broke eggs into a mixing bowl to make cookies. Pinching off pieces of the dough, they gobbled it down then licked their fingers, greasy from the butter.

No sooner than they began rolling out the dough and cutting it into shapes, Libby grew bored of the activity. Too, just watching the other children hovering about the table having so much fun, though she didn't know why, suddenly she felt resentful of their cheerfulness.

Restless, she grabbed a handful of raisins and wandered off by herself into the front parlor. Looking about, she noticed Emily's butterfly collection, propped up on the mantel. As if receiving a cue, a vague smile came to her face. She turned and briskly went to the door, slipping out onto the porch. It was a cold day, but clear and dry; the smell of woodsmoke, entrails, and fat filled the air.

Poly came hopping up the steps friskily, his tail wagging.

Expectations soaring, Libby said, "Come on, Poly. I know a place where there's lots of butterflies." No one noticed her leave the house and set off toward the woods carrying a jar, with Samuel's little puppy following close on her heels.

They walked vigorously for about fifteen minutes before coming to where a big hickory lay on its side, felled by the tornado back in July. The week before, Hiram and Wesley had cut and piled the limbs up and started sectioning the log into lengths to split for firewood. Hickory chips littered the ground.

Continuing on, Libby and Poly followed the leafy path until they reached the spot where Libby remembered there to be a patch of coneflowers in full bloom. Knowing this to be the place, she took pause and stared, panting.

At least they *had* been there, just weeks ago, back during the summer. Now, however, the once-beautiful flowers had faded. There were no flowers or any butterflies. Both lost to her. Acting on a growing sense of disenchantment, she reached out and plucked a dried seed head and rolled it between her fingers, releasing the seeds, as if in doing so, releasing herself from any expectations she'd had of catching butterflies.

Suddenly, Libby was filled with an awareness, an emptiness, that she indeed had lost something, or that something had been taken

from her, but her young mind couldn't comprehend what made her feel so.

Drawn by the smell of the creek, she inched slowly down the path toward the swimming hole. Overhead, a blue jay fluttered from one tree to the next. A gentle breezed sighed through the branches.

Libby stopped in her tracks. She thought she heard something. A voice. Or maybe someone breathing. She looked around, but there was no one there.

There it is again. That sound. Libby listened and cautiously waited. Although she didn't yet see her, some instinct told her that she was here. Libby was convinced that she'd probably been lurking in the trees all along, silently watching her.

Though the air was still, all of a sudden, Libby caught a whiff of rosewater.

"Mama?" she called out.

Even if she hadn't been so young, Libby couldn't have begun to understand the things that were happening to her lately—the troubling thoughts that invaded her mind, the images. Sometimes it was impossible for her to discern between reality and her wild imaginings.

When her mother was living, it seemed no matter how hard Libby tried, she never quite managed to earn Anna's attention. Or her love. *So why is it,* she wondered, *that now that she's dead she comes to me often, unbidden?*

The first time she had returned—that night as now—Libby had felt her presence before she'd actually seen her. Something had awakened her from a sound sleep, a sense of apprehension or some sort of noise. She had turned over, and there beside the bed stood her mama, looking more beautiful than ever in a long, flowing dress. She was smiling; she appeared to be happy at last. That night, she had gazed at Libby lovingly, sweetly, her face without the pathological hardness she'd worn so naturally in life. Lingering but a few brief

moments, she had drifted easily and weightlessly from the room, like a soft breeze...*like an angel.*

The experience had frightened Libby so, she'd wet the bed. Since then, though, she'd learned to calmly listen and watch for her, and though she'd come back a few times since, it had never again been at night.

"Mama?"

No answer. Maybe her mind was just playing tricks on her. Maybe her mama wasn't really here after all.

Libby kicked across the sandbar, drawing close to the water's edge. For a moment, she stood and watched how the sunlight shimmered upon the stream; a poignant current of melancholy eddied in her heart.

The night before, she'd had the nightmare again. It was always the same: It was in the middle of the night; she was in the creek. Her mama was holding her head under the dark, cold water. Just before she drowned, she would wake up, gulping for air, soaked with perspiration, and filled with frustration. Frustration over not being able to remember. Or was it not being able to forget? Which, Libby wasn't sure.

Remember what? Forget what? *Something.* Was it something that had really happened or something that she dreamt? The answers, like dust motes, were perpetual in motion, fleeting and elusive, impossible to grasp, leaving her in a constant cloud of confusion about it all.

Without warning, something swirled in the air around her...*like a demon.*

Libby spun around. Her stomach twisted as the swirling sound took form. There Anna was, right before her!

Filled with fear, Libby stood frozen, as though she was standing at the edge of a high bluff. Looking down at her feet, she became dizzy. She was imminently close to the edge, close to tumbling down into a psychotic abyss. She dropped to the ground and crossed her

187

arms over her knees and put her head down. She was in a private asylum, her mind tormented by a barrage of conflicting emotions, spinning around in her head like pinwheels. Her world had become one complex and frightening, one now ruled by angels and demons.

Poly sat on the sand with his head cocked, curiously watching the strange girl.

Libby heard Anna call out to her. She covered her ears, trying to shut out the sound of her voice, trying to shut out…*what?* She kept her head down, refusing to meet Anna's gaze. Her mind screamed, *Go away! Leave me alone, Mama!*

Poly bounced across the sand toward Libby. He tugged at her skirt with his teeth, wanting her to play with him.

Libby raised her head and looked out across the water again. The sun glinted off the rippling surface in a series of bright flashes, white and gold and silver. The erratic blinking movements set off a brilliant kaleidoscope of images inside her head, hundreds of them, moving too fast for her to make out, making it impossible to think. She felt a pounding at her temples.

Suddenly, everything around her seemed to take on an extraordinary energy. Libby scrambled to her feet; her legs were trembling. Possessed by an escalating sense of agitation, she grabbed Poly up and, for a moment, hugged him tightly. Anna's voice cried out in dismay, knowing, trying to make Libby stop what she was about to do. But Libby paid no heed to her. She was angry, and her anger held her in a place where she couldn't be reached. Her mind was no longer that of an ordinary child, not that of any sane person.

Then, Libby did the unthinkable.

With both her hands around Poly's neck, she plunged the puppy's head beneath the frigid water and, with surprising strength, she held him under.

A few minutes later, after a short, awful struggle, she let him go. Hardly aware of what she'd done, she stared dimly, void of emotion, as his lifeless body floated downstream, bobbing in the current.

Her face distorted with defiance, she turned and looked at Anna. "How—does—that—make—you—feel—Mama!" Each word was accentuated with a breath, spoken through clenched teeth. She picked up a pinecone and flung it at Anna.

Libby saw the pain and sadness in Anna's eyes; Anna again drifted out of sight.

As her anger slowly retreated, Libby stood and blinked in a haze of confusion, unable to comprehend why this had happened. Tears streamed down her face. Her searching gaze scanned the landscape for any sign of her mama. But her mama was again gone. Like her anger, gone. Her fear, gone. Libby lifted her hand in a gesture of farewell to all of them.

She backed away from the creek. The pounding of her heart was so loud she was afraid the others would be able to hear it all the way from the house. For a moment, she wondered what would happen if they came looking for her and discovered what she'd done.

All of a sudden, she started singing in a broken, shaky voice: "And sinners plunged beneath that flood, lose all their guilty stains...lose all their guilty stains..."

As she sang, a wonderful sense of happiness flowed into her veins and flooded her soul, cleansing her from any true feelings of what had just occurred.

"...Wash all my sins away...wash all my sins away..."

In the time it took for the tears to dry on her cheeks, Libby felt better. Thinking about the freshly baked cookies, a look of joy came into her eyes. She ran across the sand and hurried back along the path toward Addie's house, the memory of Anna's ghost and the horrible thing she'd done to Poly washed from her mind.

Lies silent in the grave...lies silent in the grave...

Soon after breakfast the following morning, Addie traveled into Oakdale, taking with her a mess of fresh meat, a sack of cracklings, a gallon of cane syrup, and a quart of huckleberry jam.

Upon seeing her pull up in the yard, Sassie ran to her for a hug. Sassie was still working at the Preacher's House most every day and her busy schedule had kept her from going out to visit them for almost a month.

"I bin missin' y'all somethin' awful!" she cried.

"We've missed you, too!" Addie smiled as she patted Sassie's growing belly. Her pregnancy was really beginning to show, being well into her fifth month. "Looks like you're doing fine, though. It'd do Stell's heart good to see you. Yesterday she bet Claire a dollar that you'd gotten round as a kettle."

This made Sassie giggle. "I wish Miz Stell an' Miz Claire could've come with you! An' Emily an' Samuel…an' ever'body else!" She missed them all and was eager to hear every scrap of news relating to them.

"Stell won't hardly go anywhere anymore except maybe to church," Addie said. "And, by her own admission, she only goes there to satisfy her craving for 'terrible singin' an' roasted preacher.'"

They looked at each other and laughed.

"Dat Miz Stell, she somethin' else," Sassie said.

Addie couldn't remember ever seeing Sassie look so happy. Marriage and pregnancy certainly agreed with her. Pointing to the box in the buggy, she said, "We butchered hogs yesterday; I brought y'all a box of goodies."

"It seem jus' like Christmas!" Sassie exclaimed. "Let's go in an' set in da ki'chen, so I can keep a watch on my pies." Obie led the way, carrying the box.

The little kitchen was cozy and warm from the heat of the stove; the wonderful aroma of apples and cinnamon filled the whole house.

"Gosh, it smells heavenly in here," Addie said.

"You want me to make some coffee?" Sassie tore into the brown paper sack to sample the cracklings. Soon as she popped one of the greasy, succulent morsels into her mouth, another sudden craving hit her. "Oh, if only I had some roast'n ears. An' a fried green tomato."

Addie smiled and shook her head at the offer for coffee. "Don't go to the trouble just for me."

It was about an hour later, when Sassie went to take the pies from the oven, that Addie got up and started putting on her coat to leave.

Sassie set a bubbling apple cobbler on the table.

"My, what a beautiful pie," Addie said. "And that dish is almost too pretty to use." Addie had not yet met Georgianne, but from everything Sassie had told her about her new friend, she sounded like quite the character.

Before she climbed onto the buggy, Addie hugged Sassie once again, saying, "We'll miss y'all tomorrow, but I trust you'll have a happy day." It sounded to her like the tensions between Rosette and Sassie at least seemed to be hitting on a lower key, so she and Obie were going to spend Thanksgiving Day with his family. "Maybe one day soon y'all can come out and spend the day with us."

"We will," Sassie said. "Tell ever'body 'Happy Thanksgivin' fo' me. An' tell Samuel I gone say a prayer fo' him to find his po' li'l puppy."

Addie smiled. "Thank you, I'll be sure to tell him, and I'll pass your message along to the others, too. Obie, you take good care of our girl now." Settling onto the seat and taking the reins, she added, "Before I head home, I promised to stop by Travis and Abigail's to pick up Sarah Beth. She's going home to spend the night and help Laura with the cooking."

Hearing that made Obie suddenly remember something. "Why, Miz Sarah Beth gone," he said.

Addie and Sassie exchanged a puzzled look. "What do you mean?" Addie asked. "Where has she gone?"

He shrugged. "I'z don't know dat, but I seed her board da stage day befo' yes'tiddy."

"Obie, iz you lyin' to us?" Sassie hit his arm. "You better not be lyin'!"

Frowning, Addie found this news peculiar. A mistake, surely. *Especially*, she thought, *since the last thing Laura said to me was, "Much obliged for going by and getting Sarah Beth for us…"* The favor was going to save Wesley from having to come into town for her later.

Obie was obviously mistaken.

Addie asked him pointedly, "Obie, are you for *certain* it was Sarah Beth you saw getting on the stage?"

He bobbed his head. "Ye'sum. I'z pretty sure it wuz her. She wuz wearin' a big ol' fluffy-lookin' hat." Looking from one of them to the other, perceiving their doubt and concern, he defended himself to Sassie, "I meant to ax you where she wuz gwine, but I forgot 'til jus' now."

Cutting short her good-byes, Addie made a quick departure.

Theirs was a marriage that suited them both, for a variety of reasons. Travis and Abigail were passionately devoted to and intrigued by each other, despite the twenty-year difference in their ages. One thing for certain, they never got bored with each other.

Travis had a son, Brandon, by his late wife, Caroline, and naturally, he had hoped his son would follow in his footsteps and become a doctor; but instead, Brandon was fascinated by law. Upon completion of law school and passing the board, he subsequently put out his shingle and, over time, had built a thriving practice. His hard work in the early years had finally paid off, for now he was a partner in one of the most prestigious law firms in Memphis.

Completely opposite from Travis's domesticated first wife, Abigail had grown up in a man's world—her late father's world— and had a respectable expertise in the field of finance. An equal part-

ner in the bank with her brother, Jonathan, Abigail had never had any inclination to have children. The bank was her baby, and she loved it.

Presently, they were in Travis's office having a glass of claret and talking animatedly about plans underway for the construction of a research hospital soon to be built in Memphis. It would be the best hospital in all of the state of Tennessee, quite possibly one of the best medical facilities in all of the country.

Still in the preliminary planning stages, Brandon's firm was handling the legal jargon and seeking out potential investors for the enormous project, and, knowing that Jonathan and Abigail had connections everywhere from New Orleans to Mobile, he had convinced them to climb on the bandwagon with them; they had all but decided to make a considerable investment in the building of it. In fact, Jonathan had gone to Memphis just this week to work alongside the attorneys and oversee the initial drafts to ensure the financial groundwork was properly laid.

Brandon had also managed to pull a few professional strings and secure Travis a promised position at the new hospital, as well as a coveted chair on the medical board. Both appointments were his for the taking; all he had to do was move to Memphis.

For the tenth time, Travis reread the latest letter from his son, which served to answer many of his questions concerning the new hospital. Abigail sat across the strewn desk from him, scrutinizing a stack of proposals that Brandon had sent along with his letter for them to review.

Years before, Travis had contemplated moving to Memphis to be closer to his son and grandchildren, but, content his whole life with being a country doctor, he'd ultimately chosen not to. Nevertheless, from time to time he'd caught himself wondering if someday he might regret not doing so. Now, it seemed the older he got the more appealing and logical the idea seemed. After all, the years were flying by, and one day in the not-so-distant future, it would be too late.

And this! What he was being offered was such a lucrative opportunity, and a challenging one. Just thinking about it made him feel more alive, almost like a kid again.

Travis drew on his cigar while he thought it over. *The legacy I could leave behind…* "Jonathan says the way it's lookin', they'll be set to break ground next summer."

He was looking at Abigail with near giddiness. Before she could comment, he added, "I think the time might be right for us to seriously consider makin' the move to Memphis."

"Oh, darling! This is so exciting!" But the truth was, she would be just as happy to stay in Oakdale if Travis decided to do so. She knew how hard he'd worked to set up his practice and how much the folks around there loved him. "Brandon would be thrilled, but what about all your patients? And our friends here? We would miss them terribly, and they us."

Travis knew that, inwardly, it would delight Abigail to no end to get back to a big city. He laughed and reminded her, "Memphis is not so far away that we couldn't come back to visit from time to time! For that matter, what of the bank…?"

"We wouldn't have to worry about the bank. Jonathan and I know any number of good people we could bring down here to run it. As for the house…"

"I've already given some thought to what we could do with the house. Miss Bernice has gone to the town council several times about needin' a bigger place for the school—"

Before he could finish his statement, their conversation was interrupted.

Having arrived at their house as quickly as she could, Addie was escorted into the room by the housemaid, Maybelle. Dispelling with niceties, not even giving anyone time to rise and offer her a chair, she addressed the both of them, "Where is Sarah Beth?"

Seeing her look of alarm, Travis said, "Why, she's not here. She went home a couple of days ago...wanted to help Laura with the bakin' an' such. I'm surprised you haven't seen her..."

Addie was shaking her head. "On the contrary, she's not there. Laura sent me to get her." She went on to tell them what Obie said about seeing her board the stage on Monday morning.

As soon as she heard that, Abigail let out a little gasp. She pushed back her chair and went running down the hall to Sarah Beth's bedroom, with Addie and Travis in close pursuit.

Abigail knocked sharply on the door. There was no answer. She turned the doorknob and entered. The curtains were closed, the bed was made, the room neat as a pin. On the washstand, they saw an envelope propped up against the mirror, addressed in Sarah Beth's loopy script: *Uncle Travis and Aunt Abigail.*

Abigail snatched the envelope up and ripped it open. She hurriedly scanned the note before passing it to Travis with a soft, "Oh, my."

Travis took it from her and read. Before it burned his fingers off, he passed it on to Addie. In all his years, this was the nearest he had ever come to being shocked.

While Addie read, Travis looked at Abigail in disbelief, thinking himself a fool. "Hell fire" was all he could say. Abigail blinked nervously and cut her eyes quickly to his face then away again. Her toes crimped in her shoes.

Nothing prepared them for this; there had been no signs of there being anything between them, absolutely nothing had given them away. Standing there, Abigail secretly doubted any gallant intentions on the part of her brother.

When Addie finished reading the note, she looked at Travis, who commented to her grimly, "I don't s'pose you'd care to deprive me the grand displeasure of passin' this news along to Wesley an' Laura... spare your ol' friend here the agony of facin' the firin' squad?" A light sweat had broken out on his forehead.

Knowing her brother and sister-in-law, she well understood Travis's dilemma. When presented this, they would forevermore pitch a royal fit. They had entrusted their daughter to him. What was it he'd said? *"Sarah Beth has a head full of sense, she just lacks direction."* More like a head full of fancy ideas. There was no wondering he dreaded telling them. For true, Travis was in a pickle.

Suddenly, Addie couldn't stop herself from laughing. After all, the girl was fine! Not kidnapped, not dead, just Sarah Beth being her silly, flighty self!

"No thanks. I'll gladly leave the honors to you! Actually, if you think about it, the firing squad might be a lot less painful than the alternative!"

Ah, life! Addie thought. *With all its strange and wonderful, complicated and terrible, unexpected twists and turns!* And for once, by some miracle, the shipwreck wasn't hers!

She could hardly wait to get home to tell Hiram what the note said.

Dear Uncle Travis and Aunt Abigail,

No doubt you all will be surprised to learn that Jonathan and I are in love—he adores me so—and we plan to be married once we reach Memphis. Please tell Mama and Father not to worry, and though I know they will miss me terribly, tell them not to come after me, for I am a grown woman now. I will write to them soon. Adieu and Happy Thanksgiving!

Love, Sarah Beth

CHAPTER 19

"And thou shalt be secure, because there is hope..." Job 11: 18

What Sassie wanted more than anything in the world was to be accepted by Rosette. Determined to yet win her mother-in-law's approval, as she went about the bedroom putting on a Sunday dress, she prayed a loud, runaway prayer that no doubt tickled the ears of the Lord.

"Lawd, bless me dis day, an' bless my apple pie, 'cause even dough Miz Rosette still like to snap at me like a loggerhead turtle, lately I bin noticin', 'specially since my belly be gittin' big, she startin' to seem a teeny bit nicer, not near as stuck-uppity as she wuz to me befo', an' las' night, I tol' Obie, 'You jus' wait an' see, dis baby gone sof'n up yo' mama's heart an'...'" Her pregnancy had become a decided advantage now that she was sensing a shift of attitude—a budding of something tender even—in Rosette.

Listening to the shouting coming from inside their house, Obie could only shake his head and smile. He thought, *First my daddy talk crazy, now my wife.* He put the pie in the wagon and, knowing what high hopes Sassie had for the day ahead—and convinced it would take a sight more than an apple pie to soften his mama'a heart—he said a silent prayer of his own, his request being that Sassie wouldn't be let down once again.

An hour later at the Quinn residence, seeing the table so loaded with food made the menfolk grunt with satisfaction. As they all gathered around the table to take their seats, unable to stop herself, Etta began to gleefully bleat the Thanksgiving menu to them like they couldn't see what was right before their own eyes: "Roasted hens, cornbread dressin', chick'n dumplin's, sweet taters, tater salad, hard-boilt eggs, collard greens, cornbread..."

Everyone was staring at the food, their eyes aglow with anticipation and greed, when someone finally hollered impatiently, "Hush yo' gabblin', li'l ninny, so we can bless dis food an' eat!"

There had been many meals at that table before, but none quite so satisfying, especially for Sassie. She could not get over how happy Rosette acted. She had never seen her in such good spirits, never heard her talk or laugh so much as she did that day. She chattered away, her mood was warm and soft, soft as butter melting on warm biscuits. Near the end of the meal, when she went to the sideboard for something sweet, taking one look at Sassie's apple cobbler, she declared, "Dis here be my fav'rit."

After Rosette scooped out a generous helping of the cobbler, Sassie watched as she lifted the blue pottery dish up and gazed at it admiringly, almost like she wished she had one like it. When she became conscious of Sassie staring at her, Rosette set the dish down jerkily, as if she had held it longer than she had intended.

Please, God, show me...

In the next instant, Sassie surprised herself more than anyone else. "Miz Quinn, I want you to have dat." The words just came out.

Rosette turned and looked at her. "What you say?"

Obie stared at Sassie wonderingly, remembering how happy she was the day old Georgianne gave her the dish. Surprise gave way to awkwardness as conversation tapered off into silence, and all the

faces around the table looked from her to Rosette expectantly, waiting to see Rosette's response.

Sassie couldn't believe what she was doing. Without consciously having planned to do so, she was giving away the dish Miz Georgianne had made just for her. It was confusing to her, how the words just seemingly rose up and came out. *Rose up in her heart...*

"Why...I couldn't...it's...too pretty..." For a moment, Rosette appeared to struggle with her feelings.

Obie looked from his mama back to Sassie.

Sassie did cherish the dish; she'd told Miz Georgianne she'd cherish it forever. And yet, she knew, she somehow just knew, this was the right thing to do, and that Miz Georgianne would somehow understand.

"I mean for you to have it," she reiterated. "It's my gift to you for—"

For what? Her mind drew a blank.

At the sideboard, Rosette's eyes went again to the dish. She held it up, inspecting it. Catching a look from Ezra, she decided there was no way to refuse graciously with everyone watching. Anyway, for some reason, she just didn't feel inspired to quarrel today. So, without further pause for debate, she yielded, ungrudgingly.

"Dis mighty kind o' you, Sassie, an' I'z much obliged."

As she stared down at her plate, Sassie felt a surge of delight pass through her soul. *Thank you, God.* In her eyes, it was a victory, small, but a victory nonetheless, and one that left a door ajar to hope. As though to reaffirm his mother's triumph, the baby inside her womb stirred, making her smile. She picked up her fork and took a bite, the taste of apple cobbler and hope mingling into one.

Knowing his mama and knowing this probably wouldn't last, Obie savored the moment for what it was. Under the table, he took Sassie's hand and squeezed it, thankful for answered prayers.

❧

Hiram bent over and spit on the ground forcefully. He shut his eyes and clenched his teeth, willing himself to stand still and endure the throbbing pain in his left hand as he pumped his fingers in and out several times.

It was after noon on Friday, the day after Thanksgiving. He and Wesley had been splitting wood for barely two hours, and he was already starting to get tired and aggravated when it happened: the hickory log had dried out; some of the wood had just about got too hard to bust. When he went to drive the wedge into a section of it, the wedge slipped, whereupon the full blow of the maul came down across the top of his hand.

Seeing what happened, Wesley swung his ax down hard, sinking the blade deep into the piece he'd been working on—half-heartedly— for the better part of an hour.

Going over to see, he hollered, "Dang, man! You all right?" knowing it had to hurt like the devil. Just the thought of it made him flinch. He didn't see how in the world Hiram could just stand there and act so calm and said as much. "That was me an' my hand, you best believe I'd be cussin' a blue streak."

Hiram opened his eyes and flicked Wesley a glance. To make his point, he spit on the ground again and indicated the spot. "You can bet your bottom dollar won't nothing ever grow there again," he replied gruffly.

Though not having been cast in jocularity—far from it—Wesley couldn't help but grin at the prophetic anecdote. Actually, it was the first time he'd felt like smiling since finding out that Sarah Beth had so thoughtlessly and insensibly run off to Memphis with Abigail's brother. The news of their daughter's elopement—rather, escapade— had hit him and Laura hard, catastrophic beyond anything they had thought might ever befall them. Shocked, angered, worried, disap- pointed—they were completely crushed, their Thanksgiving ruined.

Now, though, after consuming the better of their emotions for the past two days, it finally seemed the worst of the storm had blown itself out, as even the fiercest of storms eventually do. Once the initial tempest had passed over and the reality of the situation started sinking in, they did the only, and most difficult, thing they could: They reassembled their wits and reluctantly bowed to that which was, realizing their only consolation, if any was to be had, lay most reliably in the immemorial "time heals." They could only hope for the best. Wesley, in fact, had not made mention of the ordeal to Hiram all day, and Hiram hadn't asked.

Presently, just as Wesley went over to examine Hiram's hand, a pair of shadows glided across the ground, accompanied by a loud flapping of wings. The men looked up. They could smell the foul odor of carrion as the buzzards flew over just above their heads, so low it seemed they could have reached up and grabbed them. They watched as the giant birds descended into the tree line and disappeared.

"Must be somethin' dead," Wesley said, gesturing in that direction.

By unspoken agreement, he and Hiram advanced into the woods to investigate. The leaves underfoot were crisp as they walked through a stand of hardwood saplings along the creek bank. Within minutes, they came up on the buzzards. They were picking away at the decomposing remains of a small animal. Feasting feverishly, they paid no heed to the men.

"What you reckon happened to him?" Wesley asked quizzically as Hiram stared at what was left of the puppy.

Hiram shook his head and answered despairingly, "He must've followed the big dogs off an' got lost. Probably killed by a bobcat." It was becoming clearer by the minute he would be spared nothing this day.

Wesley paused to contemplate the theory in silence.

When they heard the report of a gun echo across the hollow, Hiram recognized it as Emily's and said, "With any luck, there's our supper bell. After all that rich food yesterday, a big mess of fried squirrel or a rabbit stew would suit me just fine."

Glancing back one time at the buzzards, down at his bruised hand, and back to Wesley's somber face, calculating in his mind their time and trouble against what little progress they'd made on splitting the hickory, Hiram resolved to call it quits. Brushing the wood chips from his beard, he said, "Brother, I 'bout had all the fun I can stand for one day. I'm fixin' to go gather up my toys an' head t'ward the house."

Wesley required little persuasion. After the chaos of the past few days, the prospect of propping his feet up on the hearth and relaxing for a while sounded like a dandy idea. He led the way as they retraced the path back to where they'd left their tools, with Hiram walking a few steps behind, thinking how he dreaded telling Samuel about Poly.

CHAPTER 20

"...stand still, and consider the wondrous works of God."
Job 37: 14

Christmas was rapidly approaching, just four days away, bringing with it all the excitement and traditions held dear. Cedar, holly, and ivy were brought in to decorate the parlor, and the smell of baking filled the house as the women seemed to spend all day in the kitchen.

"Come down to the woodshop after while. There's somethin' I want you to take a look at, somethin' Daniel's been workin' on." Hiram had said this to Addie as he was leaving the house that morning.

It was around ten o'clock, right after she slid a cake into the oven, when Addie went to Samuel's room and found he'd fallen asleep playing with his wooden blocks. Certain that he would be fine for a few minutes, she covered her napping child with a quilt, touching her lips lightly to his forehead before tiptoeing from the room.

In the hallway, she grabbed a woolen shawl from a peg and whipped it around her shoulders. Slipping quietly out of the house into the raw December day, she pulled the garment close to her body and hurried along the path in the direction of the woodshop, curious to see what it was that Daniel was making. The weather had turned off freezing cold. There had been a heavy frost the night before, and it had not yet melted away; the meadow shimmered like diamonds in the bright sunlight. Rows of icicles hung from every eave.

When Addie entered the woodshop, it was cozy inside, warmed by a pot-bellied stove. She greeted the men and casually went over to where Daniel was meticulously polishing a piece of furniture. When her eyes fell upon it and registered its meaning, for a moment she stared, taking in every detail, hardly knowing what to say or quite sure what to think. Constructed of warm, mellowed pine, the demeanor of the piece was plain and simple yet beautifully crafted. There was no doubt Daniel had taken great care, had put his heart and soul into making it.

Daniel glanced up at her, as if testing her reaction.

Addie felt a twinge of some unnamed emotion as she reached out and pushed it lightly with her fingers, setting the baby cradle into a gentle, rocking motion. "Oh, Daniel, it's—it's beautiful, truly it is."

Having made the natural assumption, she supposed congratulations were in order, but she couldn't help feeling somewhat dejected, a little crestfallen over this unexpected surprise. She felt disappointed, really. Hoping he didn't notice the hollow enthusiasm in her voice, she managed a weak smile and said, "Amelia hasn't breathed a word of it; when is she expecting?"

Daniel hesitated a moment. Weighing her words, he realized his mother had jumped to the wrong conclusion. "Amelia's not expectin'," he corrected her, but vaguely. "The cradle's for somebody else."

Avoiding her eyes, he turned and went back to work on it.

So, Daniel knew their secret!

Hiram was standing near, leaned up against a post with his arms folded across his chest. Addie flashed a quick, questioning look at him. In an exchange of eye signals, hers said, *I thought we agreed not*

to say anything just yet. But he shook his head, his expression indicating he hadn't told a soul.

A bewildered look came over Addie's face as her thoughts tumbled. *Then, how did he...?* She didn't understand. Her brow knitted in confusion, she looked back at Hiram, but he just shrugged his shoulders. He, too, was in the dark; the cradle was a total mystery.

There was a silence; Daniel could feel their eyes on him.

Addie opened her mouth to ask then closed it, waiting for Daniel to provide an explanation, wishing she could somehow read her son's mind.

Finally, Daniel cleared his throat and informed them, a little reluctantly, a little bashfully, "The cradle's for Sassie. My sister. I figure it'll come in handy here 'fore too long."

Addie put a hand to her heart. She prayed she hadn't misunderstood what he just said. For a moment, she was too taken by surprise and too overjoyed to speak. In truth, there were no words for the miracle taking form right before her eyes. *A Christmas miracle...*

There could be no other explanation. She had every confidence that God had wittingly inspired Daniel, *moved* him, to use his talent—and that He had in mind to use a humble baby cradle to work a miracle in Daniel's life, and in Sassie's.

The wonder of it filled Addie's eyes with happy tears. When at last she found her voice, she said, "Oh, Daniel! This will mean the world to Sassie!" *Thank you, Lord. This means the world to me!* She could have said so much more, but knowing her son and what a great stride this was for him, she wisely resisted. It was, after all, a start.

When she looked over at Hiram, he was standing there smiling at her. He too knew this had to be God's doing.

Addie's heart was overflowing. All of a sudden, she felt the need to get off by herself and have a good cry. Turning to go, she said, "Well, I best be getting back in case Samuel wakes up...I left a cake in the oven. If y'all find time, you're welcome to come up to the house and sample a piece."

When she stepped out into the cold air, invigorated by the sheer exultation of God's infinite power and goodness, she clapped her hands together and laughed out loud. Filled with a renewed spirit of hope, she hurried up the path toward home, rejoicing.

Rosette went to the window and looked out. Winter's shadows had fallen and the moon was just rising, but it was bright enough that she could plainly make out Ezra's silhouette across the way. He was loading sweet potatoes onto the wagon to take to market the following morning.

Supper was ready, but first she had something to say to him that she didn't want Etta hearing. Leaving the comfort of the kitchen, she stepped out the back door and pulled it to behind her. It was freezing outside. When the chill air hit her face, the cold seemed to permeate her bones, causing her to shiver. She started out across the yard, quickly making her way toward the barn.

His eyes used to the dark, Ezra saw Rosette walking in his direction, and paused from his work.

Looking out across the fields that her husband seasonally plowed and planted, tended and harvested, Rosette took a deep breath, unsure of how to start. The cold air filled her head; her words came out in puffs of smoke.

"All dis time, dem chi'ren be thankin' you'z actin' crazy, da way you go out dere ever night, walkin' an' talkin' to yo' crops. But, I jus' want you to know, Ezra Quinn, I knows you better dan dem chi'ren do, an' I knows you ain't bin talkin' to no crops…" Her voice broke with emotion. "'Cauze I know when you out dere, you be talkin' to da Lawd…mostly 'bout me." She knew Ezra had seen how far she'd strayed from God; he knew her soul was burdened and why. She knew he'd been praying for a long time for her to come back in from the wilderness.

Ezra saw tears sliding slowly down his wife's face, glistening in the moonlight; he saw something very vulnerable in her eyes, a side of her rarely seen by others. He held still as the night and listened, waiting for her to go on.

"Lately, I bin thankin' a lot about my life an' about my fam'ly. Da Lawd's convicted me, an' I bin on my knees talkin' to Him. Somewhere along da way, I los' sight o' what's impo'tant. I'z axed Him to forgive me an' give me a second chance to do what's right an' to help me, help *all* o' *us*, git beyond all dis trouble." She was tired of grappling with conflict; she wanted them all to be at peace, despite their differences. She wanted them all to be together, to be a *family*.

What Obie had said back during the summer was right. "*She caint help who her daddy wuz or what her daddy did…*" In fact, Rosette realized, *She couldn't help a lot o' thangs*. How could she not have seen this before? What a narrow-minded fool she'd been!

Ezra reached out and put an arm around her. She could feel the warmth of his hand on her shoulder, could feel the warmth of his heart, his quiet strength. She wiped her eyes and looked down at her chapped hands, her fingers stained from shelling out pecans. Even though it was too dark for him to see, she held them out to him and whispered hoarsely, "I made her a pecan pie…"

Ezra said nothing but took her and held her as she cried, "I'z so sorry, Ezra, forgive me fo' all da trouble I'z cauzed." *Please Lawd, tomorrow help me make it all right…*

"Dere, dere," Ezra hugged his wife against the cold and comforted her, and in his heart, he celebrated, as he considered the wondrous works of the Lord.

Overnight the clouds welled up thick and gray.

The weather being so inclement, that morning Wesley drove the children to the schoolhouse on his way in to Oakdale. School would be dismissing early that day, immediately following the Christmas

party, and would not resume again until after the New Year. It was winter, so there was no hurrying to get home, nothing to plant or harvest, so he planned to go and walk about the town until it came time to pick them up again.

When Wesley had stopped by their house for Emily, the instant Samuel saw his sister climbing into the bed of the buckboard with their cousins, he pitched a fit to go too. Since Wesley couldn't deny his young nephew, Addie had bundled him up in a heavy coat and mittens and off they all went, the children snug under a layer of quilts.

Now as he sat on the seat beside his uncle, Samuel leaned forward, round-eyed, as they pulled to a halt on Main Street. All the storefronts were decorated festively; the town was bustling with activity. The youngster was overcome with the almost unbearable excitement of the season, enchanted by everything he saw.

"Come on, Uncle Wesley!" He pulled at Wesley's hand, dragging him along the boardwalk, raring to explore. His eyes were dancing, his cheeks flushed.

Wesley stopped short when an old man suddenly stepped in and blocked his path. Wearing a black hat set back off his forehead, the man had a snowy mass of white curls that hung down to his shoulders. His posture was stooped, his boots shined to a fault.

"'Scuze me, son," he struck up, "I'z a-wonderin' if you might give me directions...tell me the best way to get to Collinsville from here. I ain't traveled that part of the country in I-couldn't-tell-you-when." His clear, steely-gray eyes fell on Samuel. He patted him on the head and said, "That's a fine little feller you got there."

Wesley nodded. "He's a sport. He's Addie's...my sister's boy."

Samuel looked up at the man funny. Staring at his long, white hair, he asked, "Mister, are you Santa Claus?"

The man chuckled. "No, sprout, 'fraid not, but I've run up on him a few times, an' he's a fine feller, too, just like you."

Wesley pointed and answered, "When you leave town, take Longview Road 'til it runs out. Turn south on the Monroe Road, an' it'll take you right into Collinsville."

"Much obliged," the man said. "I've got a cousin lives over that way I ain't seen in a spell. Thought I'd ease over there an' see if I can't scare him up, maybe spread a little holiday cheer."

Anxious to go, Samuel tugged at Wesley's sleeve impatiently.

"You don't say," Wesley replied. He proceeded to introduce himself to the man, giving him a hearty handshake. "Name's Wesley Warren. I grew up around Collinsville. You might've known my folks...Samuel an' Rachel Warren."

At that, a flicker of interest crossed the old man's features. "Why, do tell." Squinting, he made a quick study of Wesley's face, noting the resemblance. "I reckon that'd make you Dalton's boy then." His mouth twitched. "Begot by a true son of the Confederacy!"

Samuel couldn't be still, twisting and squirming, like he had the mad-itch.

Wesley smiled at the oldtimer. Thinking he might be a bit hard of hearing, he leaned in closer and told him again, louder, "No. My pa's name was Samuel, Samuel Warren."

Unable to contain his excitement a moment longer, Samuel took off in a scuttle, pushing and elbowing his way toward the candy shop, almost running right into a tall black lady.

"Samuel!" Wesley might as well been calling to the wind. His eyes followed the boy to be sure he didn't lose sight of him. Apologetically, he told the old man, "That young'un's wild as a buck, ain't got nothin' but a sack full of jawbreakers on his mind." Hurrying to catch up with him, he called back and reiterated, "Just follow my directions...That'll take you directly to Collinsville!... Have a Merry Christmas!"

A few seconds later, he thought about it, but it was too late. He realized he hadn't even got the man's name. Claire no doubt might have known him or, at least, might have remembered his kin.

Mentally scratching his head, the old man, Newt Knight, stared after Wesley until he and Samuel disappeared into the store. His lips moved spasmodically, silently. A Negro woman brushed right past him, but he didn't bother about stepping aside for her. Except for the twitching of his mouth, for a time he stood completely still, deep in thought, entertaining a memory from the back of his mind, or rather, one of the many ghosts lurking there.

Dalton Davis, he thought. A fellow deserter who'd served him well. A loyal friend who'd once answered to the echo of the black horn. *Boy-hidey! Me an' Dalton seen us some wild times back durin' the War!* Now, like all the others, he too was long deceased. *Shame that crazy son-of-a-gun had to go an' git hisself noosed by the Army…* Best to his recollection, not long after Dalton was hanged, Newt heard his widow-woman had married a man by the name of Warren.

Convinced of his suspicions, he exclaimed to himself, "Sure as the Devil knows my name, that man a-goin' yonder b'longed to ol' Dalton!" *Dalton and Rachel…* "An' next time I see Dalton's sister, I'll be shore to tell her I run up on some o' her kin!"

When Ezra and Rosette had arrived in town, stopping first in front of the Post Office, Rosette decided to set off on foot from there. Ezra held the pecan pie for her while she'd climbed down from the seat of the wagon.

She'd lain awake all night worrying about what she was going to say when she got to her house, and as quick as her feet touched the ground, she was attacked by a fresh onslaught of nerves. Her confidence waned as a wave of uncertainty swept through her. Taking a deep breath in an effort to calm herself, she swallowed at the lump in her throat and asked, "What if I'z waited too long, Ezra? What if it too late an' she turns me away?" …*like I did her?*

Sensing her anxiety, Ezra smiled and reassured gently, "Ain't never too late to do what's right." Handing the pie back to her, he softly urged, "Go on now." He knew what she was doing took courage, for there was no telling how this might turn out.

Willing herself to move forward, Rosette walked briskly along the boardwalk. Her thoughts so dense with purpose, she hardly noticed the little boy who almost ran headlong into her, nor did she pay particular attention when her skirts came within mere inches of brushing against the person of Newt Knight. She swished past him without either one of them taking heed of the other, not a flicker of recognition from either.

Up a ways, she turned onto Sparrow Street.

On the next block, she followed an alleyway then crossed over to the next street into the quarter. She thought about how this would change her family, *if she will forgive me...* Realizing all this time she'd yearned for this very thing, she hastened on, trying in vain to make up for lost time. *Senseless, wasted time....*

As she pressed on, tears of regret blurred her vision. So intent she was, making her way toward her destination, she almost tripped over a scampering squirrel that stopped practically under her feet, cocking his head at her inquisitively. Inwardly, she prayed, *Please God, don't let it be too late...*

Minutes later, she was there. Without pause, she went through the rusty wrought-iron gate.

Mounting the single stone step onto the porch, Rosette rapped firmly on the door. Standing stiff as a statue, she waited, battling against her nerves. A fluffy, black-and-orange cat sauntered over regally and started rubbing its head against her skirt. Glancing down at the cat, it reminded her of one she'd played with on the plantation where she'd grown up. *Knight Plantation.*

Though she'd been only three years old at the time and only another pitiful, hungry mouth for him to feed, Old John Knight had kindly bought her off the auction block in the spring of 1856 to save

her from being sold away from her mother and baby sister—*a sister Rosette bore no resemblance to, because she had a black father.* One of her earliest memories was of sitting on a three-legged stool in a corner of Master John's dining room, pulling a cord. The cord was attached to the punka, which hung from a ceiling beam and stirred the air to shoo flies from lighting on the food.

Rosette's mind unwillingly veered off course and set off on a terrible journey, down a road she'd went down time and time again: the road toward her childhood home, Knight Plantation. *Where life had been a living hell...* How she had despised the happenings that went on there. *The men...the liquor...the unspeakable acts of depravity...* She shuddered at the shame and disgrace of it all.

After what seemed like an eternity, the door opened, rescuing her from her thoughts.

Seeing her for the first time after all those years, Rosette was overtaken with emotion. Her heart went out to her sister, Georgianne Knight. In all those years, she had never forgotten her, had longed to see her and talk to her, spend time with her.

With a look of bewilderment, Georgianne stared at her, as if to say, *What is yo' biz'ness here?*

Her voice atremble, Rosette managed to say, "Hello, Georgianne...I know it bin a long time...but I...I wuz hopin' I might talk to you."

A long moment passed as Georgianne stared at her warily. Eyeing the pie Rosette clutched tightly in her hands, her curiosity finally got the best of her. She asked, "What kind o' pie dat be?"

Upon hearing her speak, Rosette gasped. She looked at her strangely and exclaimed, "Why...folks say you'z mute...dat you caint talk no mo'."

Georgianne shrugged. "Some folk say dey's a Sandy Claus!" She scoffed, "What dem ol' fools don't know iz...I *can* talk jus' fine... jus' ain't had nothin' to say da las' twenty years, not since da day my sista say she don't ever want to see or talk to me a'gin den run off like her feets on fire!"

Like an icy gale, the memory of that day blew back to Rosette with a shiver of remorse. *But God spoke to her…told her to lay apart all filthiness…He saved her…delivered her from the powers of darkness…*When she fled that wicked place, she couldn't understand why Georgianne wouldn't leave with her. She too might have been able to hire out as a laundress or house servant.

Rosette cried, "Yo' sister wuz a wretched fool…"

…I once was blind but now I see…

"But dis ol' fool's come sayin' she's sorry…an' axin' you to forgive her…even though she don't deserve yo' forgiveness."

Georgianne listened in disbelief. She heard the words but was wrought with conflicting emotions. She'd long since resigned to live out the rest of her days without ever seeing or talking to Rosette again. Now here she'd come, wanting to make amends, asking her to forgive and forget.

But it was too late.

She growled, "Ain't no use in grov'lin'…me an' you ain't got nothin' to talk about."

The hardness of life had cast a black shadow upon her; bitter sentiment had driven her heart into an obscure place of hiding. "You ain't no kin o' mine…I ain't got no kin." Twenty years in exile had made them strangers. And yet, her soul felt empty as she said, "I don't know you," and stepped back to shut the door.

The words cut sickeningly deep. Rosette felt a rush of sadness and panic sweep through her as the wind went out of her. She had expected this, or at least feared it. Such was the cost of stubborn pride, she supposed. Though standing pale and deflated, she would not yet, she decided, give up so easily after coming this far.

Surely there was something she could say, some little something left to salvage. "Wait…" She quickly uncovered the pie. "It's pecan…'cauze I remember it's yo' fav'rit…An' dis dish…soon as I

213

seen it, I knew it wuz one you made. My daughter-in-law give it to me ..." Her words were racing, running together in desperation, like her thoughts. She was rambling on, sounding like an idiot, but she didn't care.

Tears staining her cheeks, she looked at Georgianne full in the face. "My boy Obie ...he married to a girl dat make me thank o' you when you wuz her age ...I'd like you to come an' go wif me ...Dey stays jus' over on da next street an'—"

She stopped talking long enough to take a breath and try to regain control of herself. But she couldn't stop crying. She was distraught over how cruelly she'd spoken to her own sister all those years ago. "I wuz wrong, Georgianne ...I see now ...What happened way back den wasn't yo' fault. You jus' don't know how ...how sorry I am ...how bad I'z missed you." Though she wanted to, Rosette couldn't find the words to say anything more. As a last hope, she whispered, sobbing, "Please ...come go wif me."

Silently looking at her, Georgianne realized that Rosette had changed in the years since she'd last seen her. For one thing, she'd grown old. It was hard to believe this woman had once been the kinky-haired little girl whose hair she used to twist up with twine. *Back when we all lived with Newt.*

In that moment, something gave way within her; she felt an easement somewhere deep inside. Without an understanding of how or why, taking a step back, she opened the door wide. "I 'spect I look a sight ...You gone come in or not? I be needin' a minute to shine up if I'z gwine to meet my kin."

God being omnipotent, His power and knowledge of all things infinite—*'thou knowest my downsitting and mine uprising'*—that December day witnessed a Christmas miracle as twenty years became as yesterday, and were carried away as with a flood.

The next morning, Hiram awoke well before dawn. While Addie and the children were yet sleeping, he eased out of bed and went to the window, cracking open the curtain slightly to see if he was right. He remembered doing so as a boy growing up in Virginia, particularly when the clouds were somber and heavy, as they'd been the evening before. Quietly leaving the bedroom, he went down the hall and stepped out the door onto the front porch.

The moon was full and luminous, making it bright enough for him to see clearly in all directions. As he stood looking, he could think of nothing except how serene and starkly beautiful everything looked in the moonlight. It was an awe-inspiring sight. As he inhaled and exhaled deeply, his breath fogged on the frosty air.

During the night, the landscape had been transformed; a foot of snow had fallen, blanketing everything in white. Fence rails and trees were flocked, limbs draped gracefully under the weight. There was no sign of the road that ran in front of the house. The snow was pure, unmarked and unmarred by the tracks of mankind. It seemed like another world. No living thing stirred. A kind of perfect silence hung in the air, a stillness so exquisite therein a presence could be felt. Hiram knew it was the presence of the Lord.

Finding himself overcome with a deep sense of reverence, he covered his face with his hands. Thumbing his eyes, he whispered an invocation. "My God, my Father, thou art here, thou art here …"

He turned and went inside the house to wake Addie. He knew she had never seen snow, and he wanted her to see it thus, in the moonlight, peaceful and absolute, with the tranquility and holiness of the Lord God still upon it.

It was a benediction, a miracle; oh, it was!

CHAPTER 21

"The heart is deceitful above all things, and desperately wicked." Jeremiah 17: 9

All along the roads in Virginia, the embankments had erupted with ice spews. Leaving the Post Office, Wilkes pulled up the collar of his overcoat. His breath smoked in the frigid air. The ground was frozen solid and crunched under his boots. To shield himself from the wind, he stepped into the narrow alley between two buildings, where he tore open the letter from Hiram and began reading:

Dear Brother,

I bid you a hearty Christmas greeting and trust things are well with you back home. If the weather we've had so far this month is indicative of the weeks to come, this may prove to be the coldest winter on record for the state of Mississippi…

Wilkes's eyes scanned on down the page.

…fierce storm passed through less than a week after your leaving…

The words leapt up at him:

. . . Asher's wife, Anna, was discovered drowned in the creek. Whether accidental or suicide, I suppose her tragic death will forever be marked by unanswered questions . . .

Reading this, Wilkes's chest pounded harder. *Accident. Suicide.* He couldn't believe it. Thinking back, he remembered the night he met Anna Bradley. She'd had such a lovely face. When their eyes met, there just was something about her . . .

He leaned back against the side of the building while the news sank in.

In his mind, Wilkes traveled back to the morning he'd left Golden Meadow six months ago. He couldn't explain it now any more than he could explain it then, but for some reason, instead of heading north, he'd ridden off in the opposite direction and wound up in a quaint little place called Magnolia.

Located in Pike County, Magnolia was renowned as being sophisticated and unconventional, and so it proved to be. A resort-town for the wealthy, it boasted an opera house, a skating rink, and several stylish hotels. Wilkes had registered in one of the hotels under a false identity, fancying himself a rich tobacco planter there on business. Feeling important, after settling into his room, he went out and walked about the streets; he supped on beefsteak, smoked an excellent cigar, and drank a bottle of wine. He was enjoying himself immensely.

His merriment did not conclude until later that night when, in a tavern, he lost a fair share of money in a poker game to a snobbish financier from New Orleans, who had traveled to Magnolia by train with his mistress to attend a stage performance. The money Wilkes lost was money he'd counted on to see him back to Virginia.

After a fitful night of drawing counters on his ill-starred predicament, he had eventually come up with what seemed, at least at the time, to be a logical and sure-fire way to recoup his losses.

A bad storm passed through on that Wednesday. He left Magnolia and backtracked; under the cover of night, he stole a horse, a roan that he'd tried to buy off a man by the name of Rutland the week before. *Ornery ol' cuss should-a took me up on my offer while he had the chance,* he thought.

Turned out the beast was mean-spirited and unruly. Still, with some artistic salesmanship, Wilkes managed to dupe a fool into buying him for a pretty penny a couple of days later in the rivertown of Covington. Once again, he was solvent, with more than enough money in his pocket to get him back to Virginia, provided he stayed away from the gaming tables.

He then laid low for a few days in a cheap boardinghouse on the outskirts of town.

When Saturday morning came, Wilkes woke bleary-eyed and ravenously hungry. He'd passed out drunk the night before, slept for sixteen hours. He paid a dollar for a hot bath. In a restaurant down the street from the boardinghouse, he devoured a meal of tender pot roast over creamed potatoes, hot, buttered rolls, and peach cobbler. When he'd finished eating, he went back to his room and packed his belongings. The time had come for him to set off on his journey.

"Surely you ain't leavin' us so soon?" The proprietor, Merna Gallagher, was a stocky, middle-aged woman whose eyes reminded Wilkes of a ferret's. "Which way you headed, honey?"

"West, over into Texas, I reckon. Lookin' to work out the rest of the year drivin' cattle," he lied.

She'd smiled and winked at him coyly. "Well, cowboy, should you ever pass back through this neck of the woods again, stop in, an' I'll let you buy me another drink."

He had instead headed east, driven by some unexplained force, back toward Golden Meadow.

Presently, as Wilkes retraced the course of events in his mind, he could still recall the continuous humming sound made by the throng of thirsty mosquitoes that swarmed around his ears that night. He'd tied his horse to a low limb and made his way through the shadows. The air seemed so alive, so charged with energy. But then, it always did at times like that...

With predatory stealth, he'd eased close, stopped not thirty feet away from her. He'd known she'd be there, just like they'd planned. *So pathetically predictable.* Of course, he'd never intended to go back for her. The plan to elope, all the talk of a life together—all pretense and lies—nothing more than a pack of empty promises made simply to shut her up. As he'd watched her quietly, he was unable to name a reason for his return. This had not been part of his plan. He had figured on being miles away from there by then.

Wilkes pictured her now in his mind, the way she looked that night, sitting on the creek bank in the moonlight, idly sifting sand through her fingers. She was barefoot, her shoes beside her on a patch of moss. She was staring out across the water dreamily, waiting —stupidly—for her knight in shining armor to come whisk her away to fairyland.

Oh, Anna. Poor, stupid Anna.

When Anna turned her head and saw him walking toward her, she scrambled to her feet and brushed the sand off her skirt. Her eyes were sparkling. Joyful tears spilled forth as Wilkes pulled her into his powerful arms, pressing his body against her. In the days since his assumed departure, she had missed him terribly.

"I'm so happy to see you again!" she cried breathlessly. "I thought I would surely die waitin' for this night to arrive!" For a minute, she jabbered on about how they'd lost their house—everything—in the storm. No one had ever suspected that her bleakness and despair had nothing to do with any of that.

"But now that you're here and we're together again, I have every-thing I need; no, *we* have everything *we* need, you and I." She looked into his eyes. "And there's something else, Wilkes. I'm …I'm goin' to have a baby, darling, *your* baby." Anna had known she was pregnant before there were any definite signs of it. She had sensed it, and for the past few days had been able to think of little else. Motherhood was going to be different for her this time, she vowed.

Wilkes made no answer to her.

Her words echoed weirdly across the creek as he stared straight ahead into the woods, as if in a trance, digesting what she'd said, trying to settle on the choice fate was laying out before him. He was beginning to understand why he'd felt compelled, *drawn,* to come back there. Had she actually deceived herself into believing they could just ride off into the sunset and get married? That the three of them would just live happily ever after? Inwardly, he scoffed at her simplemindedness. He had no desire for a wife, and obviously she'd forgotten she already had a husband. Her incessant stupidity stained any pleasing memories he may have had of her or their affair. His scorn for her filled him with an icy rage.

Feeling his embrace stiffen, Anna drew back slightly and looked up at him. Her eyes searched his face.

Seeing his strange expression, she asked, "What's the matter?"

Her joyful demeanor gave way to confusion as he tightened his grasp and lifted her feet off the ground. She struggled to yank herself free, but was trapped in his vise-like grip. She barely managed to touch her toes to the ground, much less get solid footing. Panic seized her as Wilkes dragged her with him into the creek.

Anna fought, for she knew the moment she stopped fighting, she was going to die. As if caught up in the throes of a dreadful nightmare, she frantically thrashed her arms and kicked her legs. Her wet skirt, however, heavily weighed her efforts and hampered her movement, essentially tired her out. With every measure of strength, she strove to escape him, but to no avail.

Her struggling excited Wilkes. She looked at him pleadingly, her eyes wide with horror. Seeing the look of fear on her lovely face, seeing its loveliness turned ugly with that fear, he smiled. The look in his eyes was cold and contemptuous as he forced her head under the water. He was heartless, cruel, demonic.

Anna had always had a terrible fear of creeks and rivers, and for that reason never learned to swim. The cold, dark water that closed over her head smelled like death to her. It seeped in and filled her head, flooded her mind with unspeakable terror. The moonlight above the surface became a blinding light in her eyes as Wilkes held her under. In a futile attempt, she pushed her hands against his chest. Her lungs were bursting. She was drowning. Her nails dug into his arm as she groped, trying desperately to hold on to something.

Her strength ebbed until finally she had no strength left. No hope left. No dreams left. Energy and resolve depleted, it didn't take long for the creek to draw what was left of her life away...her baby's life was drawn away...

The last thing she saw was the moonlight coming down to her, bringing with it a wonderful feeling of lightness, freedom. Her wings poised for flight, Anna's life on the earth ended...*like a bird from prison's bars has flown*...

When it was finished, to avoid her staring, sightless gaze, Wilkes rolled her over, facedown, and surrendered Anna's limp, lifeless body to the current.

As she drifted away, he bent over and rested his hands on his knees to calm the raggedness of his breath. He was astonished at what he'd done. For several minutes, his mind was disordered. It felt like he'd taken over someone else's life or like someone else had taken over his life. He was obviously not in control of his own actions. He hadn't come here to kill Anna, at least not consciously. Had he?

The moonlight was fluttery on the water's surface. Wilkes noticed an eerie hush. Glancing up, the still woods seemed to loom around him, accusingly. He imagined the trees were standing in pious judgment of him. An old proverb flashed through his mind: *Man never knows what fate will proffer.*

Suddenly, he remembered he'd read just last year how a crazed man up in Richmond had slain his whole family: his mother-in-law, his wife, and their five children. The newspaper had described the man as going berserk. *Well, there it is,* he thought. He looked up at the trees and affirmed in his defense, "Well, gentlemen of the jury, I reckon it'd be apt to say I have just went berserk." He laughed aloud at his own insanity. "Now what say ye?"

He snapped his head to one side.

What was that? A sound. In the woods. For a moment, he listened intently. But all he heard was the drumming of his heart and the gentle rush of water.

What if...?

No. *Probably just a possum rustlin' around in the leaves,* he told himself.

Still, it unnerved him.

Careful not to leave any tracks in the sand, Wilkes waded the shallows upstream a ways, not too far. From there, he walked the creekbank, traveling at a fair pace, for how long he couldn't be sure. When he got near to where he thought he'd left his horse, he came up instead on an unwelcome sight, a broad stretch of bottomland. A swamp. Apparently, somewhere along the way he had misjudged direction and distance and got all turned around. Palmettos were everywhere; a dense undergrowth of vines crept across the ground and climbed over stumps and logs. With its moss-hung cypresses and droning insects, the place was like a spooky, infested jungle. Yet, he dared not turn back...*there was no turning back now*...nothing to do but go on through it. As he bogged through the stagnant slough, there was an underlying foulness to the slimy, sour mud that sucked at his boots; he tried to shut his mind to what kind of creatures might slither and crawl in such a vile place.

A half hour later, Wilkes emerged from the swamp a cold-blooded killer. Though it was a while before he could breathe easily again, he got on his horse and simply rode off, passed from the place without leaving a trace. Talk about crime without consequence. No one would ever know, not another living soul. Anna hadn't told anyone anything of their indiscretion, of course, and for all anyone knew, he had departed from there over a week ago.

He headed north and rode hard the rest of the night and all the next day to put some distance between himself and Golden Meadow.

Thinking about it later, he was continually astonished. Until he'd killed Anna, he'd never before tried his hand at killing, and what he discovered was that it seemed to have come relatively easy to him. Sort of like growing tobacco. Or like Hiram's ability to make furniture.

He had killed Anna and her—*his*—unborn child and felt oddly indifferent. Blameless, actually. He was bound by no ropes of guilt, not tethered by any sense of remorse, no melancholy. Nor did he perceive Anna as a victim. Lo! An impossible situation had presented itself and met with an unfortunate end. Thinking of the alternative ramifications, he'd really had no choice but to get rid of her. He merely did what had to be done, at no great loss to society.

A stupid whore, a bastard sired out of lust. Damn 'em both! he swore.

Though the invigoration of it all had dulled over time, Wilkes would never forget the look on her face right before he drowned her. *Stark terror.* Of course it had taken her a minute to grasp exactly what was happening, but the very moment her mind had awakened to his treacherous intent, he had known. In that briefest millisecond of time, he'd felt her go rigid from shock, but then an instant later, she'd come alive, fighting. Except then, it was too late.

Still, he had to admire her spirit to survive; she'd fought like a wildcat to the very end. *So alive one minute, then gone the next.* He thought it remarkable how even in death her face had looked peaceful, nearly as lovely as ever.

Wilkes finished reading the last words of the letter:

. . . I am proud to inform you Addie is with child…you will be uncle again next summer…May God continue to bless you …

Your brother,

Hiram.

For a minute, Wilkes stood with the letter in his hand; it was almost too much for him to take in. *Accident or suicide!* He felt a rush of adrenaline. It was in that moment he knew with absolute certainty that no one had suspected a thing! He had gotten away with murder! What a momentous day! In truth, it was a miracle.

Suddenly, an amused smile touched his lips, and his eyes glittered brightly with satisfaction. He had never felt so alive! He folded the letter and stuffed it into his pocket. Tipping his hat in mock salute, he jeered aloud, "An' a hearty Christmas greetin' to you an' yours, my brother. An' may God continue to bless you also."

Hearing his stomach growl, all of a sudden Wilkes realized he was starving for something to eat. He set out for the restaurant at the end of the street with a voracious craving for pot roast with creamed potatoes and juicy peach cobbler, immensely gratified that the unsavory ordeal with Anna Bradley had been laid to rest, once and for all, in the dark waters of Cedar Creek.

CHAPTER 22

"Then we which are alive and remain shall be caught up together with them in the clouds to meet the Lord in the air, and so shall we ever be with the Lord." 1Thessalonians 4: 17

The next week, the weather turned off unseasonably mild, offering a welcome reprieve from the biting January cold of days past.

Having finished breakfast, Claire shoved her arms into her coatsleeves and told Stell, "Hibernate if you've a mind to, but I be-dogged if I stay cooped up in these four walls, grim as a deacon, when the Lord's seen fit to give us such a glorious day! I've a hankerin' to go outside an' rake leaves."

Standing with her backside to the crackling fire, Stell gave Claire a look of wonder mixed with disdain. "Fiddle! I ain't *never* held a hankerin' to rake leaves! I say let the blame thangs take care of themselves!" She dragged her chair as near to the hearth as possible without setting herself on fire and plopped down. Within seconds, she was snoring.

Claire marched energetically out the front door, leaving her cold-natured companion bundled up in a quilt.

For more than an hour, Claire raked the yard with a fierce and enduring energy. Although the day was cool, as she worked, it became too warm for her heavy coat.

Out loud to herself, she said, "I reckon this'd be a sight easier if I's to shuck this bundlesome coat." So she paused to take it off.

All of a sudden, she felt winded and light-headed. Her face flushed; her legs started tingling. Her heart thudded frantically. Seeking to steady herself, she grasped the wooden handle of the rake with both hands and leaned against it for support.

Time was when I could rake and sweep my entire yard without s' much as workin' up a sweat, much less havin' to stop and rest, she thought. The very idea made her rebuke herself. *Here I've went an' gone soft from too much settin'.*

Closing her eyes, Claire stood still and sucked in several long, slow draughts of cool air, trying to lay hold of her equilibrium. Above her head, she heard the creak of a limb as it rubbed against another, heard a dead twig drop to the ground. She became aware, then, of someone calling her name. Recognizing His voice, she smiled and turned, expectantly, hoping to catch the warmth of the Son on her face.

My child, we're going home…

In the next twinkling, she was transformed and caught up with Him in the clouds.

No, there's nothing to hold me here…

Since no one saw it happen, no one would ever know how much time elapsed between then and when Stell awoke and hobbled over to the kindling box for a piece of wood and glanced through the window, discovering Claire lying peacefully dead atop a pile of leaves, her hands still holding on to the handle of the rake.

Distraught, Stell took off running in a mad panic down the lane. She managed to live long enough to make Laura understand about Claire before she, too, collapsed and died. Most would forever say that Stell Roberts's heart gave out over the loss of her one and only true friend, Claire Ellis. Though he would never say it out loud, Wesley viewed her dying as a stubborn act of will and would forever believe that Stell died that day so as not to let Claire best her.

For all the trouble and heartache Addie had come through in her life up to this point, no feeling she'd ever experienced could compare to that of losing Claire. However, as she lovingly made ready her body for burial, she gave no outward show of the overwhelming sorrow she was feeling inside. She was dry-eyed and appeared so calm she might have been struck dumb, for indeed she was.

Why, she wondered, had she felt no sense of foreboding?

Though she wondered this, of course she knew nothing could have prepared her for this hour. Even with the final and absolute physical proof lying before her, the only way she managed to make it through dressing Claire's corpse was by not allowing herself to think of her as really being gone.

Claire's going to be fine...everything's going to be fine... She repeated this mantra over and over in her mind.

Later, when there was nothing more for her to do and only one place for her to go, Addie blindly wended her way toward the path that led to the great white oak. Reaching the spot, feeling sick and empty, she leaned against the tree. Her heart was as heavy as a stone. *Claire is dead...Claire is dead...Claire is dead.* Claire was gone and nothing could bring her back. She was gone forever. With the cruel reality of it finally beginning to sink in, the pain in Addie's soul was almost too much for her to bear. Her shoulders quaked underneath the oppressive burden of it; her legs shook and gave way. With an anguished sob, she dropped to her knees, no longer trying to hold back the tears that streamed down her face.

She stayed there for a long time in the stillness of this pleasant place and mourned. She felt like she had been physically beaten. As she stared out across the pasture, she thought, *How will I make it without Claire?* The thought filled her with despair. Nothing would ever again be the same.

When at last she was able to quiet her mind and talk to God, she was reminded that He didn't promise life everlasting upon this earth, but in John 6 it is written, "Verily, verily, I say unto you, He that believeth on me hath everlasting life..."

Comforted by this promise, she wiped her face on the hem of her skirt. *Claire ate of the living bread which cometh down from heaven... she is not dead...an heir of His promise, the promise of eternal inheritance...she shall live forever...* Addie realized that Claire's passing from this earth was her reward.

For a time, Addie lingered and watched the progress of the sun as it lowered and observed as the Master used feather strokes to paint a sunset of lavender, rose, and orange. A little while later, she stood up and wrapped her shawl about herself and took a deep, cleansing breath, remembering, *Nothing is dead until it is forgotten...*

To the fading light, she whispered, "I won't ever forget you, Claire...and don't you ever forget that I love you." Claire would always live inside her heart.

In the embrace of the cold evening air, with an unfamiliar emptiness in her heart, Addie walked home.

Without a doubt, this had been one of the worst days of her life.

While there may have been singing up in Heaven, down here on earth the melody had surely faded away. It was almost impossible to fathom what had happened. The magnitude of loss was incomprehensible and almost beyond bearing.

There was no solace to be found amongst them; there was no one to comfort them, for they all needed comforting. Sharing the same loss, bearing the same burden, their faces only mirrored each other's pain and sadness. Nevertheless, in truth, aside from Addie, Sassie grieved more than any.

The next day at the double funeral, for a while Sassie's mind drifted and took her back to a time and place when she remem-

bered everything as being different, where by unspoken rule people
had customarily stayed with their own kind. Coloreds with coloreds,
whites with whites. *On second thought,* she mused, *ain't dat much
changed.*

Sassie had never been one to just sit around and wonder about a
lot of things, but once she got on smart enough to understand that
color was most times used to sort and separate and measure the
worth of people, it did make her wonder why God didn't make it
easier for all the ignorant folks and just make everybody the same.
She supposed she being mixed made it all the more confusing for
the especially ignorant ones.

However, all of that changed in some ways for her when she was
twelve years old, when she met Miz Claire, Miz Addie, and Emily.
For Sassie, that fall had been a season of discovery and acceptance.
They were the first whites she'd ever encountered who didn't seem
confined to custom and conformed to the unspoken rules of society.

Not that there was anything wrong with their eyes. They could
see perfectly well. Nor were they blind to color; they were just able
to look past it, and not in the same way of some, who simply chose
to look past colored folks like they weren't even there.

No, Claire Ellis, Addie, and Emily were the kind of people her
mama had called "precious few," the kind who sweetened the lives of
those around them with their goodness and generosity. Sassie would
always cherish the memory of the hours she spent with Emily and
Miz Claire learning to read and write. Miz Claire had also befriended her mama and had led her mama to Jesus.

When confronted with the tragic death of her mama the following spring, Sassie was forced from the world she'd known all her life
and pushed into one strange and different. Filled with despair and
uncertainty, she moved to Golden Meadow, where she lived with
Claire and Stell. Not long after coming there she found out prejudice existed everywhere, and that's when she acquired an unsuspect-
ed ally in Stell Roberts.

Though Stell never aspired to be lovable, Sassie loved that old woman dearly, and she knew without doubt Stell loved her. Inwardly, Sassie wailed, *Lawd, dey's all gone...Mama, Miz Stell, an' Miz Claire...*Oh, she would have given anything to have them back! They would never get to see her baby! It just didn't seem fair. Thinking these thoughts, she laid her head on Obie's shoulder and wept uncontrollably.

From across the aisle of the church, Addie's heart went out to Sassie. The poor girl had lost so many people she loved. *She'd surely be lost if she didn't have Obie...and thank you, Lord, that Rosette has finally made restitution...*Sassie now held her rightful place in the Quinn family. Still, it worried Addie to see her so upset, especially in her condition.

Libby was another one Addie worried about. She too had lost so much in such a short period of time: her mother, her home, and now her grandmother. To look into Libby's eyes reminded Addie of looking into an old, abandoned house. Aside from the girl's usual strange and solitary personality, lately there seemed to be an aura of despair around her, something dark. Laura was particularly concerned about Libby's frequent nightmares, and her stories of ghosts frightened Meggie.

While the eulogies were being said, in Addie's mind she pieced together a beautiful quilt from memories, precious remnants of the past. For her, Claire's death marked an ending of sorts. She couldn't remember a time when she hadn't belonged to Claire. She'd been so young, just a schoolgirl, when Claire had, in a way, adopted her and Wesley. The two of them had never felt as close to their own mother as they had Claire. Nor as loved.

Through the years, the kinship Addie and Claire held for one another flourished and was true. It was Claire, not Travis, who was there when she bore Emily into the world. It was Claire who so kindly pitched in and helped her tend to her mother Rachel, after her stroke. Addie remembered it was Claire who'd stayed at her bedside and tended her, body and soul, when she lost her baby and almost her life a few years back. Bitter and sweet, the memories flowed on...Claire quilting with her and Creenie...Claire, so beautiful as her matron of honor when she and Hiram married...Claire...*my beloved friend Claire*...

Addie smiled wistfully. She wished now she had gone ahead and told her that she was expecting. *The news would have thrilled her soul...and Stell's...*

Now Stell's little house once again stood empty.

Singing indicated that the service was nearly over. Hiram took Addie's arm and led her up the long center aisle as the crowd proceeded somberly to the cemetery.

"'The Lord is my Shepard, I shall not want. He maketh me to lie down in green pastures; He leadeth me beside the still waters. He restoreth my soul; He leadeth me in the paths of righteousness for His name's sake. Yea, though I walk through the valley of the shadow of death, I will fear no evil; for Thou art with me; thy rod and thy staff they comfort me. Thou preparest a table before me in the presence of mine enemies; Thou anointest my head with oil; my cup runneth over. Surely goodness and mercy shall follow me all the days of my life; and I will dwell in the house of the Lord forever. Amen.'"

Amos Bradley had the eternal honor of lying between the two women who had, in life, loved him. On his one side was his wife, Dinah, Stell's sister, who died in childbirth bearing Asher and Laura. On the other, they buried his sister-in-law, Stell Roberts, who helped him raise the twins and loved them as best she could as her very own. Even though Stell had seen little virtue in those around her and lived mostly to suit herself, she had indeed been loved. The church would not hold all who had come, and despite her ornery ways, she would be sorely missed and never forgotten by those who had known her.

Indeed, it was a time of great sadness and tears.

In compliance with her request, the following morning Addie, Hiram, Wesley, and Travis took Claire back to Collinsville to bury her at Eminence Cemetery beside Luke.

While the men set about digging the grave, Addie took the buggy and rode out to her old homesite on the Monroe Road. Stepping foot on the ground there again opened yet another floodgate of memories, happy and sad, vague and distinct. Once upon a time, how she had loved this place! Her very heart had lived here! Not so many years ago, she'd dreamed of raising her children here, living out her life here...*Once upon a time...*

Looking around, she took a deep, cleansing breath. It all felt so peaceful and still. Though little evidence remained of how the place looked in years past, in Addie's mind, she could envision it in every season, could see every wall and door. The old barn was still standing; Rachel's cast-iron stove—the one that Addie cooked on outside during the hot summertime—stood rusted under the lean-to adjoined to the smokehouse.

She recalled the last time she'd used that stove. It was the day Alfred, Cleve, and Ap pulled fodder in the lower field; she had been pregnant at the time. It was that very night when she and Alfred quarreled about Daniel, and Alfred shoved her down in the kitchen. Her unborn baby boy had lost his life that night.

Ap.

Addie couldn't help but smile at the thought of him. *Sweet, funny Ap.*

Ap had been a jewel of a friend to Claire, and likewise, she a treasure to him. In an unprecedented act of love and generosity, when Claire moved to Golden Meadow, she shocked not only Ap but also most of the folks around Collinsville in giving him her house and a piece of land.

Gazing out toward the road, Addie wondered, *How many times did me and Claire walk the distance between our two houses?* How many times had she heard Claire say, "The path to a friend's house is never long"?

Leaving the buggy behind, Addie set out on foot. She wanted, *needed*, to walk that path one last time.

When she reached Claire's old homestead, she paused at the edge of the yard and stood there for a moment and took in the scene. Time seemingly had not touched the place. The ground was swept. Chickens scratched here and yon, guineas protested the presence of a stranger. Off to the left of the house there was even a little garden laid out in the same spot she'd always planted. She half expected Claire to round the corner and greet her with a hoe in hand—or perhaps a mess of turnips.

Oh, how she wished!

Realizing that this would never again be, agony stabbed her heart afresh.

Just when she started toward the house, the front door opened, and Ap came out onto the porch, peering at her curiously. Waiting at the top of the step, he did not call a greeting, not recognizing her at first. As Addie approached, uncertainty turned to disbelief, which consequently turned into a gleaming smile.

"Lawd have mercy on my soul! Iz dat you, Miz Addie?" he hollered exuberantly.

Emotion washed over her as Ap reached out and grabbed both her hands in his.

Over and over, he exclaimed, "Lawd! I cain't believe my eyes! I sho caint believe my eyes! I sho iz glad to see you, Miz Addie, yes'sum, I sho am!"

Ap pumped her arms so vigorously, Addie wondered if he might jerk them out of their sockets. But she didn't care. She was just that thrilled to see him too.

"Lawd, Miz Addie, how's you bin? An' Miz Claire…tell me how iz—*where* iz—my ol' friend Miz Claire Ellis?" He cast an anticipatory look toward the road. "I sho has missed y'all…"

Addie's face gave away the truth before she could say the words. Ap's smile froze as her voice wavered. "We've brought our old friend home."

Then there were tears in his eyes. His throat constricted.

For a long moment, Addie and Ap stood with their hands clasped, neither of them wanting to let go, each comforted to hold onto another who recognized and understood the depth of their sorrow.

Finally Ap imitated sadly, "'Come on in da house. I'll put us on a fresh pot o' coffee, an' we'll have us some teacakes'."

For the next hour, in their need for each other's company, they sat in Claire's little kitchen and shared stories from days gone by. When Addie finally made ready to leave, she said, "I thought you might go with me to the cemetery…to say good-bye."

Ap jumped up. "Jus' let me get my coat."

As they walked along the gravel road, it occurred to Addie that Ap didn't know about Alfred's reappearance after they'd all believed he'd perished in the fire. So, she began telling him.

Ap stopped in the middle of the road. Standing there with his thumbs tucked into the waistband of his pants, he had a look on his face of total disbelief. "I knows you iz pullin' my leg, Miz Addie!"

She said, "I'm not! Cross my heart! He somehow escaped the fire and came back with the intent to kill us all. It was Travis who shot him and finally put an end to his meanness!"

Ap couldn't be convinced. "Now, Miz Addie, I *knows* you iz pullin' my leg!"

When they climbed into the rig, Addie handed the reins to Ap tentatively and said, "Promise me that your driving skills have improved since the last time we rode in a buggy together!"

Ap threw his head back and cackled. Slapping the reins, he warned, "You done tol' enough lies fo' us both wif dat story 'bout Mista Alfred! You best hold on!"

News of Claire's death spread quickly, whereupon during the course of the afternoon, many, both Negroes and whites, came by Eminence Cemetery to render their respects and offer their condolences. Some stood around and waited to witness her burial. Claire Ellis had lived her life in accordance to the Golden Rule, was one known for ever following that which was good in her treatment of all persons. For this exemplary trait, her reputation was preserved noble and blameless in the eyes of the community; long after she was buried, it would be remembered so in the minds of many.

While the men filled in the grave, Addie went and gathered two large bouquets of garnet camellias; the stems, she secured with twine. When it neared time to go, she placed one of the bouquets between the headstones marking the graves of her father and mother, Samuel and Rachel. She traced their names lovingly with her fingertips. On the grave of the son she would never know, the marker bearing the name Brandon Coulter, named after Travis, she laid thereon a single, perfect bloom.

From across the way, as Travis watched Addie standing beside the graves of her parents, he couldn't help thinking about all the ironies of their lives. *Dear old Samuel,* he thought. Giving way to nostalgia, he found himself trying to remember what year it had been.

He recalled it was June; corn was standing high and thick-leafed, the ears mature enough to have brown silk tassels. He, Luke, and Samuel were on the front porch of the Ellis house, smoking, laughing. Luke could always be counted on to summon laughter. Somewhere along the way the conversation had turned to the war. It was on that summer evening, while the sun set, that Samuel charged Travis with a trust, one long known to Luke. After the disclosure, the three men had stretched and yawned and sat silent for a time, smoking tobacco and listening to the crickets, the comradeship between them deepened by the secret they now shared. They had never spoken of it after that one time. Travis knew that Claire presumed the truth of Samuel's identity would die with her.

Presently, as the sun dipped below the horizon, Addie knelt soberly at the grave of her oldest and most beloved friend. Here lay the ending to a beautiful story that time had written on her heart. Tears flowed down her face; her grief dropped onto the flowers and onto her hands, leaving tiny rivers of sorrow behind. Discreetly, she reached in and took an object from her pocket. When she laid the bouquet down, she patted the dirt as gently as she would a baby's head. With one last, whispered farewell, she stood and walked away without looking back.

Lying upon the fresh mound of Claire's grave, nestled within the beautiful bunch of garnet camellias, Luke's old pipe had at last been laid to rest.

Henceforth, the following days were hard to get through; for Addie, they seemed especially blank and empty. Yet as she'd promised, Tuesday morning she went to sit with Bonnie so Amelia could ride into town with Daniel and the children to watch the last of the cane grinding.

As she crossed the corner of the front yard, she glimpsed the three of them at the barn and waved; Daniel was hitching to the wagon. She then mounted the steps to the porch and entered the house quietly without knocking.

Amelia met her with a concerned expression. "I don't know if I should leave Mama. She seems weaker today. She coughed all night…"

"Oh, go. It's such a pretty day," Addie encouraged softly. "It'll do you good to get out of the house for a while. We'll be fine here."

Through the window, Amelia glimpsed the wagon pull around with Rachel and Carson sitting on the seat beside Daniel. They were so looking forward to going to town today. Though reluctant to leave her mother, she didn't want to disappoint them.

A few minutes later, when they'd gone, Addie went down the wide central hallway that led to the sickroom. Tiptoeing into the room, a feeling both strange and familar swept over her, one of foreboding.

Her nostrils met with a particular stench. The room, whose window was kept shut to guard against a chilling draft, could stand a good airing. Beside the bed was a slop jar containing an accumulation of blood-tinged rags, proof that Bonnie had spent a miserable night coughing.

Bonnie was lying in bed, looking old and unwell. She appeared to be asleep. The skin on her face was stretched taut over her hollow cheeks. Indeed, she seemed to have suffered a decline since Addie had last seen her less than a week ago. Her frail, fading appearance reminded her of how Rachel and Creenie looked when she'd tended them. *Not long before they died.*

Putting an end to the charade, Bonnie opened her eyes and said, "This room stinks." Although knowing the answer, she looked around and asked, "Ever'body gone?"

Addie nodded as she reached for another pillow to put underneath Bonnie's head. "You must be tired of lying in bed," she said. "Wouldn't you like to sit up for a while?"

Bonnie shook her head. "*Livin's* what's come tiresome."

Waiting another moment, Addie said, "I brought a spice cake. Would you try to eat some? It might make you feel stronger."

With a frown, Bonnie grumbled, "Ain't never been partial to spice."

. . . Tribulation worketh patience . . .

Finding herself at a loss, Addie studied her grouchy companion silently for a minute, carefully reserving what she might have liked to say had Bonnie not been ailing so.

With dry deliberation, Bonnie then said, "I'm glad they're gone. Amelia stands over me wringin' her hands like an old granny. I 'spect she means well, but this mornin' her fidgetin' ain't done nothin' but hinder me from dyin'." So that there was no misunderstanding her intention, she went on to make it clear.

"I'm figurin' on dyin' before she gets back from town."

Without realizing she did it, Addie sighed heavily. Given their mutual discontent, it had become evident neither she nor Bonnie was going to be good company today. Nothing else to do, she reckoned they would merely endure each other's presence for the next few hours, dispensed of convivial banter.

As she positioned the pillows, she felt the heat of Bonnie's skin radiating through her gown and knew she was feverish. Addie's concern for her was genuine when she asked, "Bonnie, are you hurting anywhere?"

"No. Like I said before, I'm just wore out an' tired of livin'."

Addie bathed Bonnie's forehead with a cool rag and offered her a drink of water before drawing a chair near to the window and taking up her embroidery.

There was a long silence before Bonnie said, "I hated to hear about ol' lady Ellis. Best I recall, she was a right fine person."

Addie felt her eyes fill with tears. Without pausing at her stitches, she replied, "Yes, Claire was one of the best." Her voice caught on Claire's name; her throat ached with the acknowledgement of her death, her heart ached for her old friend.

"Amelia said you taken an' buried her at Collinsville."

Addie cleared her throat softly and managed to say, "That was her wish, to be buried beside Luke." She loosened and reset the wooden hoops, snapping them together in such a way that made Bonnie turn and look over at her.

Seeing her tearful expression, Bonnie turned thoughtful, as near as she could. "I'm sorry I upset you …brangin' up that she died … seein's how you an' her carried on like you'z kin." An apology, for her.

Addie thought, *Whether you'd brought it up or not, I'll always be upset about losing Claire…* "No, it's all right," she assured Bonnie.

Bonnie seemed not to be speaking directly to Addie but more to herself, or maybe even someone beyond them, perhaps out in the hallway, when she said, "Now there's a place I don't care to ever set eyes on ag'in. I didn't leave nothin' back in Collinsville, 'cept a slew of bad memories." She looked at Addie slowly, as if seeking to say more, yet at the same time not wanting to think about that which was in her mind. Taking a deep breath, she closed her eyes and mentally edged away from it, stowing her thoughts in the shadows.

To Addie, it was Bonnie's way of retreating; she could see she was wrestling with something. Regret, most likely. As she sat silently debating with herself whether or not to once again encourage her to repent of her sins and trust in the Lord, Bonnie drifted off to sleep, her cheeks rutted with tears.

While the sun climbed and the clock ticked away the hours, Addie unwittingly rocked herself to sleep. It was midafternoon when her head lolled and she woke with a start to find her embroidery had fallen from her lap and lay on the floor beside the chair. Standing up to stretch, she glanced out the window to see Daniel's wagon approaching.

All of a sudden, she heard a weird, high-pitched wheezing sound coming from the bed. Bonnie was choking!

In the dawn of her fleeting mortality, Bonnie's face filled with panic as she fought to suck air into her lungs and attempt to raise herself in bed. Addie rushed to her aide and tried to pull her upright. In her struggle, Bonnie's arm flung out and almost pushed Addie down, making her fear they might both roll off the bed.

Bonnie heaved forward and coughed, spraying Addie's sleeve and the coverlet with blood. Seizing Addie roughly by the shoulder, she

pulled her close, gripping her tightly, hurting her. With her mouth near Addie's ear, in a coarse, broken voice, she mumbled something unintelligibly. For a brief minute, her moist, ragged breath passed over Addie's neck until the words stopped abruptly in midsentence, and then her grasp loosened from Addie's arm. Her hand dropped limply to the bed; her whole body seemed to wilt as she slumped back deeply into the pillows, rendering unresponsive.

True to the words she'd spoken earlier, Bonnie Riley ceased to live.

Daniel and Amelia entered the room just as a dismayed wail burst forth from Addie's open mouth. As Amelia moved forward toward the bed, Addie staggered away from it, overcome with a feeling so sharp she had to catch her balance against the wall to keep from collapsing to the floor.

While Amelia knelt beside the bed, sobbing over the passing of her mother, Addie felt herself shrivel up like a flower withering under the heat of an August sun. She felt stricken. The color had drained out of her face; she was white as bleached-out bones. She swallowed hard against the bile that rose in her throat. For a moment, Daniel could only stare at her, perplexed by the weight of her grief for Bonnie, until he thought he knew the reason for it.

No wonder, he thought. Sympathetically, he said, "Mama, I'm sorry you had to be witness to this." *So close on the heels of losing Claire.*

Addie nodded rapidly, trying to right herself. Though she bordered on the edge of hysteria, she managed to say, "Don't mind me, I'll be all right…but Amelia's heart is breaking."

Her mind was frozen; she couldn't seem to connect her thoughts to what was happening in this room. All she wanted was to leave. Her throat thickened, and she had to fight to draw a breath. She needed some air; she needed to be alone. She watched Daniel go over and put a supportive arm around Amelia. Moving unsteadily toward the door, it was all she could do to say, "I'm so sorry, but

I must go. I'll send Hiram and Wesley with word to some of the church members. Someone will be here directly."

She was glad no one attempted to detain her as she fled the house swiftly.

CHAPTER 23

"...In the world ye shall have tribulation; but be of good
cheer, I have overcome the world." John 16: 33

Bonnie Riley was buried off to herself in the cemetery at Fellowship
Baptist Church. Little known to the people of Golden Meadow, her
funeral was lightly attended.

Bonnie's funeral. Addie had dreaded it, had not wanted to go. Nor
did she mean to offend when she offered unexpectedly, and curious
to everyone, to keep Rachel and Carson at home while the others
went to the service. Insulted by the suggestion, Amelia adamantly
replied, "You'll do no such thing! Rachel and Carson will do what's
proper and attend their grandmother's funeral with us!"

Standing beside the grave, not attuned to what the preacher was
saying, Addie held tightly to the hands of her grandchildren while
Samuel stood in front of Hiram. Looking around at the three of
them, she thought of how beautiful—*how perfect*—they all were.
Healthy children were indeed a blessing from God!

Although the day was cool and a slight wind stirred, underneath
her wool dress, she was perspiring. Her eyes wandered to Stell's

grave across the way, and it made her think of Claire. She blinked back the tears. The thoughts running through her mind made her squeeze Rachel's hand so tightly that the girl glanced up at her to see what was the matter.

The funeral sermon had been short, but not short enough to suit Addie. When it was over, she didn't stand around and talk to anyone. Had it not been so hard to explain, she would have set out walking for home instead of riding home in the buggy with everyone else.

Arriving home, Hiram helped her down from the seat and pulled her into his arms and held her close. He whispered against her hair, "Are you going to be all right?" His voice was so deep and tender.

For a moment, she melted against him, loving him. He was her best friend. She told him, "I think I'll feel better after a walk."

Studying her face, Hiram thought how her eyes looked like two blue pools of sadness. He wished in his soul he had the power to make everything all right.

"Do you want me to go with you?" he asked. He'd noticed she hadn't talked much since Bonnie's death. Yesterday she'd seemed so distracted and nervous. He'd seen her hands shaking uncontrollably during supper; she'd eaten very little and slept fitfully. He knew she was having a difficult time over losing Claire.

Losing Claire and Stell had been difficult for all of them. *Was* difficult. It was going to take time, a lot of time, and all of them leaning on each other, with all their faith and love, to get over to a place where they could accept what was and move beyond their sorrow.

Addie looked so tired.

"Are you sure you wouldn't just rather lie down for a while?" he suggested.

Noting his concerned expression, she shook her head and said, "No. I'll be fine. I just need a while to myself. I won't be long."

Before she walked away, she suddenly remembered something. She said, "Years ago, a few months before Claire moved here from

Collinsville, she and Travis came and spent Christmas here with us…"

Hiram nodded; he fondly remembered that Christmas.

"While Claire and I sat and talked, we shared an orange…Claire was telling me that Tom Dewey and Lucy James had died, and she made the statement, 'I hope the next funeral I go to is my own.' That's how I felt the day we buried her, and that's how I feel today."

When she reached the white oak and sat down, Addie drew her knees up, closed her eyes, and rested her head against the tree. She felt more alone than she ever had in her whole life. Her thoughts were troubled, yet there was not a soul she could tell of this. Though she had never doubted the wisdom of her father—or Claire or Hiram, she could never have told even them what Bonnie had told her on her deathbed. And oh, how she wished Bonnie had not told her either! The confession was too corrupt, too despairing.

Impossible as it seemed, Alfred had managed to reach up from the burning pit of hell and stab her straight through the heart yet again. She couldn't even begin to understand, would never understand, how anyone could do all that he'd done. The enormity of it was staggering. How could any one person be so evil, so vile, so depraved? Even in death, his wickedness had come back to haunt her.

The knowledge she possessed held the potential to desecrate their lives. It could turn their dreams into a nightmare, could destroy their happiness, and could very likely destroy them. She thought solemnly, *It would kill Daniel.* Yet, it could only destroy them if they knew, and they could only know if she disclosed what Bonnie had said. Only then would it have the power to destroy anyone.

Addie vowed to herself never to let that happen. She didn't intend to breathe a word of it; they would never know, no one would ever know, *must not ever know.* She would live with the atrocious secret for the sake of them all, to preserve the sanctity of her family.

In her heart, Addie knew it was fruitless to dwell on it. It would only poison her life, poison everyone's lives. She simply wouldn't allow herself to think it. It was unthinkable, beyond thinking. She thought, *I must get beyond thinking it...*

Anyway, Bonnie said even she didn't know for sure; she couldn't have been sure...Therefore, it may or may not be so. So why had she even felt compelled to tell her? Why had she burdened her with the terrible possibility of it? *Why?*

And what difference did it make now, anyway, now that they were both dead and gone? There was nothing she could do, nothing anyone could do. She looked up into the branches and wanted to scream, but instead, she cried out boldly to the Lord for help: "Lord, I know You are faithful and have promised we will not be tempted above that which we are able. Please draw me close, comfort and strengthen me, help me get beyond this thing that can only cause heartache and devastation to my family...Please help me forgive and forget this terrible admission so that I might again have peace within my heart..."

Alfred and Bonnie had been drunkards. They drank together, got drunk together. They'd got drunk and slept together...*Alfred and Bonnie...*

"...Please give me the assurance that Daniel isn't married to his half sister...Give me assurance in my heart that Amelia is not Alfred's daughter and that she didn't give birth to her own sister..."

With her soul laid bare, Addie leaned her back against the rough bark of the tree and closed her eyes. She sat there for a time—still, quiet, simply breathing and being...*resting in her Saviour.* The sun had long peaked and begun its descent in the west when the cool wind again stirred and lifted the loose tendrils of hair from about her face and neck. She opened her eyes and smiled, comforted by the quiet reassurance of God's breath moving ever so gently upon her face and, moreover still, by the awesome reassurance that His spirit moved ever so faithfully upon the earth. *'Let us hold fast the confession of our hope without wavering, for He who promised is faithful...'*

Claiming this holy and precious promise, Addie stood up and brushed off her skirts and headed for home, for the time being leaving her worries and fears behind, abandoned in the shadow of the Cross.

"The eyes of the Lord are upon the righteous, and His ears are open unto their cry... The righteous cry, and the Lord heareth, and delivereth them out of their troubles... The Lord is nigh unto them that are of a broken heart..."

EPILOGUE

In response to the whisper of spring, an alabaster flurry of snow-drops drifted across the front yard. Buttery daffodils swayed in a gentle breeze and the sunny, bell-shaped flowers of a forsythia shrub brightened one corner of the house. Red bud trees were blooming. Everywhere one looked it seemed the world had suddenly awoken and was once again teeming with life.

Less than an hour before, Travis had threatened to stuff a rag in Sassie's mouth if she didn't quit carrying on like she was dying. Now they were all crowded around the bed, excitedly craning their necks to glimpse the newest member of the Quinn family, *an heritage of the Lord* and firstborn of the next generation that would carry on their family's story, both good and bad.

As Sassie held her newborn baby in her arms, she looked down into the tiny face and crooned lovingly, "You is da purtiest baby I ever did see." Dragging her eyes away from him, for a moment she looked around the room at all the faces gathered there in celebration of this blessed occasion, at all the joy and excitement and laughter. The room spoke of nothing but love; the table was spread, the longing in her soul had at last been filled.

Beaming, she announced, her voice quivering with emotion, "Ever'body, me an' Obie is pleased for y'all to make the acquaintance of our son." She turned him slightly in her arms so they could see him better. "Dis is Obadiah Ellis Quinn."

Tears streaming down her cheeks, she smiled and looked upward and said softly to someone beyond the ceiling, "But we gone call him Ellis."

Rejoice Evermore!

NOTE FROM THE AUTHOR

In this novel, *Standing on the Promises,* the word *promise* is used many times, in a myriad of situations, solely in the interest of building a more entertaining story. However, for those of us who stand in faith, throughout the Bible—from Old Testament covenants with Noah, Abraham, Moses, and David to the very end of John's Revelation— God makes hundreds and hundreds of great and precious promises to His children, contingent upon our obedience to Him. And, unlike the sometimes quick and glib promises made by man, God always keeps His promises!

In encouraging you to study the Word and claim God's promises for yourself, below I have listed a few of my favorites to get you started:

> "Call unto me and I will answer thee, and show thee great and mighty things which thou knowest not."
>
> Jeremiah 33:3

"For ye shall go out with joy and be led forth with peace; the mountains and the hills shall break forth before you into singing and all the trees of the field shall clap their hands."

Isaiah 55:12

"Draw nigh to God and He will draw nigh to you …"

James 4:8

"Jesus said unto him, If thou canst believe, all things are possible to him that believeth."

Mark 9:23

"And all things, whatsoever ye shall ask in prayer, believing, ye shall receive."

Matthew 21:22

"If we confess our sins, He is faithful and just to forgive us our sins and to cleanse us from all unrighteousness."

1 John 1:9

"If ye abide in me, and my words abide in you, ye shall ask what ye will, and it shall be done unto you."

John 15:7

" …God is faithful, who will not suffer you to be tempted above that ye are able; but will with the temptation also make a way to escape, that ye may be able to bear it."

1 Corinthians 10:13

"God is our refuge and strength, a very present help in trouble."

Psalm 46:1

"But the Lord is faithful, who shall stablish you, and keep you from evil."

2 Thessalonians 3:3

"The Lord will give strength unto His people; the Lord will bless His people with peace."

Psalms 29:11

"I will not leave you comfortless; I will come to you."

John 14:18

"And I will make them and the places round about my hill a blessing; and I will cause the shower to come down in his season; there shall be showers of blessing."

Ezekiel 34:26

"I can do all things through Christ who strengtheneth me."

Philippians 4:13

"Trust in the Lord with all thine heart; lean not unto thine own understanding; in all thy way acknowledge Him, and He shall direct thy paths."

Proverbs 3:5,6

"And if I go and prepare a place for you, I will come again and receive you unto myself; that where I am, there ye may be also."

John 14:3

"Behold, He cometh with clouds; and every eye shall see Him…"

Revelation 1:7

May you keep yourselves in the love of God, and serve Him joyously!